DEATH IN THE RIVER

A TWISTY AMATEUR SLEUTH MURDER MYSTERY

THE BREAKFAST CLUB DETECTIVES
BOOK 2

HILARY PUGH

Housemouse Press

1

Finding a dead body was the last thing on Ivo's mind as he and Harold set off for their early morning walk. Such a glorious morning, perfect for a stroll along the riverbank. *It could be a picture on a calendar,* Ivo thought, as he locked up his cabin and climbed down the steps onto the river path that led away from *Shady Willows.* People paid a fortune for houses so close to Windsor and the river, but for nothing more than a few odd jobs around the site, Ivo lived there rent free. The homes at *Shady Willows* weren't palaces, Ivo would be the first to admit that. Not much more than caravans, really, except without the wheels. If they needed to be moved, which so far none of them had, they would have to be lifted by cranes onto massive trucks. But the people who lived in the chalets were there for the long haul. The majority were downsizers who wanted to stay in the area but were unwilling or unable to pay the exorbitant costs of retirement complexes.

Ivo looked after twenty homes, each with a tiny plot of garden and space for one car. *Shady Willows* was started by a friend of a friend who had inherited the land along with enough money to put it to good use. And the use he put it to was to provide affordable housing. Ivo had never met the man and it was all thanks to his friend, a woman called Diane James – a new age hippy type who had been involved in the murder in the Long Walk case – who had suggested Ivo for the job. He could hardly believe his luck.

Harold liked it too. It meant long walks along the river, friendly residents who as often as not had tempting snacks on offer, and plenty of interesting smells in and around the chalets. And in a way it was all because of Harold that they were there at all. Ivo had been on the verge of eviction for the second time in his life. It was not like the first time and the discovery that his mother had been months behind with the rent; a fact not discovered until after her death. His second eviction was Harold's fault. Well, not exactly his fault. Harold could hardly be blamed for being a dog. But the housing trust that Ivo rented from didn't allow dogs, or any other kind of pet. And Ivo had failed to read the contract properly. It had almost been a case of sending Harold to a dogs' home or living on the streets, also for the second time. But then Ivo met Jonny Cardew and two things changed. Harold went to live with Jonny – a temporary arrangement, both Jonny and Ivo stressed – and the Breakfast Club Detectives started. Five months ago, they had solved their first, and as yet only case. But there would be others, Katya assured them. Katya, their unelected leader because not only was she the most forceful personality, but because she was the only one of them with actual crime solving experience in her role as detective sergeant in the local force. And now she was retired, but her crime solving days were not over. In fact, she told them, retirement was only a word and her crime busting days were only just getting started.

After their walk, Ivo and Harold would have breakfast at *Jasmine's*, home to both the breakfast club and Jasmine herself – Jasmine Javadi and the fourth detective who, with Jonny Cardew, had set up the breakfast club in the café she owned with her father. Jasmine was the big sister Ivo had never had. He couldn't even remember how they'd met, but he'd been doing odd jobs in the café since he'd left school. Like Diane James and the man who set up *Shady Willows*, Jasmine was one of the *good* people. She did stuff like volunteering in the food bank, making sure the café didn't wrap their sandwiches in single-use plastic and generally keeping a sisterly eye on Ivo. And she'd founded the breakfast club with the idea of rich people getting regular breakfasts by paying a subscription which made sure that people who couldn't afford them also got to eat a decent breakfast. And Jasmine's breakfasts, all her meals in fact, were way more than decent.

Ivo looked along the riverbank at the hazy sun rising over the castle, turning the sky a pale pink. A light mist rose from the river and the ground crunched under his feet after a late frost. It would be a warm day once the cloud had burned back, but it was still only February; the nights and early mornings were cold. Ivo huddled into his coat with a sense of pride. It had been a good winter, not just his move to *Shady Willows,* but extra odd jobs for people in the town: fixing damaged door hinges; touching up paintwork; replacing broken tiles and cleaning moss from roofs. He could turn his hand to anything, no job too small. And it had paid off. He had been able to buy a new coat. His first in a very long time that had not come from a charity shop or, as had happened in the past, from the bin at the back of the charity shop where they left the stuff no one wanted. Things that were too far gone to sell. But not this time. This coat had come from a stall in the market. It had a hood and a padded lining, and the stallholder had thrown in a red and blue striped scarf. Better still, when Ivo bought the coat, there was a label fixed to the end of the zip by a thin cord with the price and the name of the company who had made it. Proof that no one had ever worn it before.

Ivo looked down at the dog trotting along beside him. Should he buy Harold a coat as well? He'd seen dogs wearing coats on walks in the park. But they'd mostly been small, pampered-looking animals and no one could say that about Harold. Rugged was a better word. Harold had been through the wars and had the scars to prove it – one ear bent at an odd angle, half a tail and a *do not mess with me* kind of expression, emphasised by an underbite that some people interpreted, wrongly, as aggressive. The idea of Harold in a coat made Ivo laugh. He already had a thick layer of black fur to keep him warm.

It was good to be on their own. Just Ivo and Harold. They'd seen a few people on the road in the distance, commuters hurrying to the station and a few more on bikes. But here on the river path there was no one. Harold barked half-heartedly at a swan standing on one leg at the edge of the water. But after a quick glance the swan had ignored them and tucked its head back under its wing. Harold lost interest and started sniffing at tufts of grass at the side of the footpath.

No need for him to be on the lead, Ivo thought, bending down to unfasten it and watching as Harold scampered off ahead of him along the path. Some dogs, Ivo had noticed in the past, leapt into the water. Not Harold. He wasn't a water lover. The closest he got was when he rolled in something, and Ivo had to hose him down. Not an activity Harold succumbed to willingly. Ivo was happy to let him run ahead, knowing he'd come back the moment he was called and wouldn't for one second think of leaping into the river as so many other dogs did.

Harold was about fifty yards ahead of Ivo when he stopped abruptly and growled at something in the water. As Ivo drew closer, he could see the dog trembling, the fur standing up in a ridge along his back. Ivo called him and slipped his lead on again, pulling him to his side. 'What is it, old fella?' he asked, stroking his dog's head reassuringly. He looked at where Harold had been standing. At what he assumed was a pile of rags, bobbing up and down in the shallow water where part of the bank had fallen away to reveal a few tree roots. He moved closer, dragging an unwilling Harold with him. He nudged the bundle cautiously with the toe of his boot. He must have dislodged something, freed it from a root that was holding it down. He watched in horror as it began to rise and turn in the water revealing a face, pale and bloated, eyes open and staring. Staring, Ivo thought, straight at him.

Ivo took a step back from the muddy bank and looked in horror and disbelief at the body rocking gently in the shallows, moving as if still alive as the river water lapped against the bank. Ivo shivered, from shock rather than cold. He shouldn't just stand there. He must do something. He reached into his pocket for his phone and with a shaking hand pressed 999. The sound of a voice, another human who was alive and well, brought Ivo to his senses. He described the scene in front of him – no, not breathing, not conscious, no sign of life at all.

The voice on the phone soothed him. There was nothing he could have done. He was told to stay where he was. Help was on the way. Police and ambulance had been alerted. All Ivo had to do was wait. Feeling uneasy about the gaze of the dead man, he pulled Harold to one side and sat on the footpath, not noticing the cold surface, with his arm around the dog for comfort.

It felt like a lifetime, but was probably no more than ten minutes, when suddenly the path, even the river itself came to life with flashing blue lights, police in heavy boots and paramedics in yellow jackets. Ivo was escorted to a police car where a young constable wrapped a blanket around him and poured him some tea from a flask. So many questions. How long had he been there? Did he know the man? Did he see anyone else? She wrote down his address and told him someone would call round and talk to him. Then she asked if there was anyone he'd like to call to be with him. *Jasmine,* he thought. *No, Katya. Or would Jonny be best?* He fumbled for his phone but found his hand was still shaking and his fingers unable to find the keys.

The constable took it from him. 'I'll do it,' she said, kindly, scrolling through his contacts.

'Katya,' he said. 'Call Katya.' The others would be kind, but Katya would know far more about what was going on. And besides, as Ivo began to regain some composure, he realised she'd never forgive him if she missed out on a real live crime scene.

The constable handed back his phone. 'She'll be here in fifteen minutes,' she told him, offering him another mug of tea, which he accepted gratefully.

2

Katya forced herself awake and glared at her phone. Six o'clock. In the bloody morning. The first time in ages she'd managed to sleep beyond five-thirty. The first time in a long while that she'd actually been woken up by something other than just not being able to sleep any longer. She looked at the name of the caller. What the hell did Ivo want at this ungodly hour? She grudgingly tapped to accept the call. 'What?' she growled, hoping Ivo hadn't been flung out of his accommodation again. But turned out it wasn't Ivo at all. It was constable someone or other. She hadn't caught the name. Ivo had had a bit of a shock and was sitting in a police car near the Eton footbridge. 'He's fine,' the constable assured her. 'Just a bit shaken. He shouldn't be on his own.'

Katya hauled herself out of bed and dragged on the first clothes that came to hand: combat trousers; a couple of sweaters and odd socks. She noticed the socks as she laced up her boots. *What the heck*, she thought. *No one's going to see them.* She opened her door to a bright but chilly morning and set off at a brisk trot. It wasn't far; short cut through the town centre, deserted at this early hour, down the hill past the theatre and over the bridge. She could see the bustle of activity from halfway across. She'd attended enough crime scenes herself in the past to recognise this as one: squad cars parked at odd angles; blue tents; flood lights and people in white hazmat suits. Organised chaos. She knew the drill.

The entrance to the footpath was cordoned off with blue and white tape and guarded by a po-faced uniform. Katya knew his type. He probably spent his time dealing with lost dogs and double-parked cars. This was likely to be the most exciting thing to have happened to him since he finished his training, and he was taking it seriously. There was no way he was letting Katya through. He was a bulky lad, useful in a closing-time brawl but possibly lacking in people skills. He stood, arms folded, one foot each side of the path blocking her way. 'Sorry, madam,' he said. 'No members of the public beyond this point.'

Members of the public? She planted her feet firmly on the footpath and glared at him with her hands on her hips. She'd show him. 'Young man,' she said in her best ex-sergeant voice. 'My name is DS Roscoff. I was called by one of your constables taking care of the person who I understand is a witness.'

'The constable's name?' he asked.

Damn, she thought. She should have made a note of it. But at least he hadn't asked for her ID.

At that moment an ambulance pulled away from the footpath and Katya saw a face she recognised. Detective Sergeant Flora Green. They'd worked together before she'd retired, when Flora was still Detective Constable Green.

Katya put her fingers between her lips and whistled, waving to Flora to attract her attention. 'Katya,' said Flora, crossing the path to join them. 'What brings you here?'

'Ma'am, I...' began the constable.

'Not now,' said Flora, holding up a hand to silence him.

'I had a call from one of your uniforms,' said Katya. 'About a young man, Ivo Dean?'

'Of course, Ivo. I thought I recognised him and his dog.'

'You know Ivo?'

'I met him a few years back. Caught a young burglar down on Meadowcroft.'

'Still working for DI Lomax?' Katya asked.

'Yeah, still working with Lugs.' Flora smiled. 'I'm his sergeant now.'

'Good for you.' Flora had been ambitious even as a rookie constable when Katya had first met her. Katya had been Lugs Lomax's sergeant herself before she retired. 'What happened to Pete?' The fourth member of the team, a timid young man Katya had never considered cut out for the police.

Flora giggled. 'He joined the vice squad.'

'Blimey,' said Katya. 'I'd never have thought he had the balls for that.'

'None of us did,' said Flora. 'But he's doing okay.'

'Must have learnt to say boo to a goose then.'

'Guess so,' said Flora.

The constable cleared his throat and started to fidget with the crime tape.

'It's okay, Jack,' said Flora, turning to face him. 'You can let Katya through. She's one of us.'

'Yes, ma'am,' he said, holding up the tape and letting Katya and Flora duck under it. 'Thanks, Jack,' said Katya. She been about to tell him what she thought of him, but the idea that she was still *one of us* softened her. 'So, what's going on here?' she asked Flora.

'Ivo reported a body in the river,' she said. 'It looks like a straight-forward case of stumbling into the water after one drink too many. He reeked of alcohol even though he'd been there for some time. But we won't know for sure until the post-mortem.'

Katya nodded. 'You won't need to keep Ivo, then.'

'We've got his contact details. If it does turn out to be a suspicious death, we'll need his fingerprints and DNA just to eliminate him. But you know all of that. He's free to go for now. We were concerned that he should have someone with him. It can be very upsetting finding a body. It's probably best if he doesn't go home alone.'

'He only lives half a mile or so upriver,' said Katya, nodding in the direction of *Shady Willows*. 'But he could probably do with something hot inside him first. I'll take him to *Jasmine's* and get him a cooked breakfast.' She could do with one herself after her unexpectedly early start. Not even time for her usual cup of strong tea to jump start her brain.

'He's in that car over there.' Flora pointed to a patrol car fifty yards away. 'Tell the constable he's free to go.'

Katya made her way over to the car, where Ivo and Harold were sitting in the back seat, looking, she thought, quite excited by all the activity. 'DS Green says he can go,' she said to the constable, who glanced in Flora's direction.

Flora gave her a thumbs up sign. 'Fine,' she said. 'He was a bit wobbly when we first got here. No surprise there, anyone would feel like that. But he's fine now.'

Ivo nodded in agreement. 'It's fascinating,' he said. 'Watching everything going on. Just like on the telly.'

'Well, we won't stay and get under their feet. I'll get all the info from Lugs later. Let's go and get breakfast. Jasmine will want to hear all about it. Jonny, too, if he's there.'

It was a short walk to *Jasmine's,* across the bridge from where there was a good view of the police activity. A crowd had gathered, staring at the footpath and taking photos of the police in action. Ivo and Katya stopped for a moment to join them, looking back at the footpath, where they could see the crime tape still fluttering in the breeze. The body had already been removed and half a dozen uniformed officers were taking photographs and searching the riverbank within the cordon.

'What do you think?' Ivo asked. 'Was it just an accident? I know he'd been drinking. I could smell it on him, but could he really have just fallen in and drowned?'

'I dunno,' said Katya. 'I suppose if he'd had a lot to drink, he could have.'

'Then why did they take all those pictures before the body was removed? And why are they searching the area?'

'They won't be sure until after the post-mortem. And once the scene is compromised it will be too late to search for evidence if it does turn out to be foul play.'

'He might have been pushed in, so they'd need to search for footprints, wouldn't they?'

'Definitely,' said Katya. 'You're starting to think like a detective.'

'Should we take some photos?'

Katya shivered in the cold breeze from the river. She quickened her pace and edged away from the crowd of rubberneckers. 'You won't get much from here. Lugs will be able to show me the pictures of the scene. But right now, it's time for breakfast.'

They continued up into the town, where things were waking up; shops opening, people hurrying to work grabbing coffees on their way. They took a short cut through the station and then turned down the steps towards the arches and towards *Jasmine's*, where Karim Javadi was standing a blackboard on the pavement. 'You're early birds this morning,' he said. He tapped the board and Katya read: *Today's specials – pancakes with sugar and lemon or cottage cheese.* 'Shrove Tuesday,' he said.

Karim and Jasmine were good like that. Always adding specials to suit whatever cultural occasion was imminent. Soon it would be hot cross buns. Karim baked them himself and served them fresh from the oven, dripping with butter. But today it was pancakes, and after the morning they'd had, Katya could think of nothing better. 'Do you fancy a pancake, Ivo? Lots of sugar – good for shock.'

He nodded enthusiastically. They went inside and sat at their favourite table by the window. It was home from home for Harold, who wriggled under the table and settled down with his head on his paws, keeping an expectant eye on the door to the kitchen.

'You two are in early,' said Jasmine, walking over to their table and reaching into the pocket of her apron for a notebook. None of those flashy apps for ordering, Katya noted approvingly. They still did things old style in here. Jasmine smiled at them. 'The pancakes are good,' she said.

'Pancakes for two, then,' said Katya.

'Sugar or cheese?'

'Sugar,' said Ivo. 'I need it for the shock.'

'Shock?' Jasmine asked, looking concerned.

'We've had a bit of excitement,' said Katya. 'We'll tell you all about it when you've got a moment. Is Jonny in this morning?'

'He's in the kitchen.'

Katya could never understand why Jonny chose to spend his time as a kitchen hand, a voluntary one at that. Okay, he'd teamed up with Jasmine to start the breakfast club, but he was also very rich. He'd been chairman of a factory in Slough – still was, she supposed – although he'd retired from actually doing any work there. And people who retired from that kind of thing, major shareholders on massive pensions, usually spent their time on posh golf courses or taking expensive cruises. But not Jonny Cardew. What he liked was solving murders – fictional mostly, but occasionally real ones. And Katya respected him for that. The world was a far better place with Jonny here overseeing the breakfast club than it would be if he was chasing a small ball across a golf course. And as she, too, was retired, she absolutely understood his need to be busy and in the company of interesting people, like herself.

Jasmine was right about the pancakes. They were hot and crisp and crunching with sugar. She and Ivo munched through a pile of them in silence, occasionally feeding scraps to Harold, who edged out from under the table and looked plaintively up at Ivo with a manufactured expression of extreme hunger.

The café was filling up now, but that would be short-lived. People dropped in for breakfast before heading off to work. Only a few stayed to linger over second cups of coffee and a browse through the newspapers. Soon Karim would tap Jasmine on the shoulder and tell her to take a break. She would pour herself a coffee and join them at their table. Jonny as well.

. . .

'WE FOUND a body in the river, me and Harold,' said Ivo excitedly, as Jonny and Jasmine joined them ten minutes later. 'Well, Harold found it first.' He leant down and patted Harold's head.

'Man or woman?' Jasmine asked.

'It was a man,' said Ivo. 'He was wearing a suit.'

'Did you call the police?' asked Jonny.

''Course he did,' said Katya. 'That's why I'm here. They called me.'

'Because it was a murder?'

'No. They wouldn't call me for that. I've retired.'

'Didn't stop you solving the man in the Long Walk case, though,' said Jonny.

That was true, Katya thought, her ex-police colleagues having shown very little interest. And she'd solve this as well if it did turn out to be a murder. If. 'They called me from Ivo's phone because he was a bit shaken, and they said he needed someone with him.'

'I just said that because I knew Katya would want to see what was going on,' Ivo told them.

'Looks like it was an accident,' said Katya. 'The bloke was drunk and fell in. They'll know more after the PM.'

'Do they know who he was?' asked Jasmine.

Katya shrugged. 'I'll get the details from Lugs later.'

'Why were you there, Ivo?' Jonny asked.

'Walking Harold. I go there most mornings. Its only twenty minutes from the *Shady Willows*.' Ivo finished his coffee and put the cup down. 'We'd better be getting back there, Harold and me. I've stuff to do.'

'I'll give you a lift,' said Jonny, reaching into his pocket for his keys. 'I need to get going myself.'

Katya watched as the three of them left. 'Jonny misses Harold, doesn't he?' she said as Jasmine poured her another coffee.

'Mixed feelings, I think,' said Jasmine. 'He's really pleased that Ivo can have Harold with him again. But he does miss having a dog. That's probably why he spends so much time here. No incentive to go for walks.'

'Does he get in your way?'

'No, not at all. He's a great help, but he's at a bit of a loose end. What he'd really like is another crime to solve.'

'He looked quite disappointed when I told him today's incident was probably an accident.'

Jasmine finished her own coffee and stood up. 'I need to get on with the lunch orders,' she said. 'But as soon as you find out this guy's name, I'll do a bit of Internet searching and see what I can find out about him. Perhaps it won't be as straightforward as it looks.'

'Just so there's something for Jonny to do?'

'Not just Jonny. I miss being a breakfast club detective as well.' She winked at Katya and headed towards the kitchen.

Very gratifying. They were a good team. And loyal. And while she'd never wish for someone to be the victim of a murder, she couldn't help hoping that there would be more to this case than the accidental death of a blameless citizen who had no secrets in his life and nothing to investigate.

3

Katya watched as Lugs bought two bottles of Knight of the Garter beer and two packets of Burt's firecracker and lobster crisps. He carried them to where she was sitting on a wire chair. The latest thing in pub furnishing, no doubt, but she'd probably have an interesting grid pattern on her backside when she stood up. Lugs put the drinks down on a table that had once been a beer barrel and which was now gentrified with a coat of pale varnish, copper-coloured hoops and topped with a circle of thick glass. Upscaling was the word that came to mind, although it wasn't a word Katya used often. In fact, she didn't think she ever had used it. There was probably scope for some upcycling of the furniture in her own flat, but she doubted she had the necessary skills for the job. Oh well, she was really quite fond of her threadbare chairs and scuffed table. She'd also been quite fond of the décor in this very pub until someone had decided to take it in hand.

'The old pub's not what it was,' she said, taking a swig of her beer and putting the bottle back on the table. 'They don't even go in for glasses. Saves on washing up, I suppose. Or beer mats,' she added, as the glass of the bottle clinked against the surface of the table in a way that set her teeth on edge. She looked around at what had once been a nice pub. The kind with a brass-topped bar and proper pumps, red plush benches and photos of Windsor in the nineteen-thirties. Last time she and Lugs had been here it was called the Rose and Crown. Now it had been renamed Rose of Windsor and the comfortingly dark red décor replaced with a shade of greenish grey.

Lugs agreed. 'Prices have doubled as well,' he said, putting his wallet back into his pocket. 'We probably need to find a new watering hole.'

Katya nodded. 'Can't imagine where, though. They've all been turned into gastro pubs or wine bars.'

'Too many tourists round here. We'd do better away from the town centre.'

'As long as you don't choose one with a massive TV screen and all-day sport.'

Lugs laughed. 'Scope for some research, then.'

'I'd be up for that,' said Katya, swallowing a handful of crisps which tasted like the prawn cocktail ones everyone ate in the nineteen-eighties but laced with unnecessary amounts of chilli powder. She took a hasty swig of beer. 'Anyway, it's good to see you. How's things? I met DS Green the other day. I hear she's your sergeant now.'

'She is. And doing very well now some of her youthful zeal has rubbed off. But I didn't ask you here to discuss my team.'

'No?' With any luck, he would have news of the body. Harold's body, as she now thought of it. 'Is it about the corpse in the river?'

'Can't get anything past you, can I? But you're right.'

'I'm all ears.'

'He was called Hugo Walsh. Sixty-five years old, self-employed upmarket carpenter – that's posh doors to you and me. Nothing interesting from the post-mortem. Cause of death was drowning. No other injuries, although he had a significant amount of alcohol in his bloodstream, which suggests he slipped, fully dressed, into the river. His next of kin is a son, Jason, who lives in Alma Road.'

'All pretty straightforward, then,' said Katya, trying not to feel disappointed. But hey, she wouldn't want to wish being murdered on anyone.

'Well,' said Lugs. 'There is one thing that's a bit of a puzzle.'

Katya pricked up her ears. Was this about to become interesting after all?

'Hugo Walsh actually died eighteen months ago along with his wife, in the Swindon train crash.'

No one would forget that in a hurry. A First Great Western train had tripped the automatic safety system at a signal on the line between Swindon and Kemble, careering into a commuter train at a junction on the Gloucester Golden Valley line. The smaller train had been catapulted off the line and down into the valley, where it landed on its roof and exploded into a fireball. Six people, including the driver, were killed outright and many more were injured. Investigations were still ongoing, questions had been asked in Parliament and an official public inquiry was scheduled to begin soon.

'Who identified Walsh after the crash?' Katya asked. Whoever it was had done a shoddy job. Even in the ruins of a train crash, the victims deserved to be properly identified. The next of kin should expect nothing less.

'That was the first question we asked,' said Lugs. 'The son identified his mother. She was holding hands with a man who must have shielded her from the worst of the fire, but he was too badly burnt himself to be recognisable. It was likely to be Mr Walsh, I suppose. There was no sign of him at their home address and no one saw him after the date of the crash. All the luggage and possessions were destroyed in the fire so there were no artifacts that would identify him. The man was the same build as Walsh, so I guess they just assumed it was him.'

'Slipshod,' said Katya. 'No dental records or DNA checks?'

'Apparently not.'

'Raises a few questions, doesn't it?'

'You're not wrong, but I'm not sure they are questions for the police. Incompetence, obviously, but I don't know if a crime has been committed. You can't accuse a dead man of impersonation. And even if you could, there's no evidence of criminal intent.'

'It leaves some interesting questions, all the same.'

'Several,' said Lugs. 'Who was the man who died in the train crash? What was he doing holding hands with Mrs Walsh? Where had Hugo Walsh been for the last eighteen months?'

'Are you sure the man in the river was Hugo Walsh?'

'We're asking for a DNA comparison with the son. But he had his passport in his pocket and a bank card in his name.'

'Can you trace where he's been through the bank card? He must have registered an address.'

'That's another puzzle. It was a card he took out as an extra on an account he'd used years ago. He cleared all the funds out of that shortly before he was believed to have died. He'd opted to go paperless, so nothing was posted to his home address.'

'And it escaped being closed down with his other bank cards. It's almost as if he was planning to disappear.'

'It does look like it was something he kept quiet about. But it could just be that he didn't want the wife to know about it, or the tax people. He'd stashed a fair bit away in the account and as I said, all funds were removed.'

'And when did he last use the card?'

'Not since he withdrew the money.'

'And the account is still open?'

'Yes, only the next of kin can close it and as it's dormant there didn't seem to be any reason to bother the son about it. I'm not sure what the position is now. Which death certificate would they accept to close it?'

'I suppose it's not all that unusual for someone to die and leave an account no one knows about.'

'Less so now, with all the money laundering protection, but yes, there will be quite a few.'

This was getting interesting. Katya wasn't sure where it was going, but something odd was happening, something she could get her teeth into. She had a nose for that sort of thing. 'Did he have a mobile phone?' she asked.

'Yes, but only a cheap pay-as-you-go one. It would be difficult and expensive to trace calls made from it. And there's nothing to suggest we need to. There's been no obvious crime committed.'

Too many bodies and not enough names to fit them. And no suggestion that the police were taking much of an interest. Just what Katya and her team needed. 'You say the son identified him?'

'He seemed sure it was his father, although you can imagine the state of shock he was in after identifying a man whose funeral he'd organised eighteen months ago.'

'Buried or cremated?'

'Cremated, I'm afraid. But the DNA result will be in soon and I'm pretty sure it will confirm his identity.'

'Hmm,' said Katya. 'I suppose the first thing you need to do is identify the bloke who was holding hands with Mrs Walsh on the train.'

'We've searched the missing person's database but it's not easy when you know nothing about the man and all the evidence has been destroyed.'

'And I don't suppose Mr Walsh's son is keen to pay for a second funeral, is he?'

'No,' said Lugs. 'And if no crime has been committed, it's hard to justify using our limited financial resources to take it any further.'

'I suppose Walsh could have been up to something illegal during the last eighteen months. Why else would he have kept himself hidden?'

'We're keeping it all quiet right now. The last thing we want is a lot of TikTok detectives digging around and making everyone's life a misery. There have been one or two compromised cases where that sort of thing's happened.'

Katya agreed. There'd been a case in the news just the other day of a missing woman. Everyone in the world, it seemed, had a theory about where she was. There was so much misinformation flying around social media that the local police didn't know whether they were coming or going. It was a mess. Even the home secretary had intervened.

'So what we need,' said Lugs, 'is someone like yourself working unobtrusively in the background. Find out what you can and pass it back to us if there's anything we can act on.'

Exactly what she was thinking. Not that she was going to let Lugs know that. 'Me?' she said, feigning surprise. 'I've retired.'

'Then you are just what we need. I've talked to the super about it and we could offer you a civilian contract. You did well with the Long Walk case.'

'I had my team,' said Katya modestly. Would she be able to use them again? It could be just what they were waiting for.

'No reason why you can't give them the odd bit of research to do. We'd need to vet them, of course.'

This was more than she'd hoped for. Up to now she'd assumed the police treated them as a bit of a nuisance; interfering amateurs just like all those TikTok people. 'You're saying you'd use a team of amateur detectives?'

'To be honest, I've discussed it with the super and we'd rather have a small group of people who know each other well and who would be answerable to us, than risk any Tom, Dick or Harry getting involved.'

What could she say? She'd hardly refuse an offer like that, would she? The alternative was a long, dull spring stretching out ahead of her. 'I'd get a proper contract?'

'We'd agree a certain number of hours and a fee. I'm afraid your team would be volunteers, though. They are all unqualified and you would have to be in charge of them. Everything they find out comes through you to us. No acting on their own. We'd need everything properly recorded and reported. And there would have to be ground rules; no talking to the press for starters.'

Katya took a thoughtful mouthful of beer. 'Jonny Cardew would be up for it. He's more or less retired and has plenty of money. He'd do it just because he's interested. Jasmine and Ivo both work.'

'But they like being in your team, and there won't be a lot of hours involved. They'd both be ideal because they are out there meeting people. They are up to speed with a lot of what goes on in the town.'

Katya was starting to feel excited about the idea. No question that she was interested. Jonny had always wanted to be a detective and would jump at it. Jasmine had IT skills and could keep on top of report writing. And Ivo was always in and out of people's houses. Handymen heard all kinds, didn't they? 'Okay,' she said. 'I'll talk to them.'

'Great,' said Lugs, scooping some remaining crisps from the packet. 'As soon as you all agree, I'll introduce you to Jason Walsh. The poor guy doesn't know if he's coming or going right now. He'll be relieved to know someone's on his side. Up to now he's got a pretty poor opinion of the police.'

'That's not really your fault, is it?'

'We've been able to support him through the ID and post-mortem findings, but like I said, there's no evidence of any crime so there's not much more we can do for him.'

THEY FINISHED their drinks and left the pub. Katya walked home through the town, which was humming with activity: early tourists; office and shop workers; even students, all of them hungry and looking for eating places. Spoilt for choice in a town like this. Katya's thoughts turned to her own evening meal. A contract and a fee, Lugs had said. She was definitely going to accept his offer. He hadn't mentioned how much the fee would be, but it would likely cover a meal out somewhere. It was still early in the evening and she was attracted by a Moroccan restaurant. Small and colourful, it was tucked away down a side street. She often looked longingly at the menu pinned up outside and this was her chance to try it. She'd bash the cost onto her credit card and blow the consequences. She'd had enough of austerity.

There were no other diners in the restaurant. Too early, she supposed. But she was greeted by a very friendly woman who showed her to a table in a corner. 'Don't look so worried, love,' said the woman. 'It'll busy up quite soon. Once they see you, they'll start coming in. People don't like to be the first, do they?'

Fancy that, Katya thought. She'd never had any hang-ups about eating. First or last, it was all the same to her. She tucked into a plate of interesting snacks while she waited for her chicken tagine and while she was nibbling, she sipped a glass of white wine, on the house, the woman had said. She found her notebook and started making lists. First, she'd need to call a meeting, set out some ground rules and a plan of action. Lugs was going to arrange an introduction to Jason Walsh. She'd take Jonny with her. He was calm and fatherly and could be just what was needed to soothe a distraught, twice – or was it three times – bereaved young man. And while they were doing that, Jasmine could start some online research; get some background on the train crash and start building a picture of what Mrs Walsh might have been up to. She tapped her pen on the table and wondered what Ivo could do. He – or rather, as he'd no doubt insist, Harold – had found the body. He'd want to be involved. Perhaps Jason Walsh was in need of a handyman. Ivo could be just the person to wheedle facts and family secrets out of him.

4

'He wants us to do an actual enquiry for the police?' Jonny would never in a million years have expected that. Proper police work. Who'd have thought it? Perhaps his ambition to be a detective wasn't such a daft one after all.

'Why wouldn't he?' Jasmine had asked. 'He knows we're good at it.'

'And retirees are often contracted as civilians,' Katya added.

Jonny suspected they paid them less that way. But he shouldn't be cynical. It was what he'd always wanted, wasn't it?

Ivo didn't have much to say about it. That was the way Ivo was, Jonny supposed. He'd tag along, not showing a lot of interest, but then suddenly come up with something none of them had thought of. Often ideas that seemed unlikely, ridiculous even, but which turned out to be rather brilliant. Like the way he'd solved the problem of how to access a secret website in their first case.

Katya had explained the first task in their latest case to them. Lugs wanted to know all about Hugo Walsh and the best way to do that would be through his son, Jason, who now lived in the family home not far from the town centre. Lugs arranged for them to visit Jason Walsh and approved of Katya's suggestion that only she and

Jonny should go to begin with. Less intimidating, they both agreed. Jasmine would find out all she could about the Walsh family on the Internet without encroaching on her working hours. 'And Ivo?' Jonny asked.

'I've got work for him once we've got to know Jason a little,' she said, without revealing exactly what she had in mind. Jonny knew better than to ask too many questions.

JASON WALSH LIVED in one of a small row of terraced houses, close to the raised stretch of railway track that curved away from the Royal Station and made its way across the meadow to join up with the main line at Slough. Trains ran every twenty minutes in both directions and Jonny wondered if, living this close, people became used to the regular rattle of wheels over the track. They were small trains that trundled the two and a half miles in six minutes, hardly the intercity express.

Jonny and Katya had arranged to meet Lugs at the end of the road. Residents only parking was rigorously enforced, so Jonny decided to walk there from his own house, which was in a more upmarket part of town. Just a few streets away but out of earshot of the railway. Katya would walk there from her own flat and Lugs from the police station. So no parking problems for any of them and all three managed to arrive within minutes of each other.

Lugs and Jonny shook hands. 'I'll not hang about,' said Lugs. 'I'll introduce you both to Jason then leave you to chat.'

They walked down the road together and Lugs rapped on the door. Jonny shifted from foot to foot nervously as they waited for an answer. How exactly did one start a conversation with someone who had lost both parents? One of them twice.

'Don't look so anxious,' said Lugs. 'Katya's well trained in interviewing, but my advice would be to keep it friendly. Don't treat it like an interrogation.'

'No good cop, bad cop, then,' said Jonny with a nervous grin.

'We're here to help him,' said Katya. 'The poor man's been

through a lot. He was in Cornwall when Walsh was fished out of the river, so there's no question of him being a suspect, even if this wasn't a cut-and-dried accident.'

'That's right,' said Lugs. 'Think of yourselves as victim support. But of course, if you do come across anything that sheds light on where his father was for the last eighteen months, make a note of it and be sure to feed it back to me.'

'So do you suspect Mr Walsh senior of being involved in something illegal?'

'His disappearance is suspicious,' said Lugs. 'But it's not against the law to go to ground for a while. We'd just like to know about it.'

While they were waiting for the door to open, a train rattled over the arches at the end of the street and Jonny decided it was the sort of sound one could live with. There was something reassuring about it, not unlike the sound of the milk float he remembered from his childhood. The Walshes, Jasmine had discovered, had lived there for more than twenty years. She'd downloaded an image from Google Earth. A confusing, murky image, but she had marked the Walshes' house with a circle and shaded an area at the back, which to Jonny looked like nothing more than a grey slab. Jasmine thought this was likely to be the flat roof of a workshop. She'd found details of Walsh's work and sent round a folder of information from adverts in the local press about plans submitted to the council planning department. Walsh specialised in bespoke doors and window frames made, Jonny assumed, in his workshop and transported to various building projects. It all looked above board. They didn't currently have access to his financial records, but there was nothing to suggest that this wasn't a thriving business and there was no apparent reason for Walsh to suddenly go to ground.

After a wait of several minutes, the door was opened by a man they knew to be in his early thirties but who looked more like an undernourished fifty-year-old. He certainly carried an air of having been through a lot. Jonny wondered if the poor man had eaten a decent meal in days. And if he had washed recently or changed his clothes. Even from the doorstep, the air in the house felt fusty and oppressive. A smell of stale food and cigarette smoke wafted from deep inside. Would it be rude, Jonny wondered, to suggest they open a few windows?

'Ah, Jason,' said Lugs, stepping into a narrow hallway and indicating to Jonny and Katya to follow him. 'I'd like to introduce Katya Roscoff and Jonny Cardew. The civilian investigators I mentioned. I'll leave you to it,' he said, patting Katya on the shoulder and beating a hasty retreat back into the less fetid air of the street. 'Call me later, okay?'

Jason scratched his head, managed a weak smile and led them into an untidy living room, where Jonny noticed a dried-up pizza still in its box and a collection of mugs with unidentifiable blobs of fur at the bottom. A small table was weighed down with piles of paper and an overflowing ashtray. Two armchairs were obscured by heaps of crumpled clothing. 'Have a seat,' said Jason, pushing some grimy shirts onto the floor. 'Sorry about the mess. It's been... I dunno, difficult.' He sat down at the table and sank his head onto his arms on a heap of papers. 'Sorry,' he muttered again.

'How about I make us a nice cup of tea?' said Katya, eyeing the chairs in a way that suggested even she would be reluctant to sit on one of them. 'Then we can have a chat and see what we can do to help you. Kitchen this way, is it?' Jason raised his head and nodded before sinking back onto the pile of papers.

A brave offer, Jonny thought. *God knows what state the kitchen will be in.* He sat down on the one chair that was free of laundry and reached into his pocket for his notebook. One of his bright red moleskin ones. He'd bought a collection of them when he first joined the breakfast club. One day he would turn all the notes he'd made into a novel. Maybe. 'Mind if I ask some questions?' he asked.

Jason lifted his head from the table, an action that seemed to drain him of any remaining energy. He stared wanly at Jonny.

'I hear you've recently returned from Cornwall?' Jonny asked, unable to think of anything else to say. 'On holiday?'

'Yeah, first time I've been away since Dad...' He let the sentence hang in the air.

They'd need to find a way round that. He and Katya were here to talk about a death that seemed to have happened twice. Jason had probably just about got his head around saying things like *since Dad died*, meaning eighteen months ago, only to discover Dad had actually died a couple of days ago. That was enough to set anyone reeling with confusion.

'I used to live in Cornwall,' Jason continued. 'In a commune.'

Jonny had assumed that communes had gone out with the seventies.

'It's a group of artists,' said Jason. 'Living off-grid on Bodmin Moor.'

'You're an artist?'

'Was,' he said. 'I came back here eighteen months ago to sort my parents' stuff. I was just about getting Dad's workroom sorted to use as a studio when all this...' he waved his arms around, 'happened.'

Katya returned with mugs of tea, which she put down on the edge of the table. 'Your milk's off,' she said. 'I made mint tea.'

Jonny picked up one of the mugs cautiously, hoping that Katya had given it a good scrub before she made the tea. He sniffed it before taking a sip. It was fine. It smelled of mint, as it was supposed to. Any other unpleasant substances that could have been lurking at the bottom had either been scrubbed out by Katya or overpowered by the mint. He had it at the back of his mind that mint was an antiseptic, so it was probably safe to drink.

'Right,' said Katya, sitting down at the table next to Jason. 'Where do we start?'

Jason shrugged. 'You tell me.'

'What's all this?' Jonny asked, indicating the piles of papers on the table.

'That's all the stuff I boxed up after Mum and Dad died. I had to go through all the will and probate business and once that was done, I'd had enough so I just stuffed it all into those boxes and shoved it up in the attic. I've been trying to go through it again in case there are any clues about what was going on around the time of the train crash.' He shuffled some pieces of paper ineffectually across the table. 'Didn't get very far, though.'

'A good place to start,' said Katya. 'Would you like some help?'

'It's in a bit of a muddle: bank statements; paperwork about Dad's carpentry stuff; a few holiday brochures, that sort of thing. Not sure what going through it again will tell me.'

Jonny felt sorry for the man. He probably just wanted to shut it all out and get on with his life. 'Are you planning to stay here or sell up?'

'They left me the house in their will. I was going to adapt the workshop into a studio and carry on painting.'

'I'm sure you can still do that,' said Jonny. 'We should check the terms of the wills, but if you were named as the sole beneficiary on both of them, I can't see that much has changed as long as your father didn't make a more recent one. Even if he did, you could probably challenge it. Have you got a good solicitor?'

Jason shook his head. 'I didn't use one. I got a book from the library about probate, and it was all quite straightforward.'

'I think we should set that aside for now,' said Katya. 'The most important thing is to find out where your father was for the last eighteen months and why he didn't come forward after the train crash.'

'We should build up a profile of him,' said Jonny. 'We'll start with this lot.' He gestured towards the papers on the table. 'And Jason can tell us everything he remembers: who were your father's friends; his business colleagues; what he did in his spare time; where he liked to go on holiday; every little detail.'

Jason looked as though he'd really rather catch the first train back to Cornwall and forget about the whole thing. And who could blame him?

'Jonny's right,' said Katya. 'We need to know a lot more about your mother as well, but we can't do it all at once.' She picked up a fistful of papers and waved them at Jason. 'I suggest we get this lot sorted into categories, separate piles for your mother and father so we can get to know them both a bit better. Then we'll go and get some lunch. You look as if you need a square meal.'

Jonny prodded a pile of clothing with his foot. 'Perhaps you should change your clothes first,' he said, imagining local eating places might object to customers with severe body odour. 'Why don't you get a load of laundry started? You do have a washing machine, I suppose?'

'There's one in the kitchen,' said Katya. 'Jason, why don't you do that while Jonny and I crack on with the papers?'

Occasionally Jonny was surprised by how sensitive Katya could be. She was right. Doing the laundry was going to be far less emotional than reading through papers about deceased parents. He and Katya settled down at the table while Jason obediently started sorting through his clothes. He was quite good at it, Jonny thought, watching as Jason sorted things into colours and sifted out jumpers, presumably for a wool wash. He also extracted a couple of tweed jackets and hung them over the back of one of the chairs. 'Dry cleaning,' he muttered.

Katya looked at her watch. 'A couple of hours,' she said. 'Then if Jason's comfortable with the idea, we'll box up anything we think might be useful and get Jasmine to do some Internet searching.'

They worked in silence, finding some cardboard boxes and packing up all the papers. Jason watched them, looking as if he cared very little about the paperwork. He seemed to find doing laundry soothing, a welcome diversion from the complications of repeat bereavements. Jonny could hear the rumble of the washing machine. Three loads in all and as Jason carried each pile into the kitchen, Jonny noticed how grimy the carpet was. He'd only seen the lounge and the entry hall but assumed the rest of the house was equally unkempt. While Jason was occupied in the kitchen, he asked Katya what she thought of the idea of getting Ivo in to give the place a good clean.

'Good idea,' she said. 'He can search around a bit as well and see if he can get a handle on what Mrs Walsh had been getting up to.'

'Is that ethical?' Jonny asked.

'Don't see why not,' said Katya. 'We'll be upfront about it. Tell Jason a disinterested outsider's view of his mother might help them find out where she'd been going on the day she died, and who was with her.'

'And if Jason objects?'

'I don't think he will, but we won't do anything he's uncomfortable about.'

Jason returned from the kitchen for the final load. 'I think I've got a clean shirt upstairs,' he said. 'I'll have a quick shower and get changed.' Anything, Jonny assumed, to get him out of doing paperwork. But it would give him and Katya a chance to nose around without Jason breathing down their necks. And a cleaner, tidier Jason was something to encourage.

BY THE TIME Jason returned from his shower, they had organised the papers into three boxes and the washing machine was rumbling to the end of its final load. Jason had no objection to the removal of his papers. In fact, the relief of being rid of them took about five years off him. A good meal, as well as the shower and some clean clothes, and he might start looking like the thirty-two-year-old he actually was, rather than the downtrodden fifty-something he'd been at the start of the morning.

'Time for something to eat,' said Katya, rubbing her hands. 'We'll carry these boxes round to *Jasmine's* and get some lunch. Jason can meet the rest of the team.'

IT WAS early afternoon when they arrived at the café and most of the lunch crowd had left. They stacked the three boxes in a corner near the counter, where Jasmine was serving.

'Jasmine, love,' said Katya. 'This is Jason Walsh. Jason, this is Jasmine Javadi. She's one of the team and will be helping us get your records in order.'

Jasmine smiled. 'Good to meet you,' she said.

Jason nodded at her.

'Any soup left?' Katya asked.

Jasmine lifted the lid from a black cauldron behind the counter and peered inside. 'A few servings,' she said. 'Carrot and coriander.'

Katya ordered for all of them. She was showing Jason who was boss, Jonny guessed. Fine by him. Carrot and coriander soup was one of his favourites. Jason didn't seem to care very much. Probably only too glad of someone to make the decision for him.

Jasmine served the soup and carried it to a table.

'Can you spare a few minutes?' Katya asked.

Jasmine looked around. 'It's quiet now,' she said, 'so I can sit down for a moment or two.'

'Those boxes,' said Katya, pointing her soup spoon towards them. 'All full of stuff from Jason's house that needs sorting. Think you can do that?'

'Happy to,' said Jasmine, to Jonny's surprise. Why would anyone be happy to do a job like that? But he'd spent most of his working life shuffling paper around. Jasmine spent most of hers on her feet serving food. A change was as good as a rest, he supposed.

'I'm allocating a couple of hours every evening for the case,' she told them.

'Don't overdo it,' said Jonny, with visions of Jasmine sitting up into the small hours and developing eye strain. 'Shout if you need any help.'

'Will do,' said Jasmine, laughing. 'It doesn't look too bad. I'll get a report done by the end of the week.'

Jonny remembered their idea of getting Ivo round to Jason's house with a van full of buckets and mops. A vacuum cleaner and a large bottle of disinfectant wouldn't be a bad idea either. 'Do you know where Ivo is today?' he asked.

'He'll be at *Shady Willows*. It's his residents' drop-in day.'

'Drop-in day?' Jonny asked, imagining Ivo sitting in his chalet dispensing wisdom.

'He gets them to list all the repairs they need on the same day. Then he can plan for the week ahead and make sure he gets the urgent stuff done first.'

'Jason,' said Katya. 'Ivo is the fourth member of our team. He's an expert at cleaning and fixing things. Would you like him to call round and do a bit of work at your house?'

Nothing like being blunt about his uselessness as a housekeeper. Jonny wondered if Jason would be too proud to accept an offer like that. Apparently not. Jason looked up and smiled at Katya. 'Great,' he said, scraping the last of the soup from his bowl.

'Another roll?' Jasmine asked, passing a basket of bread to him.

'Don't mind if I do,' said Jason, taking two.

5

I f Jasmine hadn't had a café to run, she quite fancied herself as an archivist. Much as she liked the hustle and bustle of *Jasmine's,* it was nice to work alone sometimes. No interruptions, no need to be polite to anyone and no worries about complaints. Not that she got a lot of complaints; she and her dad were far too attentive for that. But occasionally things were returned because they had too much or too little salt or the food was too hot or too cold. Inevitable, she supposed. But this evening she was all on her own. She cleared a space around the computer on her desk, pushed a couple of chairs to the edge of the room and looked with satisfaction at the space she'd created. She rubbed her hands, eager to begin.

There was so much one could learn about people from pieces of paper, from letters, bills and photographs. If one were lucky there might be diaries, invitations and postcards. Even a humble shopping list could tell a lot about a person. In this case Jasmine was going to need to keep careful records of what she discovered. This wasn't just a fun project, like the family history research she'd done in the past. It was serious work which involved the police. The idea of actually working for the police, even as a volunteer, gave her a thrill. And that reminded her of the non-disclosure agreement Lugs had emailed with a request to read it carefully, circulate copies to the rest of the team, collect their signed copies and return them all to him. She read it through slowly; no information to be passed on to anyone other than Lugs and Katya, no talking to the press and no posting on social media. She printed three copies, signed one herself and put the other two aside for Jonny and Ivo. Katya had her own contract and she had asked Jasmine to set up a simple way of recording her expenses. Not a problem for Jasmine, who already handled the café accounts and tax returns. She created an easy to use spreadsheet, ready to show Katya when they met again.

One more attachment in Lugs' email was a copy of Jason's agreement that would allow them to look at paperwork concerning his parents. Jasmine printed it out and pinned it to the wall above her desk. It gave her the right to read through anything passed on to her by Jason and to act on it as she saw fit, after discussing proposed actions with the others and filing records showing that they had all agreed to it. Ivo had sighed at the amount of paperwork involved, but she had been able to persuade him that it was safer that way. They needed to show they were legitimate and open about what they were doing. There was too much unpleasantness over so-called amateur sleuths posting things on social media, many of which amounted to conspiracy theories over particular cases, and which could make the lives of victims miserable with their false speculations.

She lifted the cardboard boxes from the table onto the floor, where there was more space, and began by sorting everything into three large box folders: one for Hugo; one for his wife, Penelope, and one for Jason. Having done that, she decided to work on Penelope's folder first. Before she started, she'd known nothing about her, barring the fact that she was married to Hugo, was the mother of Jason, and was now dead. After a couple of hours, she had built up an interesting picture of Penelope's life and could see her as a real person. She found a sheet of A3 paper, pinned it to the wall and, using a set of coloured pens, made a chart to cross-reference information that referred to all three of them. Pulling out marriage and birth certificates, she was able to draw up a timeline:

Hugo and Penelope married in January 1991 and Jason was born five months later in May. She wondered if that was significant. Not particularly interesting these days, but in 1991? She'd ask Jonny about that. He was about the same age as Hugo and would know more than she did about social attitudes to babies born to unmarried parents in the early nineties. What did surprise Jasmine was the fifteen-year age gap between Hugo and Penelope, and the fact that Penelope was only eighteen when Jason was born. It wasn't unheard of for eighteen-year-old girls to fall for men fifteen years their senior, and perhaps Hugo had been devastatingly attractive. He might have been another George Clooney for all she knew, but Jasmine couldn't help feeling that pregnant and married at eighteen had a hint of shotgun wedding about it. What had Penelope sacrificed?

She delved into the folder again and found some newspaper cuttings clipped together with a bulldog clip. Penelope had been a singer. At seventeen, in September 1990 she had won a silver rose bowl at a music festival in Guildford. There was a short account of the programme she had sung; songs by Debussy and Fauré, and a Christmas carol by John Rutter, which was possibly a favourite song since it hadn't been Christmas. There was a photograph, and congratulations from the editor that she had been awarded a place to study singing at the Royal College of Music from the following September, when she would be eighteen. *A whole year to wait and she passed the time by getting pregnant.* Presumably Jason's arrival had put paid to her studies, as there was no more news of her singing career: no graduation photo; no concert programmes or details of recordings; and no more press reviews. Jasmine looked more closely at the photo – a smiling girl with a Princess Di hairstyle wearing a Laura Ashley style dress with big sleeves and a ruffled neckline. She looked young and innocent. Prey for a man fifteen years her senior? But Jasmine knew nothing of the circumstances, and she shouldn't judge Hugo without knowing the facts. In all probability they were madly in love, Penelope only too happy to give up her career to settle down to a life of domestic bliss with a baby and the man she loved. Jasmine stared at the photo of the pretty, innocent girl and really hoped that was the case.

After that brief, arguably bittersweet glimpse into Penelope's life, Jasmine found no more about her apart from what she was able to glean from bank statements, NHS card, some receipts for household appliances and credit card statements. Penelope's credit card use was interesting. She'd signed up for it early in 2021. It had a low limit and had been used for what Jasmine considered luxury items; nothing as dull as buying petrol and groceries. Her last purchases had been from an upmarket lingerie shop, an expensive perfumery and a wine merchant, all in the city of Bath. These were dated only a week before her death. What did it say about her? That she'd been enjoying a few romantic days in the West Country? Rekindling her marriage before a tragic incident put paid to it forever. But Hugo hadn't been killed. Someone else had. She'd need to check the train schedules and routes, but could Penelope have been returning from Bath with a lover? In a train that ended both their lives in a fireball outside Swindon. But if so, why had the lover not been reported missing? And why hadn't Hugo Walsh kicked and screamed in anger and grief? Why had he disappeared? In other circumstances it could have been a revenge killing, a crime of passion. But Hugo could hardly have engineered a train crash, however much he wanted revenge.

After replacing the cuttings carefully back in the Penelope folder, Jasmine checked through Hugo's papers for bank statements. She found two. One was his business account; the other was a joint account belonging to him and Penelope, which was used for household expenses, food, council tax payments, and all the things associated with running a house. The one thing of interest was a regular standing order paid annually to a group called the Applewood Singers. Did that mean that Penelope had continued her singing? Jasmine really hoped it did. She typed *Applewood Singers* into Google and found a goldmine of useful facts. It was a small, exclusive choir for semi-professional singers and singing teachers founded by Derek Applewood in 1980; these days directed by his son, Malcolm Applewood. They rehearsed weekly in a primary school on the outskirts of

the town, but also sold recordings on Spotify and performed regularly all over the south of England. Their website had devoted a page
to Penelope following her death. Several members of the choir had
posted messages of sympathy and a recording had been made of
some of her favourite music. Even more interestingly, Jasmine found
details of a performance the choir had given in Malmesbury Abbey
two days before the train crash. She checked Google Maps and found
that Malmesbury was twenty-five miles from Bath. Further searching
told her that they had also performed in Chippenham, even closer to
Bath, three days before that.

So, thought Jasmine. *A few days away from home, ostensibly with a
respectable choir singing in concerts, but at the same time hunkering down
with sexy underwear and perfume in a cosy hotel in Bath.* Plenty to look
into there. She could talk to other choir members. It shouldn't be too
hard to find out who they were. Perhaps Penelope had a close friend
that she'd confided in. Maybe lover boy was in the choir as well. But
probably not, since he didn't get a mention on the memorial page.
Jasmine studied a photo on the website for faces she recognised.
They were local, after all, and could well have been customers at the
café. She enlarged the picture as much as she could but didn't see any
faces she knew, and no names were mentioned.

It was a pity she couldn't sing. At least not well enough to join a
choir that catered for semi-pros. Anyway, she didn't fancy the choir
uniform of ankle-length, dark red skirts and blouses the colour of
Granny Smith apples. *Santa's little helpers* came to mind and there
were limits to the lengths she was prepared to go to for the detectives.
A black velvet evening dress she might have tolerated, even enjoyed.
But apple green blouses? Definitely not.

But she knew someone who did sing. Her friend Stevie, who
volunteered with her at the food bank. The vicar's son who also
played the organ in his father's church. She was sure he could sing
well enough to at least approach the choir with a view to joining it.
He wouldn't actually have to join, of course, unless he wanted to,
which he probably didn't because his dad kept him busy with the
music in his own church. But it would give them an excuse to make

some enquiries. She could find out which evenings they rehearsed and drop in with Stevie, who would know the right kind of questions to ask. He could chat to the choirmaster or whoever ran the group, while she got to know some of the singers.

That was one idea. Her next was to track down shops in Bath and hotels that Penelope might have stayed in. Shops wouldn't be hard. She had the names from the credit card bill. They'd be upmarket places, probably in the city centre, wherever the posh shops were. She could even go and visit them herself. Bath wasn't that far. And while she was there, she could try to track down the hotels that Penelope might have stayed in. But that would be a lot harder. Other than trekking around all the hotels in Bath, she couldn't think how to do it. She checked the credit card bill again, hoping Penelope might have paid in advance, or at least paid a deposit, but there was nothing. And she might not have stayed in Bath at all. It was an attractive area for tourists and no doubt riddled with hotels. Where on earth would she start? No, the whole Bath idea was something for all of them. Jonny would know about hotels. He would have stayed in them with Belinda. Katya, too, would have experience. As a detective she must have had to ask questions in hotels. About suspicious guests, perhaps, or bodies discovered in hotel bathrooms. Ivo had probably done repair jobs in hotels and would know his way around things like back entrances and storage cellars. Katya would have some other helpful ideas – they all would. So she added it to her list of things to bring up at the next meeting. Now it was time for a mug of hot chocolate and something weepy on Netflix.

6

Ivo and Harold set off for their morning walk before getting started on the day's chores. Ivo opened the gate onto the footpath and he and Harold turned right to walk upstream. They'd done this rather than their more usual downstream route for a few days now. It was muddier and Ivo would need to hose down his wellingtons as well as Harold when they got back, but it wasn't, at least in his and Harold's experience, strewn with corpses. Finding the body had been horrifying and fascinating in equal measure, but while he was enjoying the case, looking for evidence about who Hugo Walsh was and what, if anything, he had been up to, Ivo would have preferred not to come across any more dead bodies, at least until he'd recovered from the shock of finding the first one.

They walked for fifteen minutes and then turned back to *Shady Willows* and the chores that were lined up for them. They were the usual: tidying up the site entrance, putting the bins out and sweeping the footpath that led to the river. This morning he also had a damaged door handle to fix at number sixteen, the home of Bill Sims, an eighty-nine-year-old retired mechanic, and a new washing line to put up for Mrs Jones at number three. She would want to show him the latest photos of her grandchildren sent by her daughter in

Australia and proudly displayed in an electronic photo frame. The residents were an easy-going lot, friendly and undemanding. There would be cups of tea and shared breakfasts. Sometimes Ivo wondered if they were looking after him rather than the other way around. He'd become a kind of communal grandson, and it was almost as if they were competing with each other for some grandparent of the year award.

Bill was waiting for Ivo when he arrived with his toolbox. 'Sorry to bother you, son,' he said. 'Should be able to do it myself but this arthritis is buggering up my hands.'

'No problem,' said Ivo, looking sympathetically at Jack's nobbled, bent fingers. 'It's what I'm here for.'

'I'll get the kettle on,' said Bill. 'Ready for a nice cup of tea when you're done.'

There'd be a biscuit for Harold as well. Ivo rarely needed to buy his own tea and biscuits.

Having fixed Bill's door handle and drunk his tea, and with Harold still gazing hopefully at the biscuit tin even though he'd already polished off three Hobnobs, Ivo moved on to number three, where it was a quick job to screw the washing line reel to the post thoughtfully provided by the builders. It took a bit longer to finish off the plate of bacon and scrambled egg that Mrs Jones put in front of him to eat, while a selection of grandchildren whose names Ivo tried to remember floated past in their frame on Mrs Jones' bookshelf.

HALF AN HOUR LATER, Ivo had finished tidying up the site and looked at what he'd done with satisfaction. Easy work, but a job well done and all that. He checked the time on his phone. Ten-thirty. That was good. He liked to have everything finished by mid-morning so that there was time to spend on his other clients – regular clients around the town who needed odd jobs done. He checked his list. One of his regulars, an elderly woman in Arthur Road, needed a windowpane replacing. She was a regular breaker of windows – *damn these bloody cataracts* –forever banging into the window with broom handles. But

in a way it made his work easier. He already had the measurements
so he could pop into the glass workshop and pick up what he needed.
Having the use of the van had changed his life. It belonged to the
charity who ran *Shady Willows,* and since he'd moved there last
Christmas it had made his work much easier. Before, he'd had to rely
on a friend who owned a van and that slowed him down. Good-
natured though his friend was, Ivo didn't feel he could demand van
transport whenever he needed it. That would be stretching friendship too far. Now, though, he could come and go as he pleased. A
quick trip to Slough for materials as and when he needed them did
wonders for his time management.

Ivo opened up the *Shady Willows* tool shed, another unexpected
perk of living there, a source of all manner of stuff that no one
wanted, where residents were free to leave anything they no longer
needed. One of Ivo's jobs was to clear it out every now and then and
drive its contents to the council tip. But more often than not he was
able to put the things people had abandoned to good use. That
morning he found a selection of worn-out blankets and a scruffy
duvet that would be perfect for protecting the sheet of glass in the
back of his van. And rather than risk it being broken by a few kilos of
energetic dog, Harold would be allowed to ride in the passenger seat.
A privilege he expected most days, but which was denied by Ivo, who
usually harnessed him firmly into the back of the van alongside his
toolbox. Having loaded his tools and Harold into the van and left a
sign on his door with his mobile number in case of emergencies, he
set off for the glass supplier on the Slough trading estate.

BY LATE MORNING, arriving at his client's house with the glass, he
realised that it was just around the corner from where Jason Walsh
lived. He had promised to drop in and have a chat about cleaning up
and doing some repairs. Katya would start nagging him if he didn't go
soon, so after fitting the new window glass and staying for a quick
cup of tea and a chat, he and Harold drove around the corner and
parked outside Jason's house. Parking was restricted to residents, so

Ivo put his *Handyman at Work* card on the dashboard and hoped there weren't any traffic wardens on the prowl.

Jonny was right. Jason's house was a mess. Ivo didn't think of himself as a cleaner, but somewhere under all the grime there would be repairs that needed doing, and as Katya had pointed out, cleaning and repairing would be an ideal way to get to know more about Jason. 'And you can send him your usual bill,' she had said.

'Has he got any money?' Ivo had wondered.

'Well, he inherited the house from his parents so there's no rent or mortgage to pay,' said Katya.

'And he sells some of his work,' Jonny added, having done some research into Jason Walsh and his work as an artist. 'He has a website selling personalised notebooks and greeting cards.'

And, thought Ivo, now sitting in a squalid living room while Jason was in the kitchen making him a cup of tea, *not only does he not do any housework, he also economises on clothes and personal grooming.*

Jason returned from the kitchen with two mugs, one of which he handed to Ivo. 'Forgot to buy milk,' he said. 'Sorry.'

'No problem,' said Ivo, taking a sip of his tea, which was a strange colour and had an odd taste, like burnt toast. He put the mug down without asking what kind of tea it was. 'I'll just get stuck in. What would you like me to do?'

'Dunno, really.'

Not helpful. Most people had some idea what needed doing, even if they didn't have the energy to get down to it and do it themselves. A bit of triage was required. 'Let's go through each room together and make a list of what needs doing most,' said Ivo. 'I'll just pop out to the van and get my cleaning kit.' Just as well he'd brought that. He didn't think Jason was the type to have a kitchen cupboard full of cleaning supplies. He struck Ivo as more of a grimy dishcloth sort of bloke.

'Did you park your van in the road?' Jason asked, showing more interest in Ivo's parking arrangements than his clearing up skills.

Ivo nodded.

'You'd better move it. They're buggers for parking rules round here. You could be clamped.'

Great. Just what he needed. 'Where's the nearest parking?' he asked.

'There's a car park down by the arches. Two pound fifty an hour.'

'Blimey,' said Ivo. 'I could have got a taxi for less.'

'If you go down to the end of the road,' said Jason, with the expression of someone who had just had a flash of inspiration, 'you can double back into Wise Lane and pull into the space behind my dad's workshop. He used to load up there when he was making doors and that.'

'Right,' said Ivo, fishing in his pocket for the keys to the van and wishing he'd been told about that sooner. 'I'll move it now.'

'I'll let you in the back way,' said Jason. 'Just hammer on the gate when you get there. It's got the house number painted on it.'

Ivo left his tools in the house but took Harold with him, unsure of what he might pick up in the way of rotting food if left on his own in the kitchen. He didn't want Harold throwing up in the back of the van on the way home.

As Ivo was unlocking the van, thankfully unclamped, a woman came out of the house two doors down. She reminded Ivo of a cheerful little brightly coloured bird. Late twenties, Ivo guessed, and kind of arty-looking with untidy curly hair that was doing its best to escape from a blue and white spotted headband. She kicked a flowerpot in front of the door to stop it closing behind her and approached Ivo with a beaming grin. She was a nice change from the morose Jason. 'You here to do some work on the house?' she asked.

Ivo smiled back at her. 'Just a few handyman-type jobs for Jason,' he told her, waving a bucket and mop in her direction.

'You interested in doing a few jobs for me as well? I've got a wardrobe door that sticks, and my washing line thingy is coming unscrewed from the wall.'

That would be the second washing line malfunction today, probably because it was warm and sunny for the first time this year and spring cleaning was in the air, bedspreads and curtains hanging out to dry in a brisk wind, blowing away winter cobwebs. 'Okay,' said Ivo. 'I'll be done here in a couple of hours. I'll pop in, shall I?'

'That would be great,' she said. 'I'm Poppy Cookson.' She held out her hand and Ivo shook it. 'The sun comes out and everything starts to look shabby. I'm afraid the place is beginning to feel its age. It would be really great if you could come and help me. Are you expensive?'

'I don't think so,' said Ivo, handing her one of his flyers. With any luck, Poppy's house would be less rancid than Jason's. He might get a decent cup of tea and he could pick up all the gossip about Hugo and Penelope Walsh. He guessed he was likely to learn a lot more about them from Poppy, who would hopefully be the kind of neighbour who knew everything that ever went on in the street.

Poppy read the leaflet. 'Great,' she said. 'You must be very busy, but if you could spare me an hour or two now and then...'

'Let's say an hour today. I'll do those two jobs for you, and you can call me if you think of anything else.'

'Sounds good. I'll be sure to have the kettle on in a couple of hours. Tea and biscuits for you and your dog?'

'Give Harold a biscuit and he'll be your friend for life,' said Ivo, grinning.

IVO RETURNED to the gloom of Jason's house, and after two hours he'd cleared the blocked sink, scraped and washed the kitchen floor, mended a broken window catch and cleared a clogged gas jet on the cooker. He'd also learnt that before the train crash Jason had not seen either of his parents for over a year and that as a family they didn't communicate a lot. Jason's father, he gathered, was something of a philanderer. 'Didn't just fix their doors, know what I mean?' had been Jason's exact words. And Jason's mother was, in his words, a sullen cow whose moods swung from near-catatonic idleness to over-excited exuberance at the drop of a hat. In other words, it was not a marriage made in heaven.

Ivo packed up his tools and left with a determination to stay single for ever. He moved the van down to the back of Poppy's house, parked in a small space by the garage and knocked on her kitchen door.

'Come in,' she said as she opened it. 'I've got the kettle on.'

'Okay if I bring Harold in?'

'Of course. As long as he doesn't mind cats.' She led him into a refreshingly clean and bright kitchen and told him to make himself comfortable. 'Do tell me all the goss from the house of horrors,' she said.

House of horrors? Squalid as the Walsh house might have been, it was hardly a Fred West situation. At least Ivo very much hoped it wasn't. 'Why do you call it that?' he asked.

'It's all a bit gruesome, isn't it? Poor Penny getting burnt to a cinder. But even before that it wasn't a happy place.'

Had she just asked him there to gossip? That could work both ways. And she probably had a lot more to gossip about than he had. 'Did you know them well?' he asked. *An innocent question,* he thought, *but it could lead to a torrent of useful information.*

'Penny used to drop in occasionally for a cup of tea and a chat.' The kettle boiled and Poppy reached up to a shelf for some mugs. 'Will Harold have tea?' she asked. 'He can use that bowl.' She pointed to a shallow earthenware potholder.

'Just water, thanks,' said Ivo.

Poppy filled the bowl and put it down on the floor. Then she took two teabags out of a tin with a picture of a porcelain tea service and the words *English Tea* painted in curly gold script. She put them into the mugs, which Ivo noticed were blue with white spots and matched Poppy's hairband. She poured in the boiling water, handed one to Ivo and pushed a jug of milk in his direction. Harold gave her a *didn't you mention biscuits* kind of look.

'Penny was okay,' said Poppy. 'A bit intense, if you know what I mean. Artistic temperament, I suppose.'

'You look quite artistic yourself,' said Ivo.

'Me? No. I'm more of a craft type,' said Poppy. 'Quilting,' she added, leaving Ivo not much the wiser.

'What about Mr Walsh?' Ivo asked.

Poppy opened a packet of ginger biscuits and gave one to Harold. Then she frowned. 'Hugo? Can't say I warmed to him,' she said. 'He tried to persuade me to replace all my doors. He was probably a very good workman, but I found him a bit creepy.'

Ivo looked at the two kitchen doors. Antique pine. Original features of the house, probably. 'Your doors don't need replacing,' he said. 'Not those, anyway.'

'None of them do. I don't think it was work he was after.'

'Do you live here alone?' Ivo asked, suddenly concerned for her safety.

'I own the house with my brother. He works as cabin crew for BA. Long haul, so he's away quite a lot. But don't worry. I wasn't afraid of Hugo. I can handle his type.'

She probably could. She was small, Ivo thought, but feisty.

'You should meet my brother next time he's home,' she said. 'I think you'd like each other.'

Ivo couldn't imagine why they should. Was Poppy one of those *I can see into your soul* types? 'What about Jason Walsh?' he asked, hoping to get her back on topic.

'I never saw much of him. We've only lived here for five years, and I gather Jason left home once he'd finished school. And even now he's back, he's not one for chatting to the neighbours.'

'He told me he was an artist, although I didn't see much evidence of it while I was there.'

'Watercolours,' said Poppy, with an expression that suggested watercolour painters weren't actually proper artists. 'Commercial stuff, pretty notebooks and bookmarks.'

'More of a craft then,' he said, grinning.

'Okay, fair enough. But quilting is way more complex than paintings of pretty flowers.'

The cat flap clattered, and a black and white cat strolled in. Harold eyed it nervously, edging a bit closer to Ivo. He had an unfortunate history with cats, losing half an ear in an argument with one a few years back. The cat walked around him with its tail in the air in a proprietorial way, then settled down on a cushion next to a radiator. A quilted cushion, Ivo noticed, but didn't comment. He drained his mug and carried it to the sink. 'Better get to work,' he said. 'I can't sit around drinking tea all day, although I don't charge for it. Show me what needs doing.'

Poppy led him upstairs into what Ivo assumed was the brother's room. A plain room with a few pieces of antique furniture and navy-blue curtains tied back with gold tassels. Stylish, but not Poppy some-how. He imagined her room, like the rest of the house, would be a riot of brightly coloured flowers and cushions with embroidered – or more probably quilted – covers.

Ivo adjusted the hinges on the wardrobe door and oiled them. It now opened and closed easily and without squeaking. Then he went back downstairs followed by Harold, whose claws clicked on the wood floors. The washing line only needed a couple of screws to secure it back onto the wall. 'All done,' he said, packing up his toolbox.

'How much do I owe you?' she asked.

'Fifteen pounds,' he said. 'Give me your phone number and I'll shoot you an invoice. You can pay online.'

'That's very reasonable,' she said, accepting his text and making an immediate payment with her banking app. 'I'll be calling you again,' she said. 'There's always something that needs fixing. I'll let you know when Brian's around?'

'Brian?'

'My brother.'

'Oh, yeah, right.'

That was fine by him. He'd found a useful source of gossip about the Walsh family, and he was sure there was more to discover. He might even enjoy meeting the brother, although his experience of socialising with airline staff was non-existent. Perhaps Jasmine would know all about them. Give him a heads up on what they liked to chat about.

He headed out to his van with a relieved Harold staying close to his side, keeping a wary eye out for the cat. Harold hopped into the back of the van and settled himself on the duvet Ivo had used to protect the glass. Ivo patted him fondly on the head. 'Don't get too comfortable, mate,' he said. 'We're only five minutes from home.' He secured the dog's harness then climbed into the driving seat and headed back to *Shady Willows*. It was warm enough to sit out on his patio with a glass of homemade lemonade, given to him by one of the residents. He'd make notes on everything he'd been told today. Perhaps he should buy a red moleskin notebook like the one Jonny used. He'd think about that next time he was in town.

7

'Thanks a bundle,' said Jonny, drying his hands and draping damp tea towels over a radiator. He took the box from Jasmine and rested it on the kitchen table while he put his coat on. It was a heavy, concertina-shaped file packed full of papers. All the stuff from Jason's house that he'd given them permission to look at and hopefully work out where his father had spent the eighteen months before his death. His second death, that was.

'You don't mind, do you?' asked Jasmine. 'I've sorted everything out so all the stuff in there is relevant to Hugo Walsh.' She handed him a sheet of paper with dates and coloured lines linking a collection of squares with names on them. 'This is a timeline I made. I'll share it online, but I found it was good to have a printed copy to pin up while I made notes. You can add anything interesting that you find while I set up a shared document link.'

'You've been busy,' said Jonny, admiring her handiwork. Not just a computer geek; she was artistic as well. He'd make a copy of it. One he could draw lines on without the risk of ruining what Jasmine had done.

'I've been concentrating on Penelope Walsh,' she said. 'I found out a lot about her but there are still a few things I want to follow up, so I thought it would be good if you did Hugo.'

Jonny had finished a stint of lunchtime washing up. Jasmine obviously expected him to take all this stuff home with him and work there. That made sense. He couldn't clutter up the Javadi kitchen or take up a table in the café. Home would be quiet and there was plenty of space. *Too quiet,* he thought, *and too much space.* He'd rather be here, where there was a buzz of activity. The days seemed to have got longer since he didn't have to walk Harold any more. But Belinda was out for the rest of the day on council business, and he could spend all afternoon going through the file Jasmine had just given him. He should be glad of the chance to work uninterrupted. Perhaps he'd discover something really useful and exciting about Hugo Walsh. Who said that being a detective meant always being surrounded by people? Really, he had the best of both worlds.

'I've made you a salmon and salad sandwich,' said Jasmine, placing a brown paper bag on top on the file.

He could easily have grabbed something in the café. Was she trying to get rid of him? He had been spending a lot of time there recently, and now he was being sent on his way with enough to keep him busy for the rest of the day.

'Not that we don't love having you here,' said Jasmine. 'Particularly when you do the washing up. The sandwich is just a small thank you for all your help. You can eat it in peace once you are home.'

'Thanks,' he said, hoping she didn't think he was too old to be volunteering as a washer of dishes. 'I'll be getting home then.'

'See you tomorrow?'

'Sure,' he said huffily. 'If I'm not in the way.'

Jasmine looked gratifyingly horrified. 'Don't be silly,' she said. 'We love you being here.'

'But you'd rather I worked on this at home?'

'It's just that it gets crowded in here. And it's not very private.'

'She's right,' said Karim, who had just come into the kitchen ready to roll out the dough that had been proving for the last couple of hours. 'You can't have people peering over your shoulder, not when you've all signed that non-disclosure thing.'

'We need an office,' said Jasmine. 'A crime scene room where we can spread everything out and have whiteboards with photos pinned to them like they do on the telly.' She left with a plate of muffins ready to fill the shelves behind the counter for the afternoon tea crowd.

Karim winked at Jonny. 'I've got an idea,' he said, putting a finger to his lips. 'I'll call you. Not a word to Jasmine yet.'

As Jonny walked home, he started thinking about whether or not he should get a dog of his own. He'd put on a pound or two since Harold had returned to live with Ivo. The company would be good too. And Belinda would probably like the idea because if she was elected mayor next year she'd be out even more. Mrs Gage, their cleaner, would like it as well. She'd fallen for Harold in a big way and was always asking when he was going to come and visit again.

Arriving home, he let himself in and put the file down on the hall table. The house felt empty and too large. Did he and Belinda really need all this space? But looking around, he decided they did. Belinda and Jonny both had studies, people came to stay – Belinda's cousins, and their grandson, Justin. In fact, Justin was coming more often, with Marcus and his wife travelling a lot now they were involved with international recycling schemes. They were always jetting off to some conference or other. It was great when Justin came to stay, and Jonny took over things like school runs and kicking a football around the garden. Ten-year-old boys needed space. Justin was not a restful child and always turned up with footballs and tennis rackets, multiple pairs of shoes and electronic gadgets. He needed a room of his own. Not just a spare bedroom but somewhere that felt like home. And Jonny had promised Justin that he'd look into setting up a model railway in the attic. Besides, he and Belinda had accumulated *stuff* of their own over nearly forty years of marriage, and what they'd do with it all if they moved somewhere smaller, he had no idea. No, downsizing didn't appeal in the slightest. They'd lived here since Marcus was tiny and it was better just to let things stay as they were. They liked living here and they could afford it. There was no reason to cram themselves into a house half the size, where they'd probably be at each other's throats within days.

He went into the kitchen and made himself a cup of tea, then carried the file along with Jasmine's sandwich into his study, where he spread everything out on the floor and wondered how to deal with it. He stared at it while he took a bite of his sandwich, which was delicious. Only the very best ingredients for the Javadis. No surprise that they were so popular among the lunch crowd.

Bank statements, he decided, as he brushed the last of the crumbs from his lap. An overview of what Hugo Walsh spent his money on might tell him what he had been doing the few days before the train crash and his disappearance. He sifted out anything that looked like a bank statement and discovered that Hugo had used a couple of credit cards, one in his name only and one that he shared with Penelope. There was also a joint bank account and one he used for his business. All were now closed, of course, so what had Hugo been living on since his supposed death? He recalled what Katya had told him about the credit card that had been found in Hugo's pocket. An account that had been dormant for months, so unlikely to give them much information even if they could access the records, and Jonny assumed that only the police would be able to do that.

Hugo must have known that everyone thought he had died in the crash. Had he taken advantage of that to go to ground? Or had he left home before the crash in his own bid to disappear for some other reason? None of the statements gave Jonny any helpful information about that. But what had he expected? What would Jonny do in the unlikely event that *he* wanted to disappear? Go abroad, he supposed. Hugo had his passport with him when he was fished out of the river. Perhaps that meant he had just arrived back from somewhere. He searched the bank statements for evidence of plane tickets or ferry crossings but found nothing. There were no hotel invoices or receipts for hire cars. Nothing but ordinary, everyday expenses which all came to a halt just before the date of the crash. After that, of course, it was official. Once a death certificate had been issued everything would have been closed down.

Jonny looked into the file again, pulling out the concertina pleats to see if he'd missed anything, and there, wedged into one of the compartments, he found a blue building society savings book with a zero balance. Tucked into the book was a letter from the building society confirming that the account was now closed, the interest updated and the resulting balance of twenty-three pounds and sixty-four pence waiting to be transferred once they had his new details. Assuming interest was paid monthly, and bearing in mind that interest rates had been extremely low recently, there must have been a significant amount in the account the previous month. He flicked back through the book and discovered that Hugo had withdrawn fifty-five thousand pounds the week before the train crash. Why had no one noticed? Did Jason not wonder about it? After all, if Hugo hadn't made the withdrawal, he'd now be fifty thousand pounds better off. But perhaps Jason hadn't found the book and didn't know about the money.

Jonny wondered what had happened to the card and passport that were found on the body. He searched the file again but couldn't find them, so he supposed they'd not been handed on to Jason yet. But Lugs had told them the account hadn't been used, so it wasn't likely to tell them very much about the way Hugo lived his life. That was a pity. A bank statement could have told them a lot about his final actions. So what about the passport? He'd have a word with Katya. Since Lugs had contracted her as a civilian investigator, she could probably ask to see a copy of it. If Walsh had travelled abroad in the last eighteen months, there might be a record of where he'd been. Some countries still stamped passports, didn't they?

All of that would have to wait until his next meeting with Katya. For now, he would have to make do with what Jasmine had passed on to him. He found unopened correspondence to do with Walsh's business; a reminder from HMRC about his self-assessment tax return and then a letter dated a few months later, the DVLA reminding him to renew his road tax. *Interesting,* Jonny thought. No one had mentioned a car. He looked at the letter again and noticed that Walsh was required to pay the rate for a light goods vehicle. It also gave the registration number, which meant Jonny could trace its current ownership.

Jonny was beginning to build up a picture of what could have happened and was becoming convinced that Walsh's departure had been planned in advance of the train crash. He would have known about his wife's concert tour and used it as cover for his own disappearance. Why he wanted to disappear, Jonny had yet to discover. For now, he assumed Walsh had done something he shouldn't have, or upset someone hell bent on revenge, and he needed to get away. Or perhaps he just couldn't stand the sight of Penelope a moment longer. He withdrew fifty-five thousand pounds from his building society account, presumably something he'd kept from his wife, opened a new bank account that he never got around to using, bought a cheap pay-as-you-go phone, sold or exchanged his van and strode off into the sunset. Would he have seen the news of the train crash? *Almost certainly,* Jonny thought. It was hard to avoid for days afterwards. He could have read about his own death and used it to his advantage. That made Jonny think that he'd probably not gone abroad, certainly not after news of his death was spread across the front pages of all the newspapers. He'd have been recognised at departure points or from passenger manifests. He could have gone before the train crash and slipped out of the country unnoticed, and that would make him far harder to trace now. But it would also have made it harder for him to return. Until he discovered something that suggested otherwise, Jonny would assume that he'd hunkered down somewhere in the UK. But just how he would discover where that was, he had no idea.

The *not able to stand Penelope* theory was becoming less likely. If that was Walsh's only reason for leaving, it had all worked out rather conveniently. He could merely have come home, announced that he hadn't been on the train and carried on a blameless and now single life with the added advantage of all the sympathy he would receive for having lost his faithless wife.

Jonny replaced everything in the folder and made himself a cup of coffee. He sat in the kitchen, trying to think himself into Walsh's head. Where would he go to hide? An off-grid community on Bodmin Moor came to mind, but that option had already been taken by his son. It might, however, have given Hugo an idea. Jonny found a map of the UK and checked out areas that were as far as possible from both Windsor and Bodmin Moor. Fifty-five thousand wouldn't last forever. He would need to earn money. Hugo was a carpenter. A useful skill and one that lent itself to cash-in-hand employment. Would he go for somewhere urban or rural? Or a bit of both? A peripatetic existence, constantly on the move and not staying anywhere long enough to be recognised.

There was plenty to work on and he'd make a start trying to trace Hugo's van. He found the DVLA letter and tapped the registration number into a site that promised, for a small fee, to give him the entire history of the vehicle. It made for interesting reading. Hugo's van had passed from his ownership to that of a Dan Smith in Milton Keynes and almost immediately after that to Jessie Simpson in Aylesbury. Jessie was still the registered owner and Jonny searched for her online. He'd half expected someone who bought a small second-hand van to be another Mrs Gage. A person who drove around with a van full of mops and buckets and cleaned people's houses. Not quite right, but not far off. Jessie was a travelling hairdresser, with a website that gave her contact details alongside photographs of elderly ladies with immaculately coiffed hair. Not people Jonny had experience of, but he supposed it made sense. There must be plenty of potentially housebound clients in need of haircuts. But Jessie was unlikely to know much about Hugo Walsh, so he searched instead for Dan Smith of Milton Keynes and found very little. He was beginning to think he'd have to call on Jessie and ask what she knew about the man she'd bought her van from, when a few pages in he came across a link to a Facebook page called *Never buy a car from these people*. He discovered that Dan Smith of Milton Keynes had been tagged by a disappointed car buyer, who called him a *right pain in the arse* for selling him a car with a faulty cambelt that had caused him to break down while driving his mother to a funeral and had cost him the price of a new engine.

So Dan Smith had sold at least two vehicles in the recent past, at least one of which was not in top notch condition, which led Jonny to think he could be a dodgy cash-in-hand type of second hand car salesman. And the only way of making contact with him would be to get in touch with Jessie and ask for his details. Which Jonny did right away.

Jessie's phone number was on her website, and she answered quickly so she presumably wasn't tending to a client with their head in a sink, or with half their hair in curlers. She was very chatty and happy to talk to Jonny even when he confessed that it was her van he was interested in, rather than her hairdressing skills. She told Jonny she'd met Dan Smith when out with her husband Andy at a pub called the Silver Horse, where he was playing in a darts match. 'It's a nice village pub near Wendover,' Jessie told him. 'My hubby had met Dan before at another darts match, I can't remember where that was. I'd just left *Curlers and Clippers*. Didn't get on with the manager and didn't like biking there. One of the others had her bike stolen while she was working.'

Curlers and Clippers, Jonny supposed, was the name of the salon where Jessie had been working. 'How did the topic of a van come up?' he asked.

'Well, I was saying perhaps it was time to set up on my own, but I could hardly do that on my bike, could I?'

'I suppose not,' said Jonny.

'Anyway, this Dan Smith said he had a nice little van he could sell me. Bought it off a bloke just a couple of weeks ago, he said. Hadn't got around to advertising it yet.'

'Did he say anything about this bloke? Why he wanted to sell the van?'

'I didn't ask, but he said we could have it at a knockdown price if we paid him in cash the next day. My hubby said we'd better grab it while we could and get me making money again. He'd been a bit miffed when I chucked in my job. But he reckoned I'd make much more doing cash-in-hand jobs going to clients' homes, so buying a van would pay for itself in no time.'

'Was he right about that?'

'Oh, yeah. I've never looked back. I'm taking bookings weeks ahead. Got a nice little earner at the Autumn Leaves assisted living village. There are some lovely old ladies there. They really look after me. I get a special parking slot and all the tea I can drink. They tip generously as well.'

'And the van was okay? You've not had any trouble with it?'

'It was fine. My hubby knew another bloke who resprayed it for us. It had some carpenter's logo on the side. Now it's a nice pale pink with *CURLS TO YOU* painted in those old-fashioned letters.'

Jonny could imagine Jessie, plump and curly-haired probably, in a pink apron ministering to a succession of elderly ladies, men too, perhaps, chatting over cups of coffee and plied with home-made biscuits. 'Did this Dan Smith deliver the van when you bought it?'

'No, we had to go to his house to pick it up. Well, I say house. It was more of a shack on a piece of derelict land. He said he'd buy any car and do it up to resell. But this van was already in good nick so he just wanted to move it on as soon as he could. And it had nine months MOT left so he didn't need to spend any money on it. The carpenter bloke needed to sell it quickly, Dan said, so he got it for a good price.'

'That's really helpful,' said Jonny. 'Can you give me Dan Smith's address?'

'Not sure I can remember the exact address,' she said. 'But it was off the road that goes from Milton Keynes to Bletchley, backed onto a railway line. But I can ask my hubby when he gets in and call you back.'

The road to Bletchley and near a railway line was probably enough for now. 'I wouldn't want to be any trouble,' said Jonny. 'How about I call you back if I need to?'

'Okey-dokey,' said Jessie. 'Hope you find the car you want.'

That was an idea. Could he visit Dan Smith on the pretext of looking for a second-hand car? Another thing to discuss with Katya.

Perhaps they could go together. He was sure Katya would be better at dealing with shady car salesmen than he was.

He yawned and stretched his arms to ease the stiffness in his shoulders, caused by leaning over pieces of paper all afternoon. This was the time of day when he really missed Harold. He'd enjoyed a brisk walk before his evening meal. Nothing to stop him going for a walk by himself, was there? He'd done it often enough before Harold. But it wouldn't be the same now. Not after having had the company of a dog. There would be something missing. He'd take a brisk walk around the block and then search the kitchen for ingredients with which to make one of Belinda's favourite meals that he would serve with a bottle of good wine. Suitably mellowed by good food and expensive wine, he would drop the matter of a dog into the conversation.

8

'I've found a way to help you,' said Stevie, looking pleased with himself.

Jasmine stacked the last cans of baked beans onto the shelf. It was great that people donated stuff to the food bank when doing their weekly shop, but why did everyone go for baked beans? Nothing wrong with beans on toast, of course, but surely people deserved a bit of variety. Her next project, she decided, was going to be some way of teaming up with the supermarkets and keeping a suggestions board at the entrance with a list of food ideas. At the moment there was a list at the checkout and boxes for donations. But what was the use of that? What was needed was a list of the food that people wanted at the entrance, not the exit. No one was going pay for their stuff, get to the donation drop-off, read the list that said, for example, tinned beef stew, and think, *Oh, right, I'll go and put my baked beans back on the shelf and get beef stew instead.*

She frowned at Stevie. She'd been annoyed with him and here he was, offering help when she really didn't need it. She arranged the cans in an artistic pyramid, snapped the green plastic crate they'd arrived in flat and stacked it onto the pile that was waiting for the volunteer who did the supermarket pickups. 'I don't need help now,' she said crossly. 'I'm nearly done.'

'No need to be so grumpy,' said Stevie, pulling up a chair and sitting astride it with his arms on the backrest. 'And it's not about you stacking shelves. I can see you're nearly done with that.'

'So what is it?' she asked. 'I need to get back and work on food orders for next week.'

'I've been thinking about our conversation the other day.'

'The one where you refused to do what I asked?'

'That's the one.'

'You've changed your mind?'

'No, but I might have found another way to help. That is, if you stop growling at me.'

Growling? Okay, he was right. She had been grumpy recently and she was sorry she'd snapped at him just now. But after their conversation the other day she had a right to be bad-tempered. It hadn't gone well, possibly her fault for jumping in and assuming Stevie would do whatever she asked. But he had been infuriatingly unhelpful and barely heard her out.

'Absolutely not,' Stevie had said, when she'd suggested going to have a chat with Malcolm Applewood about Stevie joining his choir and dropping in a few questions about Penelope Walsh. 'I don't want to join a choir and I've never heard of Penelope whatshername.'

Jasmine had sighed. There were times when Stevie was a disappointment. 'You don't have to actually join,' she said. 'Just show an interest and ask how they recruit singers.'

'That would be dishonest, wouldn't it?'

'Not at all. We're only going to ask how they find new members.'

'He might think I want to poach them for my own choir.'

'Your choir is just a few people who turn up to sing at weddings for a miserly fiver a go. It's half a dozen school kids and two old men who have wobbly voices and get out of breath before the end of each verse.'

'All the more reason why I might want to poach his singers.'

'Talk to him about that, then. Ask if he knows anyone who would volunteer to come in and boost your lot. There's nothing to stop people singing in two choirs, is there?'

'They're local. They'd already know I need more singers. Why do you need to know about them, anyway?'

'Because I want to find out more about someone who used to be in the choir.'

'Can't you just ask her yourself?'

'She's dead,' said Jasmine. 'Killed in a train accident.'

Stevie sighed. 'I suppose you've got yourself mixed up with those detective people again.'

'What if I have?' Was he jealous? No reason why he should be. They were just friends, and she was always here in the food bank when she was needed.

'I dunno,' he said. 'Isn't it better to leave that sort of stuff to the police?'

'We're helping the police.'

'So why do you need me?'

Exactly how exasperating could he get? 'Because you're interested in church music and choirs.'

'Yes, because I've got my own choir to run.'

For goodness' sake, she thought. *We're going round in circles.* 'Then you could ask for advice about that.'

'What kind of advice?'

'I don't know. How to make recordings and sell them, how to find different concert venues, anything.'

'Why can't you do that on your own?'

'Because I don't know enough about that sort of music.' Why was he being so difficult about it? She wasn't asking for much, just an hour or so of his time. But he obviously wasn't going to help her. Perhaps she should just take Ivo instead. Although he probably knew as little about choir music and singers as she did. Possibly even less.

'Why do you want to talk to this Malcolm Applewood, anyway? Can't you just go online and google it?'

'I've already done that, but I need to know more about Penelope Walsh and the concerts they did in Malmesbury and Chippenham.'

'So just phone and ask him.'

No, she needed to actually socialise with the choir. Just asking for information wouldn't be enough. She needed the gossip. Perhaps Stevie wasn't the right person to ask. He wasn't much of a gossiper, and would probably just be sidetracked into a discussion about acoustics and church organs. She'd have to find another way.

BUT HERE HE was now saying he'd found a way to help her. 'Okay,' she said. 'What do you have in mind?'

'It's about those choir people you wanted to go and meet,' he said.

She hoped he wasn't about to suggest using social media. She'd already tried that and drawn a blank. 'Okay,' she said. 'But I've already done a lot of Internet searching and haven't found anything useful. Nothing about individual members.'

'Well, it just so happens that I might have come across just the person you are looking for.'

'Really?' she said. He probably hadn't, but she'd humour him. He was doing his best, after all.

'Yes. This woman came into the church yesterday while I was clearing up after choir practice. She has a musical daughter, Gracie, who is grade eight piano apparently. She's started taking organ lessons as a junior at the Royal College of Music and needs somewhere to practise between lessons. Her mother asked me if she could use the organ in the church. She's going to bring Gracie for her first session tomorrow evening.'

'Good for her,' said Jasmine. 'But how does that help me?'

'Oh, I forgot to say, she's a member of the Applewood Singers. The mother, that is, not the daughter.'

'Brilliant,' said Jasmine, grinning at him. 'I could hug you.'

'Just a thank you will do,' he said. 'We don't have a hugging kind of friendship.'

Jasmine nudged him in the ribs. 'Saving yourself for the right woman?'

'Something like that.'

'You're blushing,' said Jasmine.

'No, I'm not.'

THE CAFÉ CLOSED at six and on less busy days Jasmine and her father had usually finished clearing up by seven, so if she walked fast, she could get to the church by seven-fifteen. The girl, Gracie, would be there practising from seven until eight and her mother, according to Stevie, would be there as well. Gracie was only thirteen, too young to be left on her own, so her mother would stay there with her. Probably, Jasmine hoped, only too pleased to chat to her. Listening to a teenager practising probably wasn't the most exciting way to pass an hour. The closest Jasmine had come to anything like that was when she went to a ballet class and her own mum sat with the other parents, half watching and half gossiping.

Jasmine could hear the organ playing when she crept into the back of the church. She wasn't a regular churchgoer herself, but she had occasionally been to services with her mother when she was alive. She was used to Stevie playing hymns, too, which she could hear from the food bank when she was helping out on Sunday mornings when the café opened late. The organ was tucked away to the side so she couldn't see who was playing it, but whoever it was, they were extremely good. The music was fast and very loud. That must be a change for the wheezy old instrument that for most of the time dragged reluctant congregations through hymns, with the occasional wedding march to liven things up a bit. The only other person in the church was a woman sitting in one of the side aisles, reading. Gracie's mum, Jasmine assumed. She tiptoed down the aisle and slipped into the pew in front of her. Sitting right next to her didn't seem quite right, a bit over-familiar. It felt strange, just the three of them in such a large space. Particularly when one of them was so engrossed in the music.

The woman looked up from her book and smiled at Jasmine.

'Sorry to interrupt your reading,' Jasmine said.

'That's fine,' said the woman. 'It's quite nice to have someone to talk to.'

'She's very good, your daughter,' said Jasmine. 'You are her mum, aren't you?'

'Yes, I'm Gracie's mum. Juliet,' she said.

'I'm Jasmine.'

'I guessed you might be.' She closed her book, saving her place with a leather bookmark. 'Stevie told me you wanted to talk to me about the Applewood Singers.'

'It's about someone who used to sing with them. But I don't want to disturb Gracie's practice.'

'You won't,' said Juliet. 'Nothing disturbs Gracie when she's playing. What do you want to know?'

'I wondered what you could tell me about Penelope Walsh. Did you know her?'

'Poor Penelope. Yes, I knew her, not well though. She was quite a private person. Why are you interested in her?'

'I'm doing some research for Jason, her son, about the weeks before the train crash.' *Did that sound reasonable?* Jasmine wondered. She expected to be asked why she was interested, but she knew the police were anxious not to reveal too much about the body in the river in case it caused a social media frenzy. There'd been calls for a public inquiry into the train crash, which was now scheduled to begin in a few weeks. It was likely that relatives of the victims would still be trying to find out what had happened.

'You're not a journalist, are you? Malcolm wouldn't want any kind of scandal about the choir in the papers.'

Why would there be? 'No,' Jasmine assured her. 'I'm working as a civilian investigator. With the police,' she added, in case investigator sounded as dodgy as journalist. But why had Juliet reacted that way? Was there a scandal that the Applewood Singers were already aware of? Were there things they wanted to keep quiet about? Particularly things about Penelope Walsh.

'It was tragic, of course,' said Juliet. 'We all miss Penelope's singing. But we are a respectable group.'

'Was Penelope not respectable?' Jasmine asked, having already come to the conclusion that she might not be.

'I don't want to speak ill of the dead,' said Juliet.

Which to Jasmine meant she was about to do just that.

'And I don't like to gossip.'

Jasmine sensed an enormous BUT...

'But I know Malcolm was concerned about what she was doing to our reputation. I'm afraid if she hadn't been killed in that crash, he would have asked her to leave.'

Either this Malcolm was unusually old-fashioned and strait-laced in his views, or Penelope had been up to something incredibly bad. 'Was she involved with someone in the choir?'

Juliet looked shocked. 'Oh no, Malcolm would never have put up with anything like that. This was more a suspicion that she was using choir trips as a cover for... well, staying overnight with a man who was not her husband.'

Jasmine found it hard to subdue a giggle. This sounded like Brief Encounter. Not that she approved of cheating couples, but things had moved on since the nineteen-fifties and whatever Penelope had been up to hardly affected the quality of her singing. 'Do you who know he was?' she asked.

'No,' said Juliet. 'All I know is that while the rest of us travelled to the Malmesbury and Chippenham concerts by coach and returned to Windsor every night, Penelope told us she was staying overnight in a hotel. She said coaches made her nauseous.'

'I don't suppose she told you the name of the hotel? And if she was staying there on her own?'

'I don't know where the hotel was, but I wouldn't imagine she was there on her own. Penelope was the nervous type. She didn't even go home from rehearsals on her own. Her husband always came to pick her up.'

But was it her husband who picked her up or someone else? 'Did you meet Hugo Walsh?'

'No, he waited for her outside.'

'So it might have been someone else?'

'I assumed she was telling the truth, but that's not what Malcolm thought. He was suspicious about it.'

Why should Malcolm have been suspicious? Why hadn't he taken Penelope's word for it? Or perhaps he knew it wasn't Hugo because he knew who it really was. That kind of made sense. It wasn't the reputation of the choir that worried him. It was the fact that a friend of his was becoming too involved with one of the singers in his choir. A close friend, she supposed, perhaps even a brother or a cousin.

The organ piece had finished, and they were joined by a studious-looking girl clutching some sheet music. 'Well done, darling,' said Juliet, taking the music from her daughter and wrapping her into a coat as if she were a five-year-old. 'We'd better be getting you home.' She turned towards Jasmine. 'Nice to meet you,' she said. 'I hope I've told you what you needed to know.'

'Yes, thanks, you've given me a lot to think about.' She watched as they left the church, imagining them going home for a nursery-style supper, bath and story. Thirteen? Gracie seemed much, much younger. Jasmine found herself hoping she was about to morph into an unpleasantly rebellious teenager. No, she told herself. Juliet had given her some useful information. It was none of Jasmine's business if she was an overprotective, pushy mother.

9

It felt strange to be back for the first time since she'd retired, but looking around the office, Katya didn't think anything much had changed. The same smell of over-brewed coffee hung in the air. The desks and chairs still looked worn and battered, but there seemed to be more room now, and more light. She remembered the struggle they'd had trying to fit in a third desk when she first joined the team, but now there were three desks in the room and space to walk around them. And then she realised. The filing cabinets had gone. Everything digitised now, she supposed. They had been tall cabinets, she recalled. One of them blocking the light from half the window. And now on the windowsill there was a collection of plants with glossy green leaves and a well-cared-for look. In her day, all they had was a dusty spider plant which survived, just, on neglect.

A young woman appeared with a pot of tea, two mugs and a packet of biscuits. 'You must be DS Roscoff,' she said.

'That's me,' said Katya, wondering if she was still entitled to call herself a detective sergeant. But one of her neighbours was a retired army major and generally known as *the major,* so she supposed it was fine for her to do the same.

'Flora asked me to bring this and apologise. She and DI Lomax are in a meeting with the super which has overrun.' She poured some tea into a mug and put it down on the desk in front of Katya. Then she opened the packet of biscuits, put some on a plate and passed it across the desk.

Chocolate Hobnobs, Katya noticed appreciatively. 'Thanks, love,' she said, picking one up and taking a bite. 'Are you one of the team?' she asked.

'I'm Callie. Just an admin. But they asked me to log you on and open the file of photos for you to look through.'

'The ones of the river where the body was found?' Lugs had told her he had something interesting to show her.

Callie signed Katya in as a guest on the system and opened one of the folders. Then she handed Katya the mouse. 'I'll leave you to it,' she said. 'The DI won't be long.'

Katya clicked on the first picture. She'd not had a good view of the body when she was at the river, so this was the first time she'd seen Hugo Walsh in close-up. She'd yet to read the pathologist's report, but the medical examiner who had been at the scene thought Hugo had been dead for around five to six hours when he was found. This was based on the fact that he still smelt strongly of alcohol when Ivo and Harold discovered him, six hours after the pubs closed. No bottles were found at the scene, so it was assumed that Hugo had been drinking in a pub rather than buying a bottle of something and swigging it as he walked.

Considering he'd spent all those hours in the water, Hugo was in surprisingly good condition. One of the photos showed him lying in the position in which he'd been found. The body was only partially submerged, so he must have fallen into the water near the bridge, where it was deep enough for him to drown, and then drifted down-river, washing up on a small beach where the water was shallow. She would ask Lugs about that. Forensics would have their own ideas about what had happened. Hugo was wearing a suit and tie, which Katya thought was odd. He worked with his hands, or had done until he disappeared. She didn't think he'd wear a suit for work unless he'd been through some kind of dramatic career change. Moving into a job that required suit-wearing would have been difficult, wouldn't it, if no one knew who he was or where he had come from? Perhaps he was meeting someone and wanted to make a good impression – a new customer, perhaps. He looked well fed, which suggested he'd either been earning a decent living or had someone to support him. Katya zoomed in to look at his fingernails. His hands were dirty, but his nails were unbroken. Had he not tried to scramble out onto the footpath? If he had, he would have grabbed at overhanging tree branches or handfuls of undergrowth on the bank. Both of those would have left broken nails and scratched hands, but the photo showed no evidence of either. She wondered if he'd been able to swim and if he had, why he hadn't swum for the shallows where he could have climbed out easily. Had he been too drunk to do that? Did he even realise what was happening? She must remember to check the toxicology report for the alcohol level in his blood. She found some pens on the desk and made a note of it on a scrap of paper that someone had thoughtfully left next to the computer keyboard.

So much for the body. Katya closed the photo and opened one of the riverbank itself. She was zooming in for a closer look when Lugs joined her. 'Sorry to keep you,' he said. 'Finance meeting.'

'Rather you than me,' she said. 'You been overspending again?'

'No more than usual. But whatever we spend is too much as far as the brass are concerned.' He sighed and poured himself a cup of tea. 'But enough of that. Seen anything interesting?'

'I was wondering how this guy managed to drown in what looks like about ten inches of water. I know he was drunk, but even when blotto one has some instinct of self-preservation. Did he drift there from another part of the river?'

Lugs opened one of the other photos. 'We think he probably went in here,' he said, pointing to the footpath that led down from the bridge. 'The river was running fast that night after all that rain we had. He probably drowned and was swept to the bank in the flow. When Ivo found him, he was lying on his side in the water, probably dead before he became entangled in the weeds near the bank.'

'You said you had something interesting to show me?'

'Yes,' said Lugs, opening two more photos and lining them up side by side. 'Look here,' he said, pointing with his pen to an area at the edge of one of the pictures. 'This is where we think Walsh fell. See that?'

'A footprint. Not Hugo's, I assume.'

'No. Hugo was wearing size ten brogues. This one is a hiking boot, an expensive Australian one in a size nine.'

'So someone else was there that night. Doesn't mean they were together.'

'No, it doesn't.' Lugs moved his pen to the other photo. 'But see here. Same print on the bank close to where Hugo was found.'

Katya sat back in her chair. Was Lugs suggesting Hugo had been pushed in? That would make this a murder case. And if it was, she might not be allowed to continue working on it. 'Do you think he was murdered?' she asked.

'It probably doesn't mean much. There was someone else walking along the river that night. Nothing to suggest they were together, or even there at the same time. We'd need to know a lot more before we could think of opening up a murder inquiry. Your role is safe for now, if that's what you're worried about.' Lugs picked up a biscuit and took a bite. 'How are your enquiries coming along?'

'Not bad at all,' she said. 'Jonny's on the trail of the bloke Hugo sold his van to. He's hoping it will have been a part exchange and we'll be able to track where Hugo has been through his new car. Jasmine's found out a lot about Penelope Walsh. Interesting stuff, too. She wasn't at all the good little housewife and mother she appeared at first. And Ivo's been chatting to a woman who lives in the same street as Jason. He's going back there to fix her toilet ballcock and hoping she'll be up for a bit of a gossip.'

'Good stuff,' said Lugs. 'How is Jason?'

'Happy to hand everything over to us. He seems rather out of it, to be honest, but that's not surprising given what he's had to get his head around recently. Or maybe he's always been like that. Difficult to say when I'd not met him before. Anyway, Jasmine's busy collating what we've got. She'll email it to you in a day or two. Can you send me these photos? We'll see if we can find out more about the boots.'

Lugs copied them into his email and pressed send. 'There you go,' he said. 'Do you need anything else?'

'The toxicology report would be useful. If he was as drunk as we think he was, we can start finding out where he was drinking and who with.'

'Good idea,' said Lugs. 'We know he hadn't made contact with Jason, so unless he was camping out in the shed, he might have checked into a hotel or a B&B in the town.'

'We'll look into that. And of course, if Jonny can trace a car registration in his name, we might find it abandoned somewhere, which will give us an idea of where he was staying.'

'I'll flag that up as soon as you have a registration number. There's very little street parking around here that isn't residents only or on a time restriction. If a car has been abandoned someone will notice it.'

'I suppose he might have come on the train,' said Katya. 'But if the barriers were closed his ticket would have been swallowed up by the machine.'

'There was no ticket in any of his pockets, so it doesn't look as if he was planning a return journey.'

'That's a pity,' said Katya. 'It would have told us where he'd come from. Could they be on his phone?'

'He didn't have a smartphone,' said Lugs. 'Just a cheap pay-as-you-go one.'

Yes, Katya remembered him telling her that. 'Any chance of tracing his calls?'

Lugs shook his head. 'There's a reason why criminals use burner phones,' he said. 'They're very hard to trace. We'd need a special warrant and there's not enough evidence that this was anything other than an accident.'

'Or suicide?' Katya asked.

'Getting drunk and jumping into a relatively shallow part of the river? Not very likely.'

'So you are still sure it was an accident?'

'To be honest, no I'm not. I think he was probably pushed in. I just don't have enough evidence to open a murder case.' He drained his teacup and bit into another biscuit.

'Well, we'll soldier on, me and my team,' said Katya.

'You're doing a grand job,' said Lugs. 'And so far, you've managed it keep it out of the press.'

'We're all keeping schtum,' said Katya.

'Not a word to that journo friend of yours?'

'Teddy Strang? He's moved on to higher things now. After that story about the body in the Long Walk.' Katya was quite sorry about that. Teddy had been hugely useful in that case and had even gone a long way to dispelling Katya's previously low opinion of journalists.

10

S he wasn't prepared for a reception committee, but when Katya arrived at *Jasmine's* the next morning for the detectives' meeting, Ivo and Karim were hanging around looking fidgety and excited. They followed her to her usual table by the window, smiling like a couple of idiots, she thought. 'You two are looking very pleased with yourselves,' she said, pulling off her scarf and gloves and hanging them over the back of her usual seat by the window.

'Don't leave those there,' said Ivo. 'Come and see what Karim has got for us.'

'Is it outside?' Katya asked, starting to put her gloves on again. She could do without that. Early March and it was supposed to warm up. Daffodils were out on the grass verges and in pots in the town centre. She'd even seen some primroses in the gardens near the river. And, at last, after months of darkness arriving with her afternoon cup of tea, the evenings were getting lighter. A sign, she hoped, that spring was on the way. Apparently not. Instead of mild, sunny days, the weather had turned cold again. A bitter wind blew across the river and the narrow streets and alleys were acting like wind funnels. There had even been a few flakes of snow this morning and Katya had reluctantly turned her heating on before getting dressed. The weather was one thing the government couldn't blame on the war in Ukraine, or Brexit, although no doubt they'd have a go. She pulled her hat down over her ears once more and reached for her scarf.

'It's okay,' Karim promised. 'No need to go outside again. Not until you've had a hot breakfast, at any rate. And when you see what Ivo and I have been doing you might want to stay even longer.'

The words *hot* and *breakfast* were always cheering. Jasmine's breakfast club was one of the best things to have happened this winter. That and the group of detectives that went with it. A group that now had an official police stamp of approval and better still, a group that Katya herself was in charge of. She hoped Karim wasn't about to drop a bombshell. No room for the detectives, perhaps, or worse, he and Jasmine were selling up and moving. Or the café was about to go bankrupt. But none of that would make him smile, would it? Well, leaving the area might, but that definitely wouldn't make Ivo smile and yet there he was, grinning like the Cheshire cat.

'Follow us,' said Karim, holding her by the arm, steering her around tables and chairs and leading her through the dining room towards the kitchen, with Harold and Ivo following in their wake. They passed the kitchen, no doubt to Harold's disappointment, to a small door with a key in the lock. Karim unlocked and opened the door and Katya could see a narrow flight of stairs. She'd seen the door before, of course, but she'd always assumed it was a storeroom. 'This is exciting,' she said. 'Not kidnapping me, are you?' She laughed, although it did fleetingly occur to her that this would be an excellent place to hide a kidnap victim. *Don't be so stupid,* she told herself. *Why on earth would they do that?* It wasn't as if they could demand any kind of ransom. She had nothing of any value and no one who cared where she was. 'Where are we going?'

'To the attic,' said Ivo, starting to climb the stairs, Harold following him, his claws tapping on the bare treads. 'It's a surprise. You'll really like it.'

Katya hoped he was right about that. She wasn't one for surprises. There'd been too many unpleasant ones recently. 'I didn't know you had an attic,' she said.

'We've not used it much,' said Karim. 'It's not easily reached from our flat and Jasmine and I don't need the extra space. I'd imagine that when the building was a private house, these stairs and the room in the attic would have been for a servant. Some poor girl who had easy access to the kitchen without disturbing the rest of the family.'

Katya puffed up the stairs, arriving rather breathless at another door, which Karim opened with a flourish and ushered her inside. They were in a small room, freshly painted, Katya thought, by the smell of it, with two windows set into the sloping ceiling. There were bare boards on the floor and a table around which were four chairs.

'Are you expanding the dining room?' she asked, thinking it would be inconvenient having to carry trays of food up those stairs. 'I suppose with the breakfast club now so successful you need the extra space.'

'No, no,' said Karim. 'This is not for the breakfast club. It is for the breakfast club detectives. You need somewhere you can meet without worrying about our customers overhearing and where you can keep your stuff. It's your new office. What do you think?'

Katya was speechless.

'Karim and I cleared all the rubbish out,' said Ivo. 'And I painted it and sanded the floor. I thought I'd line one of the walls with cork, so we've got somewhere to pin stuff up.'

Katya pulled them both into her arms and hugged them. 'It's perfect,' she muttered, letting go of Karim and groping into her pocket for a tissue. She wiped away a tear. *Must be the dust getting in my eyes*, she thought. 'But where are Jasmine and Jonny? Do they know about it?'

'I wanted it to be a surprise, but I had to let Ivo in on it because I needed him to do the work. But then he let it slip out and so both Jasmine and Jonny knew what we were up to.'

'Sorry,' said Ivo. 'I'm not very good at keeping secrets.'

'Don't worry about it,' said Karim, patting him on the back. 'We've still managed to surprise Katya. Jasmine's serving breakfast, but I've got help coming in soon to take over while you have your meeting. Jonny's not here yet. He said he had to do some printing for you.'

Yes, that was right. She'd emailed him and asked him to print out the photos Lugs had sent her. That shouldn't take too long, and it wouldn't be like Jonny to miss breakfast. Would he have driven to the Slough factory to do it? That would take longer, but surely he and Belinda would have a printer at home. Either way, she hoped he would be there soon. He would probably be as excited as she was to have an office of their own.

'I'd better get back to work,' said Karim. 'But you can come and go as you please. We'll get keys cut for each of you and you can come in through the back entrance without disturbing the kitchen and dining room. You can bring your food up here with you if you like.'

'I can carry it up,' said Ivo.

'It's tempting,' said Katya. 'But let's go down and wait for Jonny, and for Jasmine to finish. Then perhaps we could bring our coffee up here and launch our new office together, all four of us.' She gave Karim another hug. 'I don't know how to thank you,' she said.

'You don't need to. The four of you take up too much room down-stairs. I'll be glad to see the back of you,' he joked. 'And I know how much it all means to Jasmine. Her mum would have been proud of her, all of you.'

They started to make their way back downstairs and met Jonny on the way up. He was carrying a white box with a picture of a computer on the front. 'I thought this would be useful,' he said. 'It's from my office at CPS. But I'm hardly ever there. I keep the breakfast club funding records on it, but not much else and I can work on those just as easily from here. And we can all use it. There's no need to send each other emails any more.'

'You knew about this?' said Katya.

'I was supposed to be as surprised as you,' he said. 'But I'm afraid Ivo spilled the beans. He was talking to Karim in the kitchen about paint and kettles, and which chairs to carry up.'

'You shouldn't have been listening,' said Ivo. 'We wanted to surprise you and Katya.'

'Then you should be more careful where you chat about stuff,' said Jonny with a grin. 'Good job we're detectives, not spies.'

. . .

'What do you think?' Jasmine asked as she served Katya with a plate of warm muffins. 'It's going to be great to have an office of our own, isn't it?'

'Brilliant idea,' said Katya, reaching for the marmalade. 'Your dad is one in a million.'

'He approves of what we do,' said Jasmine. 'Well, he does now. He wasn't so sure when he thought it was all roaming round the park at night.'

'Then we'd better make sure you don't do that again,' said Katya. 'I'm not surprised he worries about you. That's a dad's job, isn't it?'

'And mine to worry about him.' Jasmine looked at the clock on the wall. 'Time for my break,' she said. 'I've made a lot of notes. I'll just pop up to my room and get them. Then I'll see you in the office. Hey, that sounds good, doesn't it?'

'It does,' said Katya. 'And I'll see you up there as soon as you're ready.' She stood up and headed for the stairs. This was going to keep her fit. Hopefully once she'd been up and down a few times she'd stop feeling so breathless.

Half an hour later, Katya sat at the head of the table, flattered that they'd given her the most comfortable chair and placed it where she had the best light from the window. She opened a folder and spread some papers out in front of her: notes she'd made during her visit to the police station, and a copy of the toxicology report that Lugs had run off for her, showing that Hugo had consumed enough alcohol to knock out an elephant.

Ivo staggered in, carrying a sheet of white melamine that he'd found in a skip. He leant it against the wall and reached into his pocket for a packet of marker pens.

'Did you find those in the skip as well?' Jonny asked.

'Bought them at the newsagents,' said Ivo.

'We all need to keep track of what we spend,' said Katya. 'I'm allowed to claim a few expenses. Seems only fair when you are all volunteering your time. I assume you didn't have to pay for that whiteboard, Ivo?'

'No one pays for stuff out of skips. I thought it would make the room look like the incident rooms you see on the telly.'

Katya took a blue pen from the packet. 'Right,' she said. 'Time to start pulling things together.' She wrote *Hugo, Penelope,* and *Man on train* across the top of the board. 'Let's start with Hugo.'

'He drew fifty-five thousand pounds out of a building society account the week before the train crash,' said Jonny, his own notes carefully spread out on the table in front of him. 'And he sold his van to a man in Milton Keynes. It now belongs to a hairdresser called Jessie Simpson. She couldn't remember the address of the guy Hugo sold it to, but she remembered where it was, so I thought I might go and talk to him. See what he remembers about Hugo and if he dropped any hints about where he was going.'

'Good,' said Katya, making some notes under Hugo's name. 'Drawing out that money the week before the crash sounds like he was already planning to leave.'

'I thought so,' said Jonny. The other two nodded in agreement.

'We also need the date he sold the van,' said Katya. 'We need to know if Hugo left home before or after the train crash.'

'I can work on that,' said Jonny, writing it down.

'In other words,' said Jasmine, 'did he know his wife was dead? And if not, when did he find out?'

Katya started another list headed *Questions to ask next.* 'Jasmine, what did you discover about Penelope Walsh?'

'I found out a lot about her,' said Jasmine, giving them a short summary of her meeting with Juliet. 'I think that this Malcolm Applewood, who runs the choir, might know who the lover was.'

'Then we need to talk to him,' said Katya. 'We'd better think about the best way to do that. He didn't come forward after the crash so he may have reasons for keeping quiet.'

'You'd think someone would have missed the guy,' said Jonny, drawing circles on his notepad. 'Even if they didn't connect him to Penelope. People don't just disappear.'

'Actually, I'm afraid they do,' said Katya. 'There's a whole database of missing persons. Lugs is going to search it for us and send me a list. Once we get that, someone will need to sift through it and look for possible matches.'

'What sort of matches?' asked Ivo. 'Men, obviously, but there'll be a lot of them.'

'That's a difficult one,' said Katya. 'We should start with anyone local and work outwards. We can probably eliminate teenagers, and there will be a lot of those.'

'And we know he was the same build as Hugo,' said Jonny.

'Good point,' said Katya, adding it to her list of questions. 'The database will give us descriptions, which I would hope include height. More action on that when we've heard from Lugs again. So, on to Jason. Ivo, how did you get on with him?'

'I don't think it was a happy family,' said Ivo. 'Jason hadn't seen his parents for years. He remembers his father as a bit of a womaniser and his mother as moody.'

'I suppose those aren't unconnected, are they?' said Jasmine. 'If Hugo was having multiple affairs, we should probably forgive Penelope for being narked about it.'

'The neighbour, Poppy, was quite helpful,' said Ivo. 'She wanted a squeaky door fixed and her washing line mended, so I popped in after I'd finished with Jason.'

'Good move,' said Jonny. 'She'd have more info than Jason. Probably able to see all their comings and goings.'

'How did you know she needed things doing in the house?' Katya asked. 'Did you just knock on the door and ask?'

'I met her in the street. She'd seen me arrive with my tools.'

'That's the kind of neighbour I like in an investigation,' said Katya. 'Always up for a bit of spying on those around them, and usually happy to spill the beans to anyone who asks. What did she tell you, Ivo?'

'She described the Walsh home as a house of horrors. She found

Hugo creepy and Penelope too intense. She doesn't know Jason well. Keeps himself to himself, is what she said.'

'That's all useful to know,' said Katya. 'Keep in touch with her. She may be able to tell us a lot more. Has she got more odd jobs for you?'

'Yes, and she wants me to meet her brother when he's home. He's cabin crew with BA.'

'Great,' said Jasmine with a wink. 'Sounds like a bit of match-making going on there.'

'Could be awkward,' said Ivo. 'I wouldn't want to be spying on friends.'

He could have a point, Katya thought. It was usually better to keep witnesses and informers at arms' length. On the other hand, Ivo's social life could probably do with a helping hand. 'Well, it's not an issue yet,' she said. 'Just play it by ear and we'll see how it goes.'

'How was your meeting with Lugs?' Jasmine asked.

'Useful,' said Katya. 'Jonny's printed some photos that Lugs gave me of where they found the body.' She held out her hand and Jonny passed them to her. She selected two of them and stuck them to the board with some masking tape. 'What do you notice?' she asked, and when no one responded she picked up a pencil and drew circles around the two footprints.

'They look the same,' said Jasmine. 'They can't be Hugo's, can they? Well, not the one on the bank where he was found. Unless he climbed out and then slipped back in again.'

'No,' said Katya. 'Lugs is pretty sure he was washed onto the bank after he drowned.'

Ivo studied the tread pattern. 'Those are from work boots,' he said. 'Hugo was wearing ordinary town shoes. Lace ups with flat soles. I noticed when the body rolled over.'

'Well spotted, Ivo,' said Katya. 'The footprints are actually from hiking boots. An Australian make, apparently.'

'So someone was there with Hugo?' Jonny asked.

'Possibly, but we shouldn't jump to conclusions. It could have been someone who was taking an evening stroll and just happened to be on the bridge and then the riverbank. And it could have been well before Hugo fell in.'

'But the one on the bank is right up close to the body and very near the water,' said Jonny. 'I suppose it could have been someone the previous evening, before the body was washed against the bank. Crossed the bridge, perhaps, and then stood at the water's edge looking back at the town. There's a good view of the castle from there.'

'But we don't know, do we?' said Jasmine. 'He could have pushed Hugo into the water, watched while the body drifted to the bank and then crossed over to check that he was dead.'

'Or he could have stood on the bank and held Hugo down with his other foot until he was sure he *was* dead,' said Ivo.

'We can't rule any of that out,' said Katya. 'Lugs said it wasn't enough evidence for a murder inquiry but it's worth looking into. Of course, if we do uncover more evidence, we have to hand it over to the police.' She picked up her pen again and wrote *Action plan* on the board. 'Suggestions?'

'I'll go to Milton Keynes and see what I can get out of Dan Smith, the car dealer,' said Jonny.

'Someone should go with you,' said Katya. 'Two heads are better than one and all that.'

'I'll go,' said Ivo. 'And Harold can have a sniff around.'

Katya wrote that down. 'Jasmine?'

'I'll go through the missing persons list as soon as you get it,' she said. 'And find out more about Malcolm Applewood. And how about contacting hotels in Bath? See if we can find where Penelope and lover boy stayed.'

'Why don't we all do that?' Jonny asked. 'It's only a couple of hours' drive. We can visit the shops Penelope went to as well.'

'It would have to be Sunday for me and Ivo,' said Jasmine. 'It's a great idea, though.'

'Excellent,' said Katya. 'Sunday's fine by me. Your car, Jonny, if that's okay with you. I don't fancy a long drive in Ivo's van and Karim has already been generous enough without lending us his car as well.'

'Sounds fun,' said Jasmine. 'I'll pack up a picnic.'

This is not meant to be fun, thought Katya. But she kept her mouth shut. She didn't want to dampen Jasmine's enthusiasm. Not when her father had been so kind. And in any case, she'd always enjoyed getting her teeth into an inquiry when she was younger. And come to think of it, things were not so very different now. So a field trip it would be. There must be worse ways to spend a Sunday.

'SOUNDS LIKE A SCHOOL TRIP,' said Belinda, laughing. She and Jonny usually spent Sundays together in the garden and he'd expected her to be a bit grumpy when he told her he would be away from home all day. But he'd overlooked the matter of the local elections in a few weeks and Belinda actually looked relieved about having the day to herself. This wasn't the moment to talk about getting a dog, though. He'd probably leave that until after the election, when Belinda would either be relieved having retained her seat and happy to agree to anything, or she'd need cheering up because she'd lost, and a dog might just take her mind off it. But right now, she was working on her election leaflets and would be glad to have the whole day to herself.

Jonny picked Katya and Jasmine up outside the café early on Sunday morning. He'd downloaded a street map of Bath with a list of car parks in the city centre. They'd be expensive and there were cheaper alternatives on the edge of the city, but they had a lot of walking to do and most of that would be in the tourist areas. He'd also filled up with petrol the previous evening to avoid an awkward discussion about who was going to pay for it. He knew Katya had a hard time making ends meet, and suspected Ivo was in a similar position. It was possible that Thames Valley Police would allow them to claim mileage, but even if they didn't, a tank of petrol was a small price to pay for a day out doing detective work. He handed the map to Katya as she settled herself in the front seat next to him. She tucked it into a plastic wallet with a list of hotels she'd made along with the addresses of the shops Penelope had visited. 'You okay in the back, love?' she asked, turning round to watch Jasmine settle herself in the back seat and clip on her seat belt. 'Enough leg room?'

Jasmine had brought a flask of coffee and bags of sandwiches, which she placed on the floor by her feet. 'Yes, thanks,' she said. 'It's a nice big car. Plenty of space for me and Ivo.'

Ivo and Harold were waiting for them at the entrance to *Shady Willows*. Harold knew his way around Jonny's car and hopped eagerly into the back when Jonny opened the tailgate for him. Jonny clipped him into the harness he'd had fitted when Harold had been a lodger at his house, and which he'd left there for when he got a dog of his own. Ivo placed a carrier bag on the floor next to him. 'I've brought his drinking bowl and a bottle of water,' he said.

'Good thinking,' said Jonny. 'I thought we'd stop on the way and give him a run. I don't think he's going to find the city sights very interesting.'

Ivo climbed into the back seat next to Jasmine, who was looking at photos of the city on her phone. 'It looks really nice,' she said. 'Any of you been there before?'

Ivo shook his head. 'I've never been anywhere much,' he said. 'Tower of London on a school trip is about all.'

'I went to a policing conference in Bath once,' said Katya. 'But it was in one of those massive corporate hotels on the outskirts and we didn't have time to look around the city.'

'It's a beautiful place,' said Jonny. 'There's an abbey and a lot of very elegant buildings. It was the setting for a few of Jane Austen's novels, so it probably features in some of the TV adaptations.'

'It says here that there's a Roman bath,' said Jasmine, looking up from her phone. 'That's how it got its name, I suppose.'

'All very interesting,' said Katya. 'But unless we manage to track down Penelope and her friend in double quick time, we're not going to be doing much sightseeing.'

I should do more day trips like this, Jonny thought, pulling the car onto the relief road and heading for the motorway. He enjoyed driving and it was nice to have company and be going somewhere interesting. He could take Ivo to the seaside one day. He wondered if there were any dog friendly beaches on the south coast.

'Is it all motorway?' asked Ivo, once they had passed Reading. He was looking out of the window at the stretch of rolling downland they were driving through.

'All but the last few miles,' said Jonny. 'We pass a hotel called Spa Gardens soon after we leave the motorway. It's probably a bit pricey for our couple, but there's a park where we could give Harold a walk. Is it on your list, Katya?' he asked, glancing at her.

'Like you said, it's rather expensive and I thought we'd concentrate on hotels in the city centre. More likely if they travelled by train. And there would have been trains to both Chippenham and Malmesbury for the concerts.'

'You don't suppose they stayed somewhere in one of those places?' Jasmine asked.

'It's possible, but the dates on Penelope's credit card bill tell us they were in Bath shopping the day before the first concert so it's likely they stayed at least one night there.'

It was a little after eight-thirty when Jonny pulled into the hotel car park. 'Since we're here,' said Katya, 'I may as well ask about Penelope at reception.'

'There's a picnic table over by the lake,' said Ivo, pointing to the far side of the car park. 'How about we meet there for coffee and sandwiches when I've walked Harold?'

'I'll come with you,' said Jonny. 'I've missed my walks recently.'

'And I'll go with Katya,' said Jasmine.

'It's going to be cold sitting by the lake,' Katya grumbled. 'Shouldn't we head for the city and get coffee there?'

'We can do that as well,' said Jonny. 'But there won't be much open this early. I've got some rugs in the car and the coffee will keep us warm.'

. . .

HALF AN HOUR later they were seated at the picnic table wrapped in rugs and using the coffee mugs to keep their hands warm.

'How did you get on?' Jonny asked, hoping to take Katya's mind off the brisk breeze that was blowing across the lake.

'I showed them the photo of Penelope that was on the choir website. No one at reception remembered her,' said Katya. 'They were very helpful and checked the registers for me, but there was no record of a Walsh staying here around then. They suggested some likely places near the shops and the abbey. Inexpensive and hidden away, they said.'

'I suppose she might have used a false name,' said Jasmine. 'But they didn't recognise the photo of her, either.'

'So what's the plan now?' Jonny asked, starting the car and heading towards the city centre.

Katya tapped the map. 'There's a long stay car park here,' she said, tapping the address into Jonny's satnav. 'We'll park there and use it as a meeting point. Jonny and Jasmine, you start with the shops.' She handed Jasmine a slip of paper. 'These are the names that were on the credit card statement. Ask if they remember Penelope, if she was with anyone and get a description if she was. I've checked which hotels are nearest, so you can drop in and ask them as well. Ivo and I will do the other hotels on the list. Meet back at the car at twelve-thirty and we'll get some lunch and check over what we've found out.'

Jonny wondered what the shop assistants would make of him and a woman young enough to be his daughter enquiring about expensive underwear and perfume. But perhaps they would think she was actually his daughter, and in any case, was it any of their business? Then it struck him that Katya was right. A portly ex-police officer and a scruffy young man with a dog asking about lingerie and perfume would be more noticeable and they were here to make discreet enquiries. Doing it in pairs was definitely a good idea. They could cover twice as much ground and would attract a lot less attention than if they'd stayed together as a group of four.

.   .   .

AFTER FINDING A PARKING SPACE, they got out of the car, stretched and yawned. Then they set off in different directions – Jonny and Jasmine heading to the shops, Ivo and Katya making for the first hotel on the list.

'Nice shops,' said Jasmine as the two of them wandered along the narrow shopping streets, looking into windows. Nothing open yet, of course, but they found the lingerie shop and sat in a nearby café with cups of tea until it opened. 'We'll probably be the first customers of the day,' said Jasmine, laughing. 'I can't imagine many people are desperate for some sexy underwear this early on a Sunday morning.'

Jonny sipped his tea. 'How are we going to do this?' he asked. 'Plunge straight in and say we're there for information, or do we pose as customers and slip in some questions on the way?'

'I don't know,' said Jasmine. 'The stuff in the window looks lovely but I'm not sure I can afford any of it. And you buying anything for me would look creepy. When's your wife's birthday?' she asked.

'April the first.'

'Really?' Jasmine laughed. 'That's unfortunate, for her I mean.'

'Oh, she's heard all the April fool jokes. Doesn't worry her too much.'

'Lucky for us, anyway.'

'Why?'

Jasmine sighed. 'It's March now. You can buy her a birthday present.'

That would be interesting. He wasn't a romantic gift buyer. Theatre tickets or exotic garden plants were more his style. He couldn't imagine how Belinda would react on opening a gift-wrapped set of sexy underwear. She'd probably assume it was an April fool joke. Interesting, though. Perhaps he would give it a try. 'Okay,' he said. 'But you will have to pretend to be my daughter and advise me.'

'It's a deal,' said Jasmine. 'I'd be honoured to be your daughter for half an hour or so.'

11

'Shouldn't we head back to the car?' Ivo asked as Katya crossed hotel number five off their list. His feet were beginning to hurt and even Harold was dragging at his lead, obviously having decided that this particular walk was not a lot of fun.

'Just one more,' said Katya, running her finger down the list. 'I'm hopeful about this one.'

'You've said that about most of them,' Ivo complained. 'What's different about this one?'

They were in a small side street, away from the shops and the tourist areas of the city. Just the place for a couple of lovers to tuck themselves away. Even the name of the hotel was hopeful. 'See what it's called,' she said as they stood outside a small hotel called *Singers' Rest*. 'Isn't that exactly the name a singer would choose when picking a hotel in an unknown city?'

'So why didn't we start with this one?' Ivo muttered.

'I planned our route so that we wouldn't have to walk too far. If we'd gone in order of most likely names we'd have zigzagged for miles. But I promise this is the last one before we stop for lunch.' To be honest, she was more than ready for a sit down herself.

They walked up the steps, through a red front door and into a reception area with a desk, some small armchairs, a tank of fish and a rack with leaflets about places to visit. There was no one behind the desk so Katya tapped the top of a small bell, one that reminded her of old-fashioned shops in the days when it was safe to leave the counter unattended.

A man appeared from a door marked *Private* and greeted them with the kind of expression that suggested checking in early on a Sunday morning was not something he encouraged. 'We don't take dogs,' he said, eyeing Harold with suspicion.

'We're not here for a room,' said Katya, flashing her ID at him and hoping he wouldn't notice that it said *Civilian Investigator* on it, wishing once again that she could have introduced herself as DS Roscoff. 'We're enquiring about a couple who may have stayed here about eighteen months ago.' She opened her notebook and showed him the dates of the two concerts.

'Name?'

'Anyone called Walsh?' said Katya.

The man tapped on a computer screen and then spent what seemed to Katya to be an excessive amount of time checking dates. He shook his head. 'No one of that name,' he said. 'A couple, you say? We had a Mr and Mrs Jameson and Mr and Mrs King on those nights. We're a small hotel. Our two other double rooms were empty, and the two singles were booked by a couple of blokes going to a conference in the Pump Room.'

'They might not have called themselves Walsh,' she explained for the fifth time that morning. 'The lady was singing in concerts in the area, in a choir that wears rather distinctive apple-green blouses and long, dark red skirts. Perhaps she was seen leaving the hotel on one of the evenings dressed like that?'

'Can't say I remember it,' he said. 'The Kings were an elderly couple celebrating their diamond wedding anniversary. I remember that because their family ordered champagne to be delivered to their room. Can't say I remember much about the other couple.' He stared at the computer screen again. 'Booked in for a week. Could have been American tourists. We get a lot of those.'

Whatever, Katya thought. It wasn't likely to have been Penelope and her man. Not if they'd booked for a week.

Ivo pulled out his phone, opened the choir website and handed it over the desk. 'This is the choir the lady was singing with,' he said.

The man stared at it for a moment then handed the phone back and shook his head. 'Doesn't ring any bells, sorry.'

Katya thanked him for his help. Not that he'd been much help, but that was no reason to forget her manners. She gave him her card and asked him to let her know if any of the staff had seen Penelope dressed in her concert gear.

'Let's go,' she said to Ivo and Harold, who were looking at the fish in the tank, and headed for the door.

'Wait a minute,' said the man. 'We did have a couple. I remember now because the lady was carrying one of those dress bags over one arm. I thought they might be headed for a dinner dance or a posh party. I guess a concert dress could be in a bag like that.'

Interesting, Katya thought, turning back to the reception desk. 'You saw them, but they didn't actually stay here?'

'They were planning to.' He scrolled though his records again. 'Ah, here it is. Booked online by a Mr Bruce Hunter. I remember it now because the credit card had been authorised when the booking was made but unfortunately, it was declined when I put the full payment through. I thought it was odd at the time.'

'People do reach their limit without realising, I suppose,' said Katya.

'No, it was odd because Hunter wasn't the name on the card.'

Katya felt a tingle of excitement. She had a feeling this was going to be their first real lead. 'Do you have the name that was on the card?' she asked, trying not to look too excited.

'Not sure, but I can check the records.' He spent another few minutes scrolling and then looked up. 'Here we go,' he said. 'Mrs Penelope Walsh. I asked if they would like me to try another card, but they decided to go somewhere else. I suppose they needed to look for somewhere cheaper.'

Ivo beamed at him. 'That's who—'

Katya interrupted him. They didn't want to give too much away. 'Do you remember what Mr Hunter looked like?' she asked.

'Not really. Pretty ordinary, I think. Middle-aged, average height. Oh, I do remember one thing. He had an accent. Australian, possibly.'

'Thank you,' said Katya. 'You've been a great help.'

'Was he wearing hiking boots?' Ivo asked.

'No idea, mate.'

'WHAT THE HELL did you ask that for?' said Katya, once they were back in the street again.

'I was thinking of those footprints on the riverbank where they found Hugo.'

Katya gave him a withering look. 'Don't tell me, you have a theory that Hugo was pushed into the river by Mr Hunter's ghost.'

'No,' said Ivo. 'That would be stupid.'

'You said it, lad.'

'But the boots on the riverbank were Australian and so was Mr Hunter. Bit of a coincidence, isn't it?'

'Mr Hunter *may* have had an Australian accent. It would be quite a stretch to say he'd turned up on the riverbank wearing the same boots as the ones in the police photos, particularly since he had been dead for eighteen months.'

'We don't know that it was Mr Hunter on the train with Penelope.'

Was she jumping to conclusions about that? 'We don't know for sure,' she said. 'But I think that's most likely. Who else could it have been?'

'Okay,' said Ivo. 'Suppose two Australian friends were over here on holiday. They split up so one of them, not the boot owner, could spend a few days in a hotel with Penelope Walsh.'

'And the bloke with the boots decides to avenge his friend's death by shoving her husband into the river eighteen months later?'

'It's a theory.'

'Highly unlikely, in my opinion. Why take it out on poor old Hugo? It wasn't his fault his wife chose to have an affair. And if he suspected it was his friend on the train and not Hugo, why didn't he come forward and say so?'

'We should see what the others think,' said Ivo stubbornly.

'If you insist,' said Katya. 'But at least we now have a name. We can start looking for Bruce Hunter.'

BACK AT THE CAR PARK, they found Jonny and Jasmine sitting in Jonny's car reading the Sunday papers. 'Been shopping?' Katya asked, eyeing a glossy, pale green carrier bag on the back seat.

'It was our cover,' said Jasmine. 'We posed as father and daughter looking for a birthday present. It's actually Mrs Cardew's birthday quite soon. We started at the lingerie shop and looked through some of their stuff. Jonny had to pretend to be a husband who was embarrassed about buying lingerie for his wife so we could get the assistant talking about other customers and see if she remembered Penelope.'

'I didn't need to pretend,' said Jonny. 'I've never been so embarrassed in my life. Jasmine did all the talking.'

'I let Jonny browse and got the saleswoman chatting. I said a friend of ours had recommended the shop and asked if she remembered Penelope, but she said she had loads of customers and only remembered individuals if they made a fuss.'

'Well, I suppose that tells us that Penelope wasn't the type to make waves, but I think we already knew that.' Katya eyed the package on the back seat. 'Either what you bought for Mrs C is very small and skimpy, or you had better luck at the perfume shop, at least with the present buying.'

'We did,' said Jasmine. 'Jonny found a gift *and* we discovered a bit more about Penelope.'

'It's a really special perfumery,' added Jonny. 'It's run by a man called Carlo. He makes bespoke perfumes to suit individual customers. It's quite scientific. All about the neurobiology of sensation and reward.'

'Sounds pricey,' said Katya. 'No wonder Penelope had maxed out her card before they got to the hotel.'

'We showed Carlo the picture of Penelope. The one that was on the choir website when she'd sung a solo and was dressed in the concert stuff. We told him that she was Jonny's wife and said she'd bought some perfume from him that she really loved and now Jonny wanted to buy her some more for her birthday but didn't want to spoil the surprise by asking what it was called.'

'And he remembered her?'

'He did when we showed him the picture. He said they'd talked about the choir and Penelope tried to sell him a ticket for one of the concerts. She'd left him with a flyer that had a photo of the choir on it, and they'd chatted about the green blouses.'

'So now we know what perfume she used?'

'He hadn't made one for her. That takes time and is very expensive, but he said it was probably one of two that he would recommend for a musician of her age and colouring. Jonny bought a small bottle of both and Carlo said he could order a bigger one online when his wife had chosen the one she liked best.'

'Is Belinda musical?' Ivo asked.

'Not particularly,' said Jonny.

'Then she'll probably hate both perfumes.'

That's the problem with amateurs, Katya thought. They're too easily sidetracked. 'Was Penelope on her own?' she asked.

'Apparently not. We didn't ask directly, because if Jonny was her husband, Carlo might have been a bit cagey about her being with another man. So we invented a cousin and Jonny said that Penelope had been showing him the city while he was visiting the UK from New York.'

'I do actually have a cousin who lives in New York,' said Jonny. 'I suggested to Carlo that he might have bought something for his own wife. But apparently he didn't.'

'We tried to look surprised when Carlo told us that and Jonny muttered something about her only buying from Saks in Fifth Avenue.'

Katya smiled. Jasmine was nothing if not imaginative.

'But then he told us something very interesting,' said Jonny. 'He said he was surprised about New York because the man with Penelope had spoken with an Australian accent. So then I had to invent a history for him that involved him having lived for years in Australia before he went to New York.'

'Carlo asked if he was into trekking because he'd been wearing these very expensive hiking boots.'

'I told you so,' said Ivo.

'What do you mean, Ivo?' Jasmine asked.

'Ivo has this hare-brained idea that Hugo was pushed into the Thames by an Australian wearing hiking boots,' said Katya.

'Well, it can't have been this man,' said Jonny. 'Because unless Penelope had two lovers on the go, he was killed in the train crash.'

'I told him that,' said Katya.

'Perhaps there were two of them,' said Ivo. 'And they fell out over Penelope.'

'And the one with the boots shoved Hugo into the river eighteen months later? Why?'

'I've not quite worked that out yet,' said Ivo. 'But we know the man's name now.'

Katya looked pleased with herself and told them what they had found out at the *Singers' Rest*.

'So we need to find a Mr Bruce Hunter,' said Jasmine, 'who speaks with an Australian accent and wears expensive hiking boots.'

And more importantly, Katya thought, *we need to discover why no one missed him after the train crash.* She looked at her watch. They'd done well and it was still only early afternoon. They should get some lunch. She'd noticed a pub close to the car park that served food until three in the afternoon, and she really fancied a nice pie and chips before they headed home. 'That's it for today,' she said. 'We'll get a late lunch and then head home. You should all make notes about what you discovered, and we'll plan where to go from here at our next meeting.'

12

Ivo opened up the back of Jonny's car. Harold jumped in and sat obediently waiting for someone to clip him into his harness. 'He's getting used to this,' said Ivo, clicking the catch into place on Harold's collar and making sure he was comfortable on the rug Jonny had provided, partly for Harold's comfort and partly to keep the back of the car free from muddy paw prints. 'He knows he's getting another day out,' said Ivo. 'I think he enjoyed Sunday – new places and new smells.'

'He enjoyed the walk around the lake,' said Jonny. 'He must have been a bit bored visiting all those hotels, though.' Jonny had enjoyed the lakeside walk as well. If he ever visited Bath again, he must remember that spot as a good place to stretch his legs after the drive. The hotel looked like somewhere that did a good meal as well. He'd suggest taking Belinda there once the election was out of the way. It would do her good to get away from Windsor, particularly if she lost her seat on the council. Not that Jonny expected that for one minute. She was well liked by her constituents and was bound to be re-elected. But she might find herself surrounded by new councillors, members of different parties, if the opinion polls were anything to go by.

'The hotels were a bit dull for a dog,' said Ivo as he climbed into the passenger seat. 'But he liked the pub.'

Of course he did. The helpings were large and Harold had done well from punters who had more than they could eat. 'A bit like being in *Jasmine's*, I suppose,' said Jonny. 'A table to sit under and people feeding him scraps.'

'How far is it?' Ivo asked as he clipped on his seat belt and adjusted the seat to give him a bit more leg room. Katya had been the last person to use it and she was quite a bit shorter than Ivo.

'About fifty miles,' said Jonny, handing him a plastic folder. 'I've written down some directions in case the satnav doesn't recognise the place. I called Jessie and she got the address from her husband, but he only remembered the name of the road that leads to this bit of land. I'm not sure it even has a postcode. It's just wasteland with a few temporary huts. It's probably waiting for planning permission, so I hope the car dealer is still there. I checked it out on Google Earth and printed some pictures. They're in the folder.'

Ivo opened the folder and pulled out the screenshot of a row of what looked like shipping containers on some derelict ground. In the background, he could see the railway line with a rough track running alongside it. 'How often do they update Google Earth?' he asked.

'About once a year,' said Jonny. 'But not over the winter. Unless they cleared it this winter it should still be there. I checked out building plans for the area and couldn't find anything for this particular spot.'

'A wasted journey if it's all been cleared away.'

'Yes,' said Jonny. He'd thought the same, but the only way to know was to drive there and have a look. 'Even if it's gone, we can still give Harold a good walk and get a nice lunch somewhere. And there may be people still on the site who know where he moved to.' He tapped the name of the road into his satnav. It would be easy enough to find the place from there, he hoped.

Ivo put the photos back into the folder and took out some more pieces of paper; the registration number of Hugo's van and a photograph of it that Jonny had found on a website of local businesses. The van was white with *H. Walsh Bespoke Joiner* stencilled on both sides in brown letters. There was a web address and phone number on the back door in the same brown letters. Jonny knew from Jessie that the van was now pale pink and with Jessie's logo and *Curls to You* painted underneath in dark pink, but he assumed the change had happened after Jessie's husband's deal with Dan Smith, who only bought and sold cars. Jonny didn't think he also resprayed them to order. In any case, it didn't matter. All he wanted from Dan was information about Hugo Walsh. Had he bought another car? If so, that was going to be very helpful in tracing his whereabouts.

The second-hand car lot looked scruffy on the pictures Jonny had found, but to his relief Dan Smith's paperwork was in order. At least it was where Hugo's van was concerned. It had been easy to trace it through DVLA records. What Jonny wanted to find out was first, whether Dan remembered Hugo, and then if he knew where he'd been headed for after he sold the van.

The satnav guided them to the road that led to the car lot, and Jonny was alarmed to see a builder's board at the end of it stating that the land was being cleared for the construction of industrial units. There was a barrier across the road and beyond it a wooden hut. Jonny drove the car as close as he could to the barrier and stared over it. As far as he could see, the shipping containers were still in place but there were few signs of life and no cars parked outside them.

'What now?' Ivo asked.

Jonny wasn't sure, but before he could decide, the door of the hut opened and a man came out carrying a teapot, which he emptied onto a patch of grass. 'I'll go and talk to him,' said Jonny. 'See if he knows where they've all gone.'

He climbed out of the car, ducked under the barrier and rapped on the door of the hut. 'What?' said teapot man, opening the door a crack and peering round it.

'Sorry to bother you,' said Jonny, 'but I'm looking for Dan Smith. He used to sell second-hand cars here.'

'Well, he's not here now, is he? They all cleared out last week.'

'I can see that. I wondered if you knew where he'd gone.'

'Nothing to do with me.' He started closing the door and then watched as Jonny reached into his pocket, took out his wallet and edged out the corner of a twenty-pound note. The man opened the door a little wider, and without taking his eyes off the money, he said, 'Of course, you might try the Railway Tavern. Some of the lads meet up there for a pint around lunchtime.'

'Is it far?'

'Nah, just follow the railway track and it's about a mile back down the road. You can't miss it. Used to be the station before they closed the branch line, so it looks like, well, it looks like a station.'

'Thank you, that's very helpful,' said Jonny, letting the money flutter to the ground and walking back to the car.

He climbed into the driving seat and looked at the clock on the dashboard. Eleven-thirty. A bit early for a pub lunch, but there was no point in hanging around here. He turned the car round and started to drive back along the road.

'Any luck?' Ivo asked.

'Kind of.' He pulled off the road and parked by a gateway into a field. 'There's a pub near here where we might meet some of the men who used to work in the containers. They were moved out last week, but the chap in the hut reckons they still meet for a lunchtime pint. It's probably not open yet so we'll give Harold a walk first and then drop in for a drink and see if we can grab lunch there.'

Ivo got out of the car and stretched. Then he opened the tailgate and freed Harold from his harness, letting him jump out onto the grass verge. He sniffed the air and headed for the gate. Ivo followed him and, staring warily over the gate, clipped on his lead.

Jonny locked the car and joined them. It looked like a good place for a walk. He could see a stile at the far end of the field, so he checked the map on his phone and noticed there was a right of way across to it, and on the other side of the stile there was a short foot-path to a canal. They could walk along the towpath, maybe see some ducks or even boats. He lifted the heavy metal latch on the gate and went through it into the field.

Ivo waited where he was on the verge, watching him. 'Can we take

Harold in there?' he asked, looking worried. 'There might be animals.'

Harold obviously didn't think that was a problem. He tugged on the lead, trying to follow Jonny.

'I can't see any animals,' said Jonny, amused by Ivo's caution. He really needed to get out into the countryside a bit more. 'It's marked on the map as a public footpath. We can cross the field and walk along by the canal.'

'I can't see a canal,' said Ivo, looking at the stile hesitantly but allowing Harold to pull him into the field.

Jonny clicked on Maps on his phone and handed it to Ivo. 'It's just over there,' he said, setting off across the grass with Harold at his heels, dragging a still-reluctant Ivo behind him. 'You see,' he said as they arrived at the stile a few moments later. 'Not an animal in sight.'

Stiles were not designed with dogs in mind, Jonny decided. Harold blinked at it and then sat down. Ivo tried to coax him onto the wooden step, but getting all four legs onto it was more than Harold could manage. 'You go over,' said Jonny. 'And he might follow you.' But there was no way Harold was going to follow Ivo. Instead, he gazed up at Jonny with an expression that seemed to say, *I'm not going over there, not if you pay me.* 'Oh, come on, Harold,' said Jonny, after a few more minutes of coaxing him. He lifted him up and passed him over the stile to Ivo, who took him in both arms and set him down on the footpath. Jonny climbed over and jumped down to join them, catching his breath after the exertion of lifting several kilos of dog over the stile and brushing the mud from Harold's paws off his jumper. Harold scampered off ahead of them along the path, the indignity of the stile forgotten.

At a bend in the path Harold stopped suddenly. He'd reached the canal and Jonny was thankful for the dog's aversion to water. He hadn't brought a towel and didn't want his car reeking of wet dog.

'It's nice here,' said Ivo, looking along the canal to where some narrowboats were moored against the bank. 'Looks like there are people living in them.'

He's probably right, thought Jonny. The boats had a lived-in look to them, wooden boxes of flowers on the roofs, smoke coming from small chimneys and washing hanging on lines strung across decks. As if to confirm it, a woman emerged from a hatch on one of the boats, climbed out onto the bank carrying a brightly decorated can and started watering the pots on the roof of the boat. She smiled at them. 'Nice day,' she said. Harold sensed a friend and scampered towards her, wagging his tail. 'Hello, doggie.' She patted Harold on the head. 'What's your name?'

'It's Harold,' said Ivo, following him to where the boat was moored. 'I'm Ivo.'

Jonny stepped forward to join them. 'And I'm Jonny,' he said, reaching across the deck to shake her hand.

'Pleased to meet you,' she said. 'We don't see many dog walkers along here. I'm Dot.'

'Do you live here?' Ivo asked, craning his neck to try to see inside the cabin.

'I do, same as those two over there.' She nodded towards two other boats tied up further along the canal. 'But we move around. This is a good spot to stay between March and September and we've spent several summers here. It's one of the less sought after summer moorings, so it's not too expensive. We usually move on to more popular places once the tourist season ends and the price drops. We like to winter in a town. Last year we went all the way up to Chester.' She finished watering her plants, put the can down and perched on the roof of the cabin. 'What brings you here?' she asked. 'Like I said, it's a bit off the rambler routes, too industrial.'

'We're looking for someone who used to work over there,' said Jonny, nodding back across the field to where he could just see the gate to the bit of land where the containers had been parked. 'Seems we just missed him because everyone was moved away last week. I was told he might be in the pub at lunchtime, so we're giving Harold a walk before we go there.'

'We've been to it a few times,' said Dot. 'What's this bloke's name?'

'Dan Smith,' said Ivo. 'A second-hand car dealer.'

'Can't say I know him,' said Dot. 'Doesn't mean he won't be there, though.'

'We're actually trying to trace someone who sold him a van about eighteen months ago.'

'There were all sorts working from those containers. We didn't have much to do with them,' she said. 'There was a guy who did some welding for us once, but I've not much need of a car, none of us boaters have. Eighteen months ago, September? We'd have been getting ready to move off this mooring for the winter. But good luck at the pub. Hope you find him.' She upended the watering can, tipping the dregs into the canal and went back on board and down into the cabin, sliding the hatch closed behind her.

JONNY ORDERED a Coke for Ivo and, having unsuccessfully scanned options for low alcohol beer, a lemonade shandy for himself. He picked up a grimy laminated menu and read it.

'Most of that's off,' said the barman, wiping the bar with a damp cloth and pulling the beer with an old-fashioned pump handle. 'I can do pie and chips or cheese toasties.'

'What kind of pie?' Jonny liked the old-fashioned pumps, but apart from that the pub had definitely seen better days.

'Meat.'

'I'll have two toasties,' said Jonny, having decided not to enquire too closely into the kind of meat on offer. He picked up the glasses and carried them to a table where Ivo and Harold had installed themselves.

'Do you think he's one of those over there?' Ivo asked, nodding towards a group of four men huddled around a table in the corner, clutching pint glasses and packets of crisps.

'They look the most likely,' Jonny agreed. The only other people in the pub were an elderly couple and a young man with acne.

One of the men went to the bar for a refill just as a woman appeared from the kitchen with their toasties. Jonny stood up and walked over to collect them. He smiled at her. She looked a lot more friendly than either the barman or the other punters. 'There you go, love,' she said. 'Ketchup and that over there in the wire basket.' She pointed to the end of the bar close to where the man was standing. Jonny moved over and started studying the various sachets of ketchup, mustard and brown sauce. 'What can I do for you, Dan?' she asked, turning to the other customer. *Clearly a regular,* Jonny thought. Was this their man? He had the right name, but Dan was not an uncommon name.

'Another pint,' said Dan. 'And a cheese sarnie.'

'Are you Dan Smith?' Jonny asked as he selected two packets of ketchup.

'Who's asking?'

'Let me get that,' said Jonny, getting out his wallet and nodding at Dan's pint. 'I'm looking for Dan Smith the car dealer.'

'Thanks, guv,' he said, swallowing a swig of beer. 'Yeah, I'm Dan Smith. What do you want?'

He looked aggressive, Jonny thought. But if the Facebook page he'd found could be believed, Dan probably had a lot of disgruntled customers seeking him out. 'Just wondering if we could have a word,' said Jonny. He picked up the toasties as well as Dan's cheese sandwich and headed back to the table, Dan following him looking reluctant. He pulled up a chair and sat down. He was a big man with an armful of tattoos and several days' stubble. Jonny was glad he had Ivo and Harold with him, especially Harold, who appeared from under the table and bared his teeth at Dan. Jonny knew that Harold was a generally friendly dog, and baring his teeth wasn't a gesture of aggression, merely the result of a fight followed by some bad dentistry. Dan wouldn't know that, of course, which as far as Jonny was concerned made him feel safer.

'So what is it you want?' Dan asked. 'I don't do returns and I've no motors available, not since we was closed down by the builders. Hoping to find a new place soon if you want to wait a week or two.'

'No, I don't want to buy a car,' said Jonny.

'Your mate then?' he said, nodding at Ivo.

'I've already got a van,' said Ivo.

'Then...'

'I hear you're a darts player,' said Jonny.

Dan suddenly looked relieved and a lot less aggressive. 'Oh yeah, you come to fix up a match?'

'No, but I talked to one of your fellow darts players, Andy Simpson. Bought a van from you for his wife.'

'Nothing wrong with that van,' said Dan, becoming defensive again. 'A nice little runner, nine months MOT and tax. All the paperwork was kosher.'

'I'm sure it was,' said Jonny. 'Jessie seems very pleased with it.'

'Not much chance of another one that good, if that's what you're after.'

'No, it's not. We're interested in the man you bought it from.'

'I gave him a good price for it.'

Jonny only had Dan's word for that, and Hugo was not in a position to argue. 'What do you remember about him?'

'Not much. Must be over a year ago.'

'Another pint?' Jonny asked.

'Don't mind if I do.' He pushed his glass towards Jonny.

'I'll get it,' said Ivo, jumping up with his own glass.

'Tell you what,' said Dan, pushing his now empty plate in Ivo's direction. 'Another sarnie might just jog my memory.'

'Tell them to put it on my tab,' said Jonny, hoping the day wasn't going to involve much more bribery. Did police detectives get a budget for that kind of thing? Not that he couldn't afford to stump up for a bit of information, but he seemed to have landed in the kind of culture that didn't believe in something for nothing.

'He wanted cash,' said Dan, his memory returning now another free pint was on the way, not to mention a second sandwich. 'And he was in a hurry.'

'How did he find you?' Jonny asked, wondering if Hugo had sought out somewhere isolated to discreetly sell his van. This was hardly a spur of the moment kind of place that you'd come across while driving around looking for somewhere to raise a quick bit of cash.

'I advertise in the local paper. No idea why he came all the way up here to sell his van, though. Came from Windsor way. Must be plenty of other dealers there.'

Perhaps Hugo had been heading north anyway, and once well away from home, stopped to buy a local paper to search for someone who'd take his van off his hands without attracting too much attention.

Ivo returned from the bar with the drinks and a sandwich.

'Thanks,' said Dan, taking a bite of it. 'Not having one yourself?'

Ivo shook his head. He still had the remains of his toastie, which Harold was eyeing hungrily.

'Did he tell you he was coming?' Jonny asked, finishing his own toastie. 'Or did he just turn up?'

'Called me about half an hour before he arrived.'

That would fit in. A stop for coffee, perhaps, a read of the paper and a quick phone call to a likely dealer. 'Was he on his own?' Jonny asked.

'Yeah.'

So not doing a runner with a lady friend. From what he'd learnt about Hugo Walsh, that surprised Jonny. But all it told him was that Hugo didn't leave with a woman who had lived in the Windsor area. Perhaps he'd arranged a meeting well away from home. Selling his van was just a first step to cover his tracks. 'Did you sell him another car?' Jonny asked.

'Nope.'

Did that mean Hugo had been holed up somewhere around here? 'So how did he leave? You're a bit off the beaten track.'

'Walked into town, I suppose.'

'Did he say where he was going?'

'None of my business.'

It crossed Jonny's mind that Hugo's van might have been stolen, or that Hugo had already passed it on to someone else. Perhaps he wasn't the guy Dan had met. He wouldn't rule out Dan Smith as a handler of stolen vehicles. 'Are you sure the man you met was the registered owner, Hugo Walsh?'

'Didn't ask for his passport, if that's what you mean. But there was no reason to think he wasn't who he said he was.'

'Can you describe him?' Jonny asked, hoping Dan wasn't about to lose his memory again.

'Sixtyish, medium build, ordinary looking.'

Jonny fished into his plastic wallet and pulled out a picture he'd downloaded from Hugo's website. 'This him?'

'Yeah, I reckon that's him. Friend of yours, is he?'

'Never met him,' said Jonny. 'We're making enquiries about where he might have been for the last eighteen months.'

'Can't help you there,' said Dan. 'Never saw him again.'

'Did he have much with him?'

Dan thought about that for a moment. 'Just a backpack, as far as I remember.'

'Didn't you think that odd?'

'None of my business, was it? He'd left the van clean and tidy. Can't ask more than that.'

'So you've no idea where he was headed?'

'I offered to drop him off near the station, but he said he wasn't going that way.'

'And he didn't leave any contact details?'

'Just the address on the logbook. Why would he need to do more than that?'

'You'll have the number he called you from.'

'Can't help you there, I'm afraid. Got a new phone and didn't bother copying the call history.'

Jonny sighed. This was like pulling teeth. If Hugo had deliberately covered his tracks, Dan Smith had been a gift.

'Tell you what,' said Dan. 'I like to be helpful, so give me your number and I'll call you if he turns up here again.'

'He's dead,' said Ivo, speaking for the first time since Dan had joined them.

'Weren't me, guv,' said Dan with a chuckle, holding his hands up in a way that suggested he was not hiding any lethal weapons. 'Only joking,' he added. 'But I'd better be getting back to my mates.'

Jonny settled his tab – thankfully, this was very much at the bargain end of pub catering – and he and Ivo returned to the car followed by Harold, who paused only to clear up a few crumbs that had found their way under the table.

'Are we going anywhere else?' Ivo asked as they settled into the car once again.

'I think we've done enough for today,' said Jonny. He reached under his seat and found a road atlas. He'd not used it for several years, satnavs being easier, but it wouldn't have changed that much. Motorways had become smart but still went to the same places. He handed it to Ivo. 'See if you can work out where Hugo might have been going,' he said. 'He didn't have a car, but he might have got himself to the motorway and hitched a lift.'

Ivo frowned at him. 'He could be anywhere,' he said. 'I can stare at the map all you want, but without a few clues there's no way we are going to find him.'

He was probably right. Jonny took the atlas from him and pushed it back under the seat.

'But hey,' said Ivo, 'we know what he did with his van and that he didn't buy another car. And the canal was nice. I'd really like to live on a boat like one of those.'

'We knew about the van before,' Jonny grumbled, wondering if they had just wasted a whole day. A day that had cost him twenty pounds in backhanders along with two pints of beer and a cheese sandwich. The only plus he could think of was that Harold had had a nice walk by the canal and Ivo had discovered an ambition to live on a boat.

13

Katya sat down at the head of the table and beamed at everyone. They'd had a successful day out in Bath tracking down Penelope and they had all sent her notes about the people they were following up. Katya spread these out now on the table in front of her. Jasmine had spoken to one of the singers, who suspected that Penelope was having an affair. Ivo had learnt a lot about Hugo and Penelope from Jason and a woman called Poppy Cookson, who was one of his neighbours. Jonny had found some interesting facts about Hugo's finances, as well as his movements concerning the sale of his van a few days before the train crash that had supposedly killed him.

She cleared the board, picked up a pen and drew three columns headed *Penelope Walsh*, *Hugo Walsh*, and *Bruce Hunter*.

'Let's start with Penelope,' she said. Under her name she wrote:

Married Hugo when eighteen and pregnant
Appears to have given up a promising career as a singer
Not happily married according to both Jason and neighbour
Suspected of having an affair
Seen in Bath a few days before the train crash
Body identified as a crash victim

'Anything to add?' she asked.

'We now know she was with a man called Bruce Hunter, who had an Australian accent,' said Jasmine.

'We do,' said Katya. 'Now we need to find out all we can about him. We've got a description of sorts that might help.' She picked up her pen again and under Bruce Hunter's name she wrote:

Australian accent

Can any of the choir identify him?

Described as medium build – same as Hugo

Wearing expensive hiking boots

Was he the man on the train with Penelope?

'What about my idea that he was with a friend who also wore boots that match the police photo?' said Ivo.

Katya sighed. She still thought it was a crazy idea, but not wanting to upset Ivo, she added *Boot prints?* to the bottom of the list.

'I could contact Juliet again and see if the name Bruce Hunter means anything to her,' said Jasmine. 'She was the one who told me Penelope was having an affair, so she may be able to give me a description even if the name means nothing. And other members of the choir might have seen them together and remember what he looked like, or know where he lived.'

Katya agreed that someone must have seen the two of them together after choir rehearsals or concerts. 'Check the electoral register and local directories as well,' she said. 'See if he lived around here, although I don't think that's likely. He'd have been missed after the train crash and someone would have connected his disappearance to Penelope's death.'

'Any luck with the missing persons list Lugs gave you?' asked Jonny.

'No one on it called Hunter,' said Katya, taking the list out of her folder and passing it to him.

'Probably from abroad, then,' said Jonny. 'There are always plenty of tourists in Windsor and that could account for why no one reported him missing. Would it be worth checking hotels in the area?'

Katya added the words *Foreign tourist* to the list. 'Good idea,' she said. 'Can I leave that with you, Jonny?' He nodded and wrote it down.

'Which leaves Hugo,' said Katya.

'We know he was planning to leave,' said Jonny. 'He withdrew fifty-five thousand from his savings account a few days before Penelope's concert tour. It looks like he was planning to disappear for a while. He could have lived on that for quite a long time if he chose cheap places. Plus, there would have been some money from the sale of his car.'

'Anything useful from your car salesman?' Katya asked.

'We're fairly sure Hugo sold the van himself,' said Ivo. 'He matches the description Dan Smith gave us of the man he bought it from. So it hadn't been stolen or in any kind of chain.'

'The paperwork was all present and correct, according to Dan Smith,' Jonny added. 'And the date he sold it suggests he left home while Penelope was away in Bath. We also know he didn't exchange the van for another car, not from Dan Smith anyway. After that he just disappeared. He was alone when he sold the van, so there was no one to give him a lift. Smith's container office was off the beaten track, and he was a long way from any kind of transport link. He could have walked the hour or so into Milton Keynes and caught a train, although Smith said he'd offered Hugo a lift to the station, but he told him he wasn't going that way.'

'He could have been lying, I suppose,' said Katya. 'Perhaps he didn't want anyone to know where he was headed. I'll ask Lugs if we can get CCTV footage from the station in Milton Keynes for that day.' She made some notes under Hugo's name:

Planning his escape – why?

Running away from a threat?

Seen at station after selling his car?

Walked to train or coach station?

Where did he spend the last eighteen months?

Why did he return to Windsor?

'Anything in his paperwork that suggests he was being threatened, Jonny?'

Jonny shook his head. 'I'll go through it again, but I don't recall anything. There was nothing personal at all.'

Katya wondered if that was unusual. Had Hugo carefully gone through everything before he left home and destroyed anything that might give a clue about why he was leaving and where he was going? Driving fifty miles to sell his van was odd, unless he was trying to cover his tracks, and the isolated venue of Dan Smith's business suggested he might have been. The paperwork from DVLA with Dan Smith's name, and Jessie's, would have arrived long after Hugo had disappeared, so would have been no use in tracing him. This definitely had the feel of someone not wanting to be discovered. But why? Katya sat back in her chair and mulled it over. There were two possible reasons, she thought. Either Hugo had done something illegal and wanted to get away before it was discovered, or he thought he was in danger from someone. The second was more likely. If he'd been involved in a crime, there would be traces of it. Crimes that are serious enough to need an escape were usually noticed. Lugs would have flagged it up when they thought Hugo was a victim of the train crash.

Jasmine interrupted Katya's thoughts. 'If anyone was threatening Hugo, wouldn't Penelope be top of the list of suspects?'

'That's right,' said Ivo. 'They weren't happily married, and if Penelope was having an affair, well...'

'She'd certainly be a contender, but that doesn't explain why Hugo didn't return after her death.' Although Jasmine could have a point, if perhaps Hugo had been living so far off grid that he didn't know Penelope had died, or even that she was on the train. And presumably he didn't know that he'd supposedly died himself. But was there anywhere these days that was so completely out of touch with the world? And even if Hugo *did* know about it, wouldn't that work to his advantage? He could have changed his name and created a whole new life for himself. In which case why return when he did? Or at all?

Katya looked at her watch. She'd promised to keep meetings short because Ivo and Jasmine had to work. 'That will do for now,' she said.

'You two need to get off to work.' She and Jonny were the lucky ones. It was one of the few times she actually appreciated having retired. They both had all the time in the world to think about what might have happened and to search for evidence. And now they had this room, there was no reason for her to rush off anywhere. She looked around appreciatively at the crime board with its photos and print-outs, at their list of persons of interest. Not so different from incident rooms she had worked in before she'd retired. 'Jonny,' she said. 'Have you got a map handy?'

'A map of where?'

'The whole country, I suppose. I want to think about where Hugo might have been heading for.'

'Ivo and I tried to work that out, but we didn't get very far. Milton Keynes is north of Windsor, which might mean he was heading north or for the Midlands. But he might as easily having been setting a false trail.'

'There must be parts of the country that are more amenable to off-grid living than others. We should check train and coach routes.'

'I've a map in the car, but I walked here this morning. Why don't I go and get us coffee and buns and we can do a bit of Google searching right here? I bet there are websites for people who want to get away from it all.' He turned on the computer and tapped in *Off grid locations in the UK*. Then he went downstairs for elevenses, leaving Katya to search for likely locations.

'Scotland or Northumberland,' said Katya, as Jonny returned with two coffees and a plate of Karim's finest pastries, which he put down in front of her. She picked up an apricot Danish and took a bite. 'Or West Country, Devon or Cornwall possibly. Even parts of Somerset,' she added. 'Although going to Milton Keynes doesn't suggest he was travelling west. He'd want to go as far as he dared before selling his car, even if he was travelling light. If he was picking up lifts after selling the van, he'd need to be as far as possible from where anyone might recognise him. Going north and then heading back south again wouldn't make sense.'

Jonny chose a chocolate croissant. 'He could have been on the move. In a camper van, perhaps, although that would have left a big hole in his fifty-five thousand. I don't suppose he got all that much for the van.'

'You know,' said Katya, wiping sugar from her fingers, eyeing the remaining bun and clicking out of Google. 'We're probably not going to find where he went. Do you think we should focus on why he came back?'

'To visit Jason?'

'And break the news that he was still alive? But why now?'

'Out of cash?' Jonny suggested.

'It would have given Jason a hell of a shock to have his dead father turn up out of the blue, demanding money. Hugo would have realised that, so perhaps he got himself drunk to psych himself up to see Jason, but then slipped into the river before he got there.'

'Or,' said Jonny, 'and this theory is probably as off the wall as Ivo's two Australians idea – perhaps Jason's been lying and Hugo had already been to see him. Jason got him drunk and pushed him into the river to protect his inheritance.'

Katya couldn't resist the final bun any longer. She picked up a knife and looked at Jonny, who shook his head and made a gesture that suggested it was all hers. 'It's a nice theory,' she said. 'It's just got two holes in it. First, is Jason capable of planning something like that, when it takes all he's got just to turn the washing machine on and change his clothes now and then? Second, does he wear expensive hiking boots in a size nine?'

'I expect you're right,' said Jonny. 'Jason's tallish so he probably has quite big feet. And anyway, I can't see him saying "Okay, Dad, let's go for a drink on the way to the cash machine and how about a walk by the river?"'

Katya laughed. 'Jason's not going to work as a suspect, is he? Much as we might want him to.'

'He does have a motive,' said Jonny.

'If you're going to be a real detective,' said Katya, 'you need to remember he also needs the means and the opportunity.'

'Do we know he was in Cornwall that night? Hugo suddenly turning up would be an opportunity. Jason might have lied about where he was.'

'And I suppose the river is a handy means of disposing of some-one. Okay, we'll not rule him out yet.'

14

Ivo emerged from the cupboard under Poppy's sink, clutching a wrench and rubbing his shoulders to ease the stiffness caused by being bent double in a confined space. He stood up, stretched and opened the window above the sink to let in some fresh air. Clearing blocked U-bends was one of his least favourite jobs involving working in small, dark and usually smelly spaces. He put the wrench back into his toolbox and returned to the cupboard to remove a bucket of filthy water. He scooped out a disgusting mix of tea leaves, potato peelings, hair and some unidentifiable blobs of rancid fat, which he wrapped in newspaper and dropped into the kitchen bin. He turned on the tap and he and Poppy watched with pleasure as the water swirled freely down the drain.

'You're a hero,' she said. 'Cup of tea?'

'Lovely,' said Ivo. 'I'll just get rid of this.' He picked up the bucket and carried it through to Poppy's back yard, where there was an outside tap and a drain. He emptied and rinsed the bucket while peering across two gardens for signs of Jason. He should call round and see if he needed any help, at the same time asking if he had any clues about where his father might have disappeared to. Did he, for instance, have any friends in the Milton Keynes area?

Returning to Poppy's kitchen, he found she'd made the tea and set out a teapot and some mugs, both blue and decorated with brightly coloured flowers. Roses. Ivo didn't know a lot about flowers, but he recognised a rose when he saw one. Poppy, he already knew, was a fan of bright colours and decorations, whether it was what she wore or the contents of her house. Last time he was here it was polka dots, today flowers. Blue seemed to be an ongoing theme. Her flower-strewn shirt was a good match for the mugs, and both reminded Ivo of the flowerpots that Dot had been watering on the roof of her canal boat. The same blue background painted with coloured roses. 'Nice tea set,' Ivo said.

Poppy smiled. 'I don't get to use it a lot,' she said. 'My brother hates it. He's more of a fine white china sort of person.'

Makes sense, Ivo thought, thinking of the starkly furnished bedroom with the navy blue curtains. His own décor owed more to what was available in charity shops. Apart from Harold's water bowl, which he'd bought at Tesco in a moment of extravagance after his first *Shady Willows* pay cheque, everything in his cabin was second hand, carefully chosen item by item when he spotted something he liked after a lucrative repair job.

'I bought it at a craft fair at the Brocas a couple of years ago,' said Poppy. 'There was a canal artist there, selling her work. I loved the style and could have spent a fortune.'

Canal, thought Ivo, something suddenly sparking his brain into action. Why hadn't he and Jonny thought of that before? 'It's an actual style, is it?' he asked. 'Canal art?'

'Absolutely. The families that lived on the narrowboats covered just about everything they owned with roses like these. It was a way of displaying their identity, I suppose. They would have passed the designs down the generations.'

'And she always paints household objects like these?'

'She paints on just about anything: pottery; plant pots; wooden boxes; even narrowboat doors. I checked her out online and looked at her other work. It's a distinctive style. You can see it on canal boats all over the country.'

Interesting, Ivo thought, wondering if carpentry counted as a craft. 'What else did they have there?'

'So many things. Quilted jackets; painted silk scarves; handmade candles; wooden boxes and toys. I think Hugo Walsh might have been there with some cupboards. I know I'd seen him somewhere selling them.'

This was getting very interesting. Ivo was starting to make connections – craft fair, canals, an artist. 'Do you remember the name of the artist?'

'Now you're asking. It was a couple of years ago and I'm no good with names. Sorry.'

'No problem,' said Ivo. 'I can Google it.'

He finished his tea and put the rest of his tools away. Poppy picked up the teapot ready to rinse the tea leaves down the drain.

'That's why it keeps getting blocked,' said Ivo as she headed for the sink he'd just cleared. Had she never heard of teabags? 'If you're going to use leaves, you need to get one of those drainer plugs. I've got some at home. I'll bring you one next time I'm in the area. Let me rinse that out in the yard for you.'

Poppy handed him the teapot and he went out to the tap in the yard to rinse it. He swilled the tea leaves round and tipped them into the drain, which was protected by a grid. He scooped the leaves out and dropped them into a dustbin. There was no point in blocking the outside drain as well. Having got rid of the tea leaves, he ran some water into the teapot to give it a rinse. Then he turned it upside down to empty it. On the bottom he found some black writing, very small and in a script that made it hard to read. He held the teapot carefully in one hand. Poppy would never forgive him if he dropped it on the stone paving slabs. Once he had a secure grip, he fumbled for his phone and took a photo. Then he returned to the kitchen to pick up his tools and collect Harold, who had stayed inside, probably in the hope of a biscuit.

Poppy rinsed the mugs and dried the teapot on a Harry and Meghan tea towel. Then she put them on a shelf on the dresser alongside several more brightly coloured mugs. She paid Ivo for the work he'd done using her phone and assured him that she would be more careful about what she washed down the sink.

Ivo left the van parked at Poppy's back gate while he and Harold walked the short distance to Jason's house. Before he knocked on the door, he paused to check his phone for messages, and not finding any, he looked at the photo he had taken of the bottom of the teapot. He pinched it with his thumb and forefinger to enlarge it. As he had hoped, the writing was now easy to read. Betsy Blake. The name, he assumed, of the artist who had made and painted it. He wondered if Jason knew anything about her, both being artists, or were they craft people? Did they call themselves craftists? It wasn't a word he'd ever heard, but then he wasn't really into crafts, or art.

He knocked on Jason's door and waited. He was knocking for the third time when Jason appeared looking dishevelled and barely half awake. He yawned and gaped at Ivo.

'I've just unblocked Poppy's sink,' said Ivo. 'Anything you need doing while I'm here?'

'Dunno. Come in,' said Jason, leading Harold and Ivo into the kitchen, which appeared to have reverted to its pre-Ivo clean-up.

Ivo sighed. 'I've not got long,' he said. 'I could wash those pots for you if you like.'

'Nah, you're all right. I was just going to make a start on them myself.'

Ivo thought that extremely unlikely, but if Jason liked living in a tip who was he to argue? It wasn't what he'd come for, anyway. He was there after an odd request from Jonny, who wanted to know Jason's shoe size. He glanced down at Jason's feet, which were wearing only socks. *Average size,* Ivo thought, which probably wouldn't be much use to Jonny, who, in Ivo's opinion, was way off the mark if he thought Jason was responsible for the footprints on the riverbank. But if a job's worth doing... 'You need to put some shoes on,' said Ivo. 'You don't want to get splinters in your feet or tread on broken glass.' *Or bits of rotting food,* he might have added.

Jason stared down at his feet and looked surprised by their unshod state. He stared helplessly around. 'Now, where...?'

'Here,' said Ivo, reaching for a pair of scruffy trainers that had been left on the sofa.

'Oh, yeah,' said Jason. 'Must have taken them off when I was watching the telly.'

Ivo passed them to him, glancing inside to see they were a size ten. 'Nice trainers,' he said as Jason started to put them on.

'I wear them all the time,' he said. 'The only pair I own.'

'So you don't have any others? Hiking boots, for instance?'

'Nah, why would I have hiking boots?'

'Just wondered. You'd need them on Bodmin Moor, wouldn't you?'

'Where?'

'Bodmin Moor. Isn't that where you used to live?'

'Long time ago,' he said. 'We didn't go out much.'

So much for Jonny's theory, Ivo thought as he and Harold left. Although Jason might have been lying. He'd never thought of Jason as a suspect, although Jonny obviously did. If Jason had wanted to get rid of his father, all he had to do was invite him round for a meal and wait for food poisoning to take hold.

LATER THAT EVENING, Ivo searched the Internet for all he could find about Betsy Blake and canal art. He made several pages of notes ready for the next meeting. But then he remembered the way Katya had dismissed his ideas, and he decided to talk them through with Jasmine first. If she thought it was a daft theory then he would keep quiet about it.

15

J asmine looked out of her bedroom window at the rain beating against it. *Just my luck,* she thought. It had been dry for weeks and now, on her day off, a day she'd set aside for a run in the park followed by some girly time with her best friend from school, it was torrentially wet. Shopping would be okay, she supposed. They could go to Westfield at Shepherd's Bush, which was under cover and only forty minutes or so up the motorway. They could get their hair and nails done and look at wedding dresses, because her friend was getting married soon. Jasmine's dad would be working in the café all day so they could borrow his car. Driving in heavy rain wasn't much fun but it was probably better than sitting here all day watching it through her window. She stared hopefully out into the street again but the rain showed no sign of letting up, so a run was out of the question. She definitely didn't want to run in the rain and her friend worked until midday, so what could Jasmine do this morning? If she stayed here, she'd probably be roped in as a kitchen hand. Living and working in the same place was sometimes a bad idea. She had to be tough and not give up her free day. But she needed something to do, so she decided to work in the detective office. She'd have it to herself with sole use of Jonny's posh desktop computer and also of the coffee machine that he'd donated, saying he was never at CPS long enough to need coffee. Pop down to the café and grab a couple of croissants and she'd be set up for the morning. She would search for men called Hunter.

WHERE TO START? she wondered as she turned on the computer. Jonny had set them all up with their own usernames and her first thought was that her personal login page was rather dull. She spent some time changing the wallpaper. Apple, she discovered, had a colourful selection to choose from. She picked pastel colours and set them to change every few minutes. Then she discovered an app for making coloured folders. She downloaded it and then realised she didn't actually have any folders. Plenty on her laptop, but none on the detective computer. Some of the stuff on her laptop was relevant to their cases so she AirDropped them across and played around with different coloured folders. She chose a deep magenta colour, labelled it *Body in Long Walk Archive,* and dragged all the notes she'd made into it. For their current case she should have some folders that she could save information in to share with the others. She chose bright yellow for a main folder, which she called *Death in the River*. Then she added more, each one a different colour, which she labelled *Hugo, Penelope, Jason, Police info* and finally, the one she was hoping to fill that morning – *Hunter*.

That was enough playing around. It was time to get down to work and do some proper research. What should she search for? Hunter on its own brought up about a million suggestions, Bruce Hunter only slightly fewer. He had an accent, probably Australian, so she typed in *Bruce Hunter Australia* which wasn't much better. What did she actually know about the mysterious Mr Hunter? Very little. She tried *Hunter and Bath* and discovered a firm of estate agents in the city. She chewed at her croissant and tapped in *Applewood Choir Bruce Hunter* with no results at all. This was getting her nowhere. Perhaps she should concentrate on the boots instead. What was it Katya had said about them? The only thing she could remember was that they were Australian and expensive so she tried *expensive Australian hiking boots* and was shown a selection that she might want to buy.

Glancing at the photo of the footprints that was pinned to the board, she wondered if there was something distinctive about the tread pattern. That was how the police had identified the boots as Australian. She looked at the various websites involved, luckily not too many of them, and studied the different views of the boots. It was useful that sellers of footwear often displayed their boots in a way that allowed her to look at them from different angles. She could manipulate the images, turning them around, many through 180 degrees, enabling her to study the soles and match them against the police photo. Finding one that looked very much like the photo, she visited the seller's Facebook page. With any luck, people would have left comments. They might also have left a clue about where they were from, and anyone within a twenty-mile radius of Windsor would be worth exploring as a possible witness. Someone who had been walking along the riverbank the night Hugo died.

She glanced at the time at the top of the screen. She needed to leave at twelve and it was now eleven-fifteen, so she had a little time to scroll down and read some of the comments. There were plenty of happy-looking hikers wearing the boots and commenting on their comfort. *Why bother posting that?* she thought. *You pay for expensive boots, you expect them to be comfortable. Why waste time posting on Facebook when you could be yomping around the countryside actually using them?*

She was about to shut down the computer and write off the morning's searching as a waste of time, when she noticed a tab for reviews. She clicked on it and again scrolled through a long list of comments, eventually finding an entry that said *Share a tinny with these guys.* This one had a collection of photos and had been added by a user called Clive Longlegs, who had written an account of a hiking holiday he had taken in Western Australia. One photo in particular caught Jasmine's attention. Clive – she knew from the other pictures that it was him – was standing in front of a log cabin with his arms around the shoulders of two other men. Brothers, possibly; they looked similar. But there was an obvious age gap, so perhaps they were father and son. They all looked like what she imagined were stereotypical Australian men – stocky, rugged, suntanned and jovial. All three were clutching cans of beer – *another stereotype,* Jasmine thought. Surely there must be some nerdy, bespectacled men in Australia. Although they lived in a country with almost permanent sunshine and on a diet of steak, so perhaps not. Anyway, she was looking for those that wore expensive hiking boots, and your average nerd probably didn't. All three of these men were wearing identical boots – those that were sold by the people who ran the Facebook page. And which had very similar treads to the police photo. The picture was captioned *My thanks to the Hunters for this rip snorter of a hiking trip.* Since all three were grinning, Jasmine assumed that *rip snorter* was a compliment.

Could this be who she was looking for? The older of the two men could be the Mr Hunter described by the hotel manager, although his description could also fit hundreds of other men. And what on earth was he doing first at a hotel in Bath, and eighteen months later on the banks of the River Thames? Perhaps Ivo's theory was not so daft after all. Dad could have been on holiday, met Penelope and then died in a train crash. Son travelled here eighteen months later to avenge his father's death by pushing Hugo Walsh into the river. *No,* she thought. There was no way that would add up. It was way too complicated and posed far too many questions. Most of which they had already asked. It just brought in even more people who knew nothing about the man on the train. The man supposedly known as Hugo Walsh.

She closed down the page, making sure she had bookmarked it, and searched *Hunter hiking trips Western Australia.* And there they were, Bruce and Mervyn Hunter – yes, there really were Australian men called Bruce and Mervyn, another stereotype to add to her list. They were a father and son company who offered guided and unguided hikes, special interest hikes, which seemed to involve visits to wineries to sample the produce, art hikes, which provided trans-port for art materials, and many others.

She clicked on a tab labelled *News,* hoping the news might include a trip to the UK by one or other of the Hunters, or perhaps an interest in singing and northern hemisphere choirs. But there was no mention of either of them being in the least interested in travelling or music of any kind. She did discover that Mervyn, at the age of sixteen, had been Western Australia's junior rock-climbing champion, and that his wife had recently given birth to a son called Leo. So he was unlikely to have been in the UK pushing people into rivers. Another blow to Ivo's theory.

Jasmine bookmarked the site. She'd print out some of the pages later and pin them to the board before the next meeting, and see if Katya and the others thought she might be onto something. Right now, she needed to clear her head. And there was nothing better for that than a bit of retail therapy.

16

Arriving at the back entrance to *Jasmine's,* Ivo rubbed an unwilling Harold down with a towel that Karim handed him through the kitchen window. 'Think yourself lucky we didn't walk here in the rain,' said Ivo as Harold cowered at his feet, wearing a hard done by expression. They always walked the twenty minutes from *Shady Willows* to *Jasmine's* because parking was hard in this part of town, and anyway, the exercise was good for both of them. Ivo had promised Karim that he would drop in and fix a dripping tap in the kitchen. He did jobs like these once his on-site chores were done, but his morning had been busy and he was running a bit late. It had been pouring with rain since early morning. A couple of the cabins had leaking skylights and Ivo had been called out first thing – first to find buckets to catch the water and then to patch them up. One of the paths had flooded and he'd had to find a pump before any of the residents needed to get out. He'd looked anxiously at the river that ran close to one or two of the cabins. It was flowing faster than usual but there'd been little rain in the last month and there was still a way to go before it broke the bank. All the same, he decided to be ready in case the worst happened. He unlocked the shed and found a stack of sandbags, which he laid in a double layer along the bank that bordered the site. They probably wouldn't be needed but, although they were heavy and would all have to be put back in the shed once the rain stopped, it would be better than dealing with a full-scale flood; homes knee-deep in water with ruined carpets and furniture would be far worse to deal with.

Having installed the sandbags, he went to see how the pump was doing. It was still raining but the path was now clear. He turned it off and watched for a while to see if it flooded again, but after twenty minutes the rain had eased and the path remained free of water. Now soaking wet himself, Ivo returned to his own cabin where he found Harold curled up on the sofa. Normally he did the rounds with Ivo, but one of them getting soaked through was enough and Harold didn't like rain. He was happier staying in the cabin and watching Ivo through the window. Once Ivo had changed out of his wet work clothes, and now the rain had stopped, he decided to walk to *Jasmine's* to fix the dripping tap in the kitchen. He also wanted to talk to Jasmine, and early afternoons when she'd finished serving lunch was a good time to do it.

The rain might have stopped but it still lay in deep puddles along the road and at a point where the pavement narrowed, a lorry passed them. The driver ignored the near flood in the gutter and soaked Harold to the skin. Harold hated being wet and immediately sat down, refusing to take another step and gazing longingly back the way they had come. 'We're closer to the café,' Ivo told him, tugging gently on the lead. Harold refused to budge. 'There'll be sausages,' said Ivo. Harold was highly intelligent, or so Ivo had always thought. He knew food words like sausages and, encouraged either by that or the fact that he was sitting on a damp, gritty footpath, he stood up and trotted along beside Ivo, making sure he stayed on the inside, as far away as he could from passing traffic.

Once Harold had dried off, they found Jonny sitting at his favourite table with a cup of coffee and an iced bun, and Karim and his assistant serving lunches. There was no sign of Jasmine, and Ivo remembered that it was her day off. Agreeing with Karim that the dripping tap could wait until after the lunchtime rush, Ivo bought a sausage sandwich and he and Harold joined Jonny at the table by the window.

'Can I talk to you about something?' Ivo asked.

'Of course,' said Jonny.

Jonny would do just as well as Jasmine for what Ivo wanted to talk about. Better, perhaps, as they had both seen the canal boats when they'd visited Dan Smith, and it was the boats that had given Ivo his idea. 'I don't want to talk to Katya yet,' he said. 'She never takes my ideas seriously. Well, not the idea about Bruce Hunter being the person with the boots, anyway.'

'Katya can be a bit brusque,' Jonny agreed. 'But that's just the way she is.'

'I had this idea,' said Ivo, taking a bite of his sandwich and extracting a piece of sausage for Harold. 'I unblocked Poppy's sink the other day.'

'That's nice,' said Jonny. 'Who's Poppy?'

'She lives next door but one to Jason.'

'Yes, of course. I'd forgotten. And did unblocking her sink give you an insight into our case?'

'She made me a cup of tea when I'd finished, and the teapot she used was painted by someone who does canal art.'

'We saw some, didn't we?' said Jonny. 'Painted planters on the boat. Was it like those? All bright coloured roses and castles?'

Ivo nodded, telling Jonny about Poppy's visit to the craft fair where she'd bought the teapot and some mugs. 'She thought Hugo Walsh was there selling some of his cupboards,' said Ivo. 'It made me think that perhaps he knew about the canal boats close to where he sold his van and maybe he hitched a ride on one of them. That's why he didn't need a lift to the station.'

'That's an excellent theory,' said Jonny. 'Do we need to go back to the canal and ask?'

Ivo shook his head. 'I think Dot said there were a lot of boats coming and going at the beginning and end of the holiday season. There were probably any number of boats on that stretch of the canal that September. Going back there could be a wasted trip.'

'It could still be worth a try,' said Jonny. 'I don't mind driving up there again. But you're right, unless Dot actually remembers Hugo it could be quite hard to track him down. The trouble is, I don't know how else we can find out where he was going.'

'I've got an idea,' said Ivo. 'Poppy told me a bit about the craft fair and the kind of things they had there. She mentioned wooden furniture and painted doors. If Hugo was there selling some of his cupboards, he and the painter could have met. So if we can find the artist, we might also find where Hugo spent the last eighteen months.'

'That's possible,' said Jonny. 'I don't suppose Poppy knew the name of the artist?'

Ivo grinned at him, feeling pleased with himself. 'It was painted on the bottom of the teapot,' he said. 'She's called Betsy Blake. I checked her out online and she has a website with loads of photos of her work. She lives on a narrowboat near Banbury and sells stuff at a shop on the canal bank. There's a photo of her boat on the website. It has wooden doors that she decorated.' He pulled up Hugo's website and showed it to Jonny. 'Hugo made doors,' he said. 'Look. His doors are very like these ones here.' He flicked back to the picture on Betsy's website and passed his phone to Jonny.

Jonny put his glasses on and looked closely at the two pictures, scrolling from one to the other, pinching them with his fingers to enlarge them. 'You're definitely onto something here,' he said. 'So how do you think it all hangs together?'

'I think Hugo met Betsy at the craft fair, saw the things she'd painted and got talking about him making doors for her boat. That means they'd probably have got to know each other quite well. Perhaps he even visited her on her boat.'

'And then when he wanted an escape, he found a place close to a canal where he could sell his car. A short walk down the road and he could hitch a lift on a boat to, where did you say it was?'

'Banbury,' said Ivo. He fished a piece of paper from his pocket and spread it out in front of Jonny. 'He'd have gone up the Grand Union to this place here.' Ivo jabbed his finger onto the map at a place called Braunston. 'Then down the Oxford Canal to Banbury.'

'It's a long way,' said Jonny.

'I looked that up as well,' said Ivo. 'Canal boats go very slowly, only about three miles an hour. And then there are locks where the boats usually have to wait. It probably took him weeks.'

'A good way to hide,' said Jonny. 'And most likely out of touch with the news. It could have been a while before he found out that everyone thought he was dead.'

'And if he was running away from something, that would suit him very well.'

The café was still busy with lunchtime customers, and since Ivo was going to have to hang around a bit longer, he suggested that he and Jonny might go to the office and do a bit more research on the whole canal boat idea.

IT WAS INTERESTING, Jonny thought, that Ivo had brought his idea to him rather than Katya. But he could sympathise. Katya did tend to treat Ivo like a child, which was a pity. Ivo might be the youngest of the four of them, but he was no fool. He was observant and came up with some good ideas among the slightly off the wall ones.

Karim told them it would be another hour before the kitchen was empty enough for Ivo to fix the tap. He'd call up the stairs for him when the decks were clear, and they'd finished with the tap. Jonny decided he and Ivo should do some further research and have a plan in place for when they next saw Katya. That way, she was less likely to argue with them. He turned on the computer and searched for Betsy Blake's website. He downloaded the photo from her home page and wished they had a printer up there. *I must see what I can do about that.* For now, he enlarged the picture and saved it to the desktop. He and Ivo looked at the photo, a woman in her mid-fifties, with unruly hair held back with a red and white spotted scarf, and wearing a blue artist's smock over paint-spattered leggings.

'She looks arty, doesn't she?' said Jonny, thinking that if he'd been asked to come up with a visual of a canal painter who went to craft fairs and had a shop in Banbury, this was pretty much what it would have looked like.

'Do you think she's a suspect?' Ivo asked. 'She looks too friendly.'

Jonny smiled. 'I should think killers would want to look friendly in their photos, same as the rest of us. Anyway, are we looking for a suspect? As far as we know, Hugo's death was an accident and Penelope's death definitely was.'

'I think someone pushed him,' said Ivo. 'There were the footprints on the bank where he probably went into the water. And more where his body was found.'

'Lugs told Katya that was not enough to treat it as murder, and we should probably keep an open mind about it. But I don't see how Betsy Blake can possibly be a suspect. Even if she hated the way Hugo had made her doors, it's hardly a motive. And anyway, if she wanted to drown him, she could have pushed him into the canal.'

'Canals aren't deep enough,' said Ivo.

'So you think she lured him to Windsor so she could get him drunk and then push him into the river?' Jonny was beginning to think Katya might have a point about Ivo's theories. On the other hand, if Betsy had known Hugo, she might have some useful information about him. 'We should still go and talk to her. If she did know Hugo, she might be able to give us some background about why he left home suddenly. Even why he returned eighteen months later.' He opened Google Maps. Banbury was a drive of around an hour and a quarter from Windsor. If they went that afternoon, they could be back by early evening and if things went well, they might have some very useful information to pass on to Katya in the morning. He looked out of the window. The rain had stopped, he had nothing in particular planned for the rest of the day, so why not go straight away? 'Let's go,' he said, grabbing his car keys.

'You mean go and talk to Betsy Blake now?'

Jonny nodded. 'No time like the present.'

'What about Karim's tap?'

'How long will it take you to fix it?' he asked.

'Only about ten minutes.'

'You go and do that, and I'll drop an email to Katya to tell her what we're doing.'

NOT ONLY HAD it stopped raining, but the sun had also come out by the time they reached Banbury. They parked near the canal, put Harold on his lead and walked towards a collection of narrowboats moored along the bank. It was a lot busier than the stretch of canal they'd seen at Milton Keynes. There was a boatyard and a shop selling equipment and gas cylinders. A lot of the boats had people working on them, preparing for the Easter holiday and the start of the season. Canal boating was obviously a popular holiday. On the opposite side of the canal was a modern, red-brick shopping centre and further out of town, a lock. They stood and watched a couple of boats going through and then walked on towards some smaller buildings, where they found Betsy Blake's shop and narrowboat. The boat was red and blue with *Lady Elizabeth* painted in an arch shape on a blue panel in a shadowed script, framed with red roses.

Jonny recognised Betsy from her website photo, a recent one apparently. She was sitting on the roof of her boat with a mug of coffee and dressed in the same navy-blue smock, her hair tied up with a scarf. Not red with white spots today. This one was green with a design of yellow hummingbirds. She watched as Jonny and Ivo looked into the window of her shop, which was empty of people. Too early in the year for many customers, Jonny supposed.

'Want to go in and have a look?' Betsy called out to them, reaching into the pocket of her smock for a bunch of keys and jumping down onto the towpath. 'Not many customers this afternoon, but the shop is open.'

'Thanks,' said Jonny. 'We'd like that.'

'Can we bring the dog in?' Ivo asked. 'I don't mind waiting out here with him.'

'No, no,' said Betsy. 'Bring him in. I have some dog bowls you can look at, or decorated leads.'

Betsy must have had a busy winter stocking up for the holiday season. The shop was crammed full of painted crockery, plant pots, trays, coffee pots and buckets, all decorated with traditional canal designs featuring roses and castles, narrowboats and horses, one of which was carrying Lady Godiva. A local connection, Jonny supposed, being quite close to Coventry. He wondered if this might be another chance to find a birthday present for Belinda. He was unsure how the perfume would be received. She'd be happier with something for the garden. A half barrel perhaps, or a window box. Then he spotted some wooden wall cupboards. He nudged Ivo, who nodded. Apart from being covered with painted roses, they were the same as one they'd seen in Jason's living room.

'We sell a lot of those,' said Betsy, noticing their interest. 'At least, we did until the bastard who made them disappeared.'

Jonny was suddenly alert. But he shouldn't jump to conclusions. Although this was an unusual design, certainly not one Jonny had seen anywhere else, there could still be other people who made them. 'It wasn't Hugo Walsh, was it?' he asked.

Betsy looked at him in surprise. 'You know him?' she asked.

'I know of him,' said Jonny, thinking that he couldn't just come out with it and tell her Hugo was dead, even if she had just called him a bastard. 'Actually, we've come to talk to you about him.'

'Is he in trouble?' she asked, frowning. 'Do you know where he is?'

Probably best not to let her know that yes, he did know where he was. It might not be the best moment to tell her that right now Hugo was in the mortuary at a hospital in Slough, while decisions were made about who should be responsible for disposing of his remains. Or more to the point, who should pay for their disposal. Better break it to her gently. 'It's not good news, I'm afraid,' said Jonny. He glanced at Ivo, hoping that he was not about to blurt out the circumstances of Hugo's death. But Ivo was at the far side of the shop looking at dog leads. 'Is there somewhere we could sit down and talk?' Jonny asked.

'I'd better close the shop. We can talk in the boat.'

Did she have any idea what Jonny was about to tell her? If she did, she was taking it very calmly, and Jonny wondered if that was because she didn't know Hugo very well or if what had happened to him was not entirely unexpected. He still didn't go along with Ivo's idea that she'd killed Hugo. He was still in two minds about whether or not he had been murdered. But she would be able to throw some light on where Hugo had been and what he had been up to.

Betsy locked the shop and invited them into the cabin of the boat. They walked across the footpath and up a short gangplank. Harold took some coaxing, but Ivo had come prepared with a few dog treats in his pocket. Betsy unfastened a padlock and slid back the hatch so that they could step down into the cabin.

'Wow,' said Ivo, looking around. 'I wish I lived on a boat.'

It was beautiful; a room with a polished wooden table and cabinets with brass handles, some comfortable seats with bright coloured cushions close to a wood-burning stove. Beyond the room they were in, Jonny could see a galley kitchen and further along, a bedroom.

'I like it,' said Betsy. 'But I've lived on the canal all my life.' She boiled a kettle and made them cups of tea. 'So what did you want to tell me about Hugo? Gone back to his wife, has he?'

'I'm afraid he's dead,' said Jonny. 'They both are. Penelope died eighteen months ago in a train crash. Hugo drowned in the Thames quite recently.'

Betsy sat down suddenly. From shock, surprise or even guilt, Jonny couldn't tell. It was hard to know. People reacted to bad news in different ways.

'Penelope died eighteen months ago?' she said.

Jonny nodded, thinking it was odd that she was more interested in Penelope's death than Hugo's.

'The bastard,' she said angrily. 'He told me she was refusing to divorce him. Then he just upped and left me. No warning, and nothing since. Not even a note to explain what was going on and when he'd be back.'

'You knew him well, then?'

'He's been living here for... oh my God, for eighteen months.' She'd turned suddenly pale. 'He didn't... How did you say his wife died?'

Jonny reached for her hand, hoping he looked sympathetic. 'No,' he said kindly. 'There's no question of him killing Penelope. She died in a train crash. He was in no way responsible and in any case, he'd already left home when she was killed.'

'And you say he drowned? An accident?'

'That's what the police are saying at the moment. That he was drunk and slipped into the river.'

'They did find footprints on the riverbank,' said Ivo. 'So they've not ruled out—'

Jonny shushed him before he could say any more. 'We've been asked to trace his movements,' he said.

'You're police?'

'No, we're civilian investigators. Just here to get some background.'

'Okay,' said Betsy. 'I'll help any way I can.'

'Tell us how you knew Hugo,' said Jonny.

'I met him at a craft fair, maybe two years ago. He was interested in my painting because he had some commissions for narrowboat doors, and he thought his customer might like a traditional decoration on them. We kept in touch and he came up here a few times and, well, we fell in love. At least, I thought we had.' She dabbed her eyes with a tissue. 'Looks like it could have been rather one-sided. Anyway, Hugo told me he and his wife didn't get along.'

The age-old *my wife doesn't understand me,* Jonny supposed. Assuming that Betsy knew nothing of Hugo's womanising reputation.

'He told me he wanted a divorce,' Betsy continued. 'But he said she was being difficult about it, and we might need to wait out the two years before he could go ahead with it and marry me. It didn't bother me that much. Marriage is just a piece of paper. It was what we felt for each other that mattered, and we were able to spend a lot of time together.'

'Where did you meet?' Jonny asked.

'Sometimes he came here. He'd drive his cupboards here in his van then stay a few days. Other times we'd meet in a hotel on the M40. Then he turned up here suddenly one day, saying he'd left his wife for good. He'd cashed in all his savings and sold his van. He got a lift down here with a friend of mine on her narrowboat. He said he didn't want anyone to know where he was.'

'Did he say why?'

'I assumed it was because he didn't want his wife to find him.'

'And he was here for the whole eighteen months?'

'Yes, he did a bit of work in the boatyard and made a few things for the shop. The cupboards you were looking at and some window boxes.'

'You don't have a TV,' said Ivo suddenly.

Betsy looked surprised by his statement. 'No, I get all I need from my computer.' She nodded at a laptop that was sitting on one of the cabinets.

'Did Hugo use the laptop as well?' Ivo asked.

'No, he wasn't interested.'

'Not even to sell his stuff?'

'He was very off-grid, worked from hand to mouth, cash only.'

'Didn't that surprise you?' asked Jonny.

'Not really. A lot of canal people are like that. They keep themselves to themselves. Why are you asking?'

'I'm just wondering if it's possible that he didn't know his wife was dead. Did he ever say anything to suggest he did?'

'Not a word. He just said she was being difficult about the divorce.'

'And he left suddenly? Did he give you any idea where he was going?'

'He picked up a lift on one of the boats that was heading south. Said he'd be back in a couple of days and that he needed to meet his son. Which was odd. He'd not mentioned a son before.'

'Had he been in touch with anyone?'

'No idea. Someone could have phoned or texted him, I suppose, but he only had a cheap phone. No email or WhatsApp. He may have used his email at the boatyard and had post delivered there.'

'No visitors?'

'I don't think so. He might have met someone in the pub. We weren't joined at the hip.'

'And he'd told you nothing about his son?'

'No. Not that I asked. His life before he came here was not important to me.'

All the same, discovering that the man she was living with had a son must have come as a bit of a shock. And Jason had a few questions to answer. Jonny didn't think they'd learn any more. At least they now knew where Hugo had been. It was just a slightly grubby case of a middle-aged man leaving home to live with his lover. What he and Ivo needed to do now was discover how Jason had found his father and how he had persuaded him to return home. Jonny stood up. 'I'm so sorry to have brought you bad news,' he said. 'We need to get back. Is there anyone who could stay with you for a while? All this must have been a shock for you.' That sounded very abrupt, but Betsy showed no sign that she couldn't cope with the news or that she wanted them to stay.

'No, I'm fine on my own,' she said. 'And to be honest, I was getting a bit sick of Hugo. Not that I wanted him dead,' she added, suddenly looking shocked by what she'd said.

'Of course not,' said Jonny.

'Poor Hugo.' She reached for a tissue and dabbed at her eyes. 'What a horrible thing to happen.'

He handed her a slip of paper with his email and phone number. 'Get in touch if you think of anything else or if you need anything.'

JONNY, Ivo and Harold walked back to the car. 'We need to talk to Jason, don't we?' Ivo asked.

'He's definitely got some explaining to do,' said Jonny, heading away from town and towards the motorway. Why had Jason said nothing about knowing where his father was? How had he even found him? It seemed to Jonny that young Mr Walsh was a lot less gormless than he wanted them to believe.

'You've got to admit he's a suspect now,' said Ivo.

It certainly looked that way. He went through Katya's three conditions in his head. Motive – a tick for that. If Hugo was alive, Jason would lose everything he had inherited. Opportunity – had he somehow persuaded his father to return to Windsor? Either to come to some arrangement about the house and the money, or quite simply to push him into the river? Means – Jonny had to think about that. Alcohol and enough strength to push a well-built man into the water. That was the weakest of the three. Jason was a not too healthy, five-foot-ten weakling. Would he have had the strength to push Hugo into the river?

He asked Ivo what he thought.

'Must have had an accomplice,' said Ivo. 'Someone with size nine hiking boots.'

17

'Your name Katya Ross?'

'Why?' said Katya crossly. She'd not slept well and it was still cold. She'd come to *Jasmine's* for a bit of warmth and a quiet breakfast. The last thing she needed was some interfering woman who couldn't even be bothered to get her name right.

'They said I'd find you here.'

'Who did?' Katya bit into her toast and scowled at the woman. Didn't she realise it was rude to interrupt a person's breakfast?

'Them at the police station. Sergeant Florence somebody and an inspector chap.'

'DI Lomax? And DS Green? Flora, she's called.' This woman obviously had a problem with names.

'That's them. Said I should talk to Katya Ross.'

'Roscoff,' Katya corrected. 'DS Roscoff, retired.'

'Whatever.'

Katya knew she could be impatient, but she didn't often take against people on sight. This woman must be an exception. Katya didn't like her, whoever she was. Skinny, mouth like a chicken's backside and grey curls that looked like they'd been painted on. She'd had a doll once that had painted hair. She'd never liked it. Never liked dolls, full stop. And this woman had a doll-like quality, with her pursed red lips and buttoned-up expression. 'What do you want?'

'It's about him in the river.'

'You mean the man who was found drowned?'

'Yeah. I reckon someone bumped him off.'

Since Katya was beginning to think the same, the least she could do was hear the woman out. The police still weren't taking the case seriously, otherwise they wouldn't have palmed the woman off on her. But perhaps she'd come to confess. Finding a body always brought a stream of nutters queueing up to own up to crimes they imagined they'd committed. She could understand Flora and Lugs needed to get rid of people like that, but sending the woman in Katya's direction was a bit much. It would serve them right if this *was* the murderer. Katya glanced hopefully down at the woman's feet. No more than a size six, if Katya was any judge of shoes. And definitely not hiking boots. But she might have been a witness. It would be one in the eye for her ex-colleagues if Katya and her team not only proved Hugo Walsh's death was murder, but also solved the case and got all the credit. *Dream on*, she told herself. *Not a chance of that.* But the woman was here. She'd better listen to what she had to say. She fished into her bag for a notebook and pen, which she placed on the table in front of her. 'You think he was murdered?' she asked, her pen poised over a blank page in the notebook.

The woman nodded enthusiastically. 'And I know who done it.'

Were Lugs and Flora having a laugh? Katya wouldn't be surprised. But she couldn't take that chance. If this woman had evidence, Katya needed to know about it. 'What's your name?' she asked.

'Elaine Johnson. Miss.'

The *miss* didn't surprise her. Although Katya, a lifelong singleton, was hardly in a position to criticise. She'd never considered marriage herself, even if she had been a bit of a goer in her prime. 'And you knew the man who drowned?'

'Never seen him in me life.'

'Then what makes you think he was murdered?'

'Something I overheard,' she said, tapping the side of her nose in a way that Katya found irritating, not to say sinister.

Was she going to elaborate? This was like pulling teeth. 'Perhaps you'd better start from the beginning,' said Katya, realising she could be stuck with her for some time. 'Why don't you sit down and have a coffee?'

'Thanks. Don't mind if I do.'

She pulled out a chair, sat down opposite Katya with her handbag on her lap and looked at her hopefully, in a way similar to Harold when he was hoping for a biscuit.

Did she expect Katya to go and buy her coffee herself? Obviously she did. Katya caught Jasmine's attention and made what she hoped was a coffee cup type gesture. Jasmine must have understood because a moment or two later, she appeared at the table with a cup of coffee and a small jug of milk. Should she invite Jasmine to join them? Katya wondered. Probably best not to. Jasmine was busy with customers and Elaine Johnson looked like the type to embroider a few details if she thought she had an audience. Katya could update Jasmine later. That is, if the woman's story actually made any sense and wasn't just another loony theory. There'd been plenty of those when she was working. Any high-profile case and they came crawling out of the woodwork.

'Right,' said Katya. 'What's the story?'

Elaine poured some milk into her coffee and stirred it slowly. Then she took a delicate sip, her little finger held aloft. She pulled a face and dabbed the corners of her mouth with a lace handkerchief she extracted from the sleeve of her cardigan. 'Too strong,' she said, shovelling in a large amount of sugar.

Katya sighed and tapped her pen on the table. 'You were telling me you overheard something.'

'I did,' she said, leaning towards Katya in a conspiratorial way and lowering her voice. 'It was one evening. Must be more than a year ago now. I was working late.'

'Where do you work?'

'At the junior school in Long Lane. I'm an admin worker there.

People think we work school hours and go home when the kiddies finish, but they're wrong. We're short-staffed and often have to stay late.'

Long Lane Junior School. Why did that sound familiar? 'And you were working late when you overheard... what? Someone planning a murder?' It was probably a bit lonely working late in a school office on her own. Easy to imagine things.

'That's right.'

'You were working on your own?'

'I was, yes.'

'But there were other people there?'

'Of course. How could I hear people talking if I was on my own? I didn't make it up.'

Katya wasn't so sure about that.

'It was a rehearsal evening. You know, the choir.'

Of course, that was the school where the Applewood Singers rehearsed. Suddenly Katya's interest was piqued. Perhaps the woman was onto something after all.

'I have to stay until they've finished singing so I can lock up. But I usually work in the office and they probably don't know I'm there. Well, this was an evening just a few days before they all went off to sing in some abbey, West Country, I think. And then that poor woman was killed. Don't stand a chance, do you, not in a fire like that?'

Katya nodded sadly, wondering where this was going.

'When I heard about the crash, my first thought was at least the poor woman's husband wouldn't get murdered after all. Some said he died in the crash along with his wife, but some of the others said she hadn't been with her husband, and the man with her must have been her bit on the side.'

'What exactly did you overhear?' Katya asked, trying to get Elaine back on track.

'I'm telling you, aren't I? That Penelope Walsh and her fancy man were planning to get rid of her husband.'

'Tell me exactly what you heard. Word for word, if you can.'

'He said, "We'll do it as soon as we get back from Bath." Then she said, "We'll get an earlier train and be back before the choir coach. We'll get him drunk. A quick push and it'll just look like an accident." Then she sort of giggled and they must have left after that. I didn't hear anything else.'

'You didn't tell anyone what you'd heard?'

'Didn't really take it seriously. Thought they were just having a laugh. Then like I said, she was killed in the train crash. It wouldn't have been right to start accusing her of planning murder, would it?'

'What made you come forward now, eighteen months later?'

'It was reading about that poor man who was found drowned in the river and then finding out his name was Walsh, same as the lady on the train.'

Katya felt they were going round in circles. 'But if it was Penelope Walsh you overheard and she was planning to kill her husband, well, it can't have been anything to do with her. She's been dead eighteen months. Hugo Walsh died recently.'

Elaine thought about that for a moment. 'Doesn't mean whoever she was plotting with couldn't have done it.'

'But why would he? If, as you say, he was Penelope's fancy man, he was too late. She was already dead, so why bother?'

'He might have had a different reason for wanting him dead.'

She was, Katya decided, a loony of the most determined kind. She'd be having words with Lugs next time she saw him. Why couldn't the police deal with their own weirdos? They had specialist people to take care of that sort. With a list of their names and phone numbers so they could spot the regulars. 'What exactly did the police say to you when you reported it?'

'Oh, they were ever so kind and helpful. They said they knew just the person to listen to me.'

I bet they did, thought Katya. Lugs was going to owe her a couple of pints for this, if not a full pub meal. But suppose the woman had something important to say? Katya would look a proper prat if it turned out Elaine really did have information that could alter the case. 'Do you get to know the singers?' she asked. 'They must have coffee breaks when they socialise.'

'Some of them like to chat,' said Elaine. 'There's always gossip when choir members are up to a bit of no good with each other, if you take my meaning.'

'Was Penelope getting up to no good with another choir member? Is that who you overheard?'

'No, this was a friend of Mr Applewood's.' Elaine leaned towards Katya in a way that suggested she was about to reveal a dark secret. 'Mr A was not too pleased about it, I can tell you.'

Ah, they might just be getting somewhere. 'Do you know his name, Mr Applewood's friend?'

'No. Didn't see a lot of him. He just popped into rehearsals a few times. S'pose that's how he met Mrs Walsh.'

'Can you describe him?'

'Kind of ordinary, mid-height, brown hair, quite suntanned.'

'Suntanned?'

'Yes, like he worked outdoors.'

'Have you seen him recently?'

Elaine had to think about that. She shook her head slowly. 'I don't think I've seen him in months, maybe more than a year.'

'Since Mrs Walsh died?'

'You know, I don't think I have, no. I did hear one of the singers ask after him and Mr Applewood scowled and said it was none of her business, but if she really wanted to know, he'd just gone off without so much as a goodbye.'

Katya was scribbling all of this down in her notebook. Elaine tried to peer across at what she was writing. 'What are you going to do now?' she asked. 'Will you arrest him?'

'I don't think there's enough evidence for that, and anyway I can't arrest him unless I know who he is.'

Elaine looked disappointed. Perhaps she was hoping for her moment in court. 'You should ask Mr Applewood,' she said. 'He'd be able to give you all the details if they were friends.'

He would indeed, and that was something Katya was planning to do. But she didn't want Elaine poking her nose in any further. 'Thank you for bringing this to my attention,' she said, standing up and hoping that Elaine would take the hint that the interview was at an end. She held out her hand at an angle that meant Elaine had to stand up to shake it.

But Elaine wasn't finished yet. She fished into her pocket and handed Katya a card. 'You'll keep me informed,' she said. Katya felt this was a demand rather than a request.

Bloomin' cheek. 'I'll contact you, if necessary,' she said coldly, hoping that she never had to clap eyes on Elaine Johnson again. She watched as Elaine pulled a headscarf out of her pocket, tied it over her hair and headed for the door. Then she sat down with relief as she watched the woman close the door behind her.

'You look like you need another,' said Jasmine, arriving at the table with a pot of fresh coffee. 'Who was that?'

'An infuriating woman,' said Katya. 'Glad to see the back of her.' She took a grateful gulp of coffee. 'Except... except I think she might just have given me some really useful information.'

Jasmine laughed. 'How maddening,' she said. 'Wouldn't you much rather get information from someone you liked?'

Katya laughed too. 'I suppose so. Unless it's someone I like confessing to murder.'

Jasmine looked startled and peered through the window to see if Elaine was still there. 'Did she commit murder? Did she push Hugo into the river?'

'I wish,' said Katya. 'That would make our case so much easier, and I'd be quite cheerful at the thought of locking the woman up for many years. She had nothing to do with it, I'm afraid. But she's given me an idea who can tell us about the elusive Mr Hunter. You and I need to pay a visit to young Applewood when you've finished with the lunches.'

∿

THEY FOUND Malcolm Applewood's contact details on the choir website, where he also advertised himself as a teacher of singing and piano. It gave them his address, which, when Jasmine checked on Google Maps, was only a short walk from the town centre. 'Should we call him first?' Jasmine asked, wondering how they could catch him between students and thinking it wouldn't exactly help them if Applewood was less amenable to chatting to them because they'd disturbed one of his lessons.

'Better to take him by surprise,' said Katya. 'If he's in the middle of a lesson we'll wait until he's finished.'

'How will we know if he's in the middle of a lesson?' Jasmine asked.

'We'll hear, won't we?'

Only if he taught in his front room, Jasmine thought. But Katya was in charge, and she was definitely more experienced. It was possible people gave more away if they were taken by surprise. Katya would know about that, so Jasmine didn't feel she was in a position to argue.

The Applewood residence was in a quiet avenue of small, detached houses and Jasmine was glad they hadn't come by car. Every space in the road was marked for residents only from nine in the morning until five in the evening. Too easy for shoppers to park there and not pay car park charges in town, Jasmine supposed. It was even worse outside the café. They had a small yard at the back, just big enough for her father's car. Although it was obviously not part of the road, people still tried to use it when he was out or when Jasmine borrowed his car. He and Jasmine had put up signs asking people not to park there but with little effect. Ivo had now fitted a chain with a board saying *PRIVATE* hanging from it. The Applewood house had a small, paved front garden with parking space for two cars, one of which said *STUDENTS ONLY.* Both spaces were currently unoccupied. Perhaps no one was at home and they'd had a wasted journey.

'Good,' said Katya when Jasmine pointed out the lack of cars. 'That means he won't be in the middle of a lesson.'

'It might mean there's no one here,' said Jasmine.

'Not necessarily,' said Katya, marching up a small ramp to the front door and ringing the bell. And Katya was right, there was someone in. The door was answered by a woman Jasmine guessed was in her forties. She was dressed in leggings and a loose jumper. Mrs Applewood, Jasmine assumed.

'I'm Katya Roscoff and this is Jasmine Javadi,' said Katya. 'We'd like to speak to Mr Applewood.'

'I'm afraid he's not here,' said the woman. 'Can I help? Is it about lessons?'

'It's to do with the choir. Mrs Applewood?'

'Miss. I'm Malcolm's sister, Clara.' She held the door open and led them into a small entrance hall, made smaller by a stairlift with a seat at the bottom of a staircase. Jasmine wondered if they had an elderly parent living with them. Clara showed them into a sparsely furnished room with a small grand piano, a long bench, a coffee table and shelves of sheet music. On the wall was a photo of a group of singers standing in front of a tall mullioned window. *A church,* Jasmine thought, moving closer to look at it.

'That was taken in Malmesbury Abbey,' said Clara. 'Just before poor Penelope Walsh was killed. That's her,' she said, pointing to a woman in the front row.

'And your brother isn't in the photo?' *Why not?* she wondered. But perhaps he was the one taking the picture.

'No,' said Clara. 'Malcolm doesn't like to be photographed.'

Jasmine stared at it. She realised they didn't have a recent photo of Penelope, although the woman in the picture was recognisably similar to the news cutting they'd seen of Penelope at seventeen. She wondered if it would be okay to take a photo of it. Probably not, at least until Clara knew why they were there. 'This isn't on the choir website, is it?' Jasmine asked, wondering why it wasn't.

'No,' said Clara. 'They were going to put it on the tribute page, but Malcolm persuaded them not to. He said it didn't seem right.'

'Why not?' Katya asked.

'I don't like to gossip about it,' said Clara. 'I think Malcolm was being unreasonable. He...' She stopped mid-sentence. 'You're not journalists, are you?'

'No,' Katya assured her. 'We're actually working with Thames Valley Police on an inquiry into a recent death.'

'And you think Malcolm was involved somehow?' She stared at them in surprise. 'Have you met him?'

'No,' said Katya. 'And we don't think he was involved. We'd just like some information about someone we think he knew.'

'Well, you'd better talk to him yourself. He'll be back soon. Would you like some tea while you wait?'

'That would be very nice,' said Katya, sitting down on the piano bench as Clara made her way towards the kitchen.

While she was out of the room, Jasmine whisked out her phone and took a photo of the choir. It would enlarge enough for her to cut out Penelope's face and paste it into a photo they could use when asking questions. She'd just put the phone back in her pocket when the door swung open, revealing a man in an electric wheelchair.

'Can I help you?' he asked, steering himself into the room as Clara returned with a tray of tea and biscuits. She'd brought four cups, Jasmine noticed, so she must have heard him arrive. They weren't going to get to talk to Malcolm on his own. But they were only there to find out about his friend and there was nothing confidential about that. Clara might even be able to help.

Clara introduced Katya and Jasmine and passed round mugs of tea. 'They are working for the police,' she said, squeezing his shoulder in a way that Jasmine thought looked painful. *Some sort of warning?* she wondered, although she couldn't imagine why he would need to be warned. 'They want to ask you some questions,' Clara continued. 'About a death.'

Jasmine wasn't sure but she thought she noticed Malcolm flinch slightly at the word *death*. He reached up and removed Clara's hand from his shoulder. Was he nervous or was it because she was hurting him? Was *she* nervous? Unaware of the strength of her grip, perhaps?

'We'd like to know about a Mr Bruce Hunter,' said Katya, burrowing in her bag for her trusty notepad.

'Bruce?' asked Malcolm, spluttering into his tea. 'Bastard,' he added.

'We gather you knew him. We talked to someone who described you as friends.'

'Well,' said Malcolm. 'I can assure you that whoever you spoke to was mistaken. Bruce Hunter wouldn't be a friend if he was the last person on earth.'

'But you do know him?'

'I prefer not to talk about it,' he said, his hand beginning to shake.

'Calm down, Malcolm,' said Clara, taking the cup from him and putting it down safely on the table. 'Let me explain,' she said, turning to face Katya while at the same time avoiding Malcolm's warning glance. 'Malcolm and Bruce knew each other from way back when they were students and went on a rock-climbing course together in Australia. There was an accident. Malcolm was flown home for treatment. He was in hospital for months and then another year at a rehab centre. When he eventually came home, he discovered that an inquiry had been held in Australia and he'd known nothing about it. It was written off as an accident and no one was blamed.' She was clearly furious about what had happened, and Jasmine couldn't help wondering if it was out of love for her brother or because she'd spent the last thirty or so years caring for him.

'I'm so sorry,' she said, reaching out and holding Malcolm's hand in her own. 'What happened?'

Malcolm managed to smile weakly at her. 'It was a faulty piece of equipment. Bruce was supposed to have checked it but obviously he hadn't. I fell forty feet onto some rocks. I was lucky not to be killed. If you can call it luck to be left like this.'

'And Bruce Hunter was cleared of any negligence?' Katya asked.

'It all happened on the other side of the world,' said Clara. 'An obvious cover-up, but what could we do? Malcolm came home and concentrated on his music, rebuilt his life around that. Luckily Dad was there to help. He was a professional musician himself, you see. Plenty of contacts and opportunities that he could hand on to Malcolm.'

'Is your father still in the area?' Jasmine asked.

'Retired,' said Clara. 'He and Mum moved down to the south

coast. Dad still potters around doing bits of accompanying and teaching.'

'I was doing okay,' said Malcolm. 'I had plenty of work and Dad left me to run the choir. The nightmares had stopped, and I was beginning to feel human again and then...'

'Then Bruce Hunter turned up and it brought it all back,' Clara interrupted. 'Would you believe it? He said he wanted to make amends.' She snorted in a way that reminded Jasmine of when Harold had found a raw chili on the floor and bitten into it.

'I told him to get lost,' said Malcolm. 'But he started turning up at choir rehearsals. He hung around for three or four weeks. Started an affair with one of my singers.'

'And you disapproved?' Katya asked.

'Of course I bloody disapproved. Penelope Walsh was one of my best singers and a married woman. Bruce had ruined my life and now looked set to ruin Penelope's marriage as well.'

'Do you know where Bruce Hunter is now?' Katya asked.

'Back in Australia, I suppose. As far as I'm concerned, the further away the better.'

'When was the last time you saw him?' Jasmine asked.

'I... I don't remember.'

Surely if he hated the man so much, he'd remember when they'd last met. 'Did you see him after the Malmesbury concert?'

'It was all chaotic around then,' said Clara defensively, jumping in before Malcolm had a chance to answer. 'Everyone was upset about Penelope and it's hard to remember what else was going on.'

'Do you know why Penelope didn't travel on the coach with the rest of the choir?'

'I'm not sure,' said Malcolm. 'I think she said she was going to visit friends near Bath.'

'More likely she was planning to spend a night or two with Bruce,' said Clara, her dislike of Bruce obvious.

'Is it usual for choir members to travel separately?' Katya asked.

'It's not unusual,' said Malcolm. 'Some prefer to make their own way to concerts. Frankly, as long as they turn up when they're supposed to, I don't care how they travel.'

'But Penelope told you she was visiting friends,' said Katya. 'I don't suppose you know who they were?'

'I told you,' said Clara. 'I don't think there were any friends. She didn't tell you anything about them, did she, Malcolm?'

He shook his head. 'We were barely speaking by then.'

Clara was becoming impatient. She looked at her watch. 'I'm afraid Malcolm has a lesson in ten minutes, and he needs to prepare.'

Katya drained her cup. 'We won't keep you any longer, then.' Jasmine remembered her saying that the art of interviewing was knowing when to stop. She had reached that point now and Jasmine thought she was right. They were not going to get anything more from Clara or Malcolm. Katya handed Clara a card. 'Let me know if you remember anything else, and thank you for your help.'

They left Malcolm to prepare for his lesson and Clara showed them out, squeezing past the lift at the bottom of the stairs.

As they turned into the road outside the house, Jasmine glanced back. Malcolm was at the window, staring at them. There was something odd about it and Jasmine couldn't quite work out what it was. A young girl passed them carrying a music case. Malcolm's next student, she supposed.

KATYA AND JASMINE walked back into town. 'What did you make of him?' Katya asked.

'I felt sorry for him,' said Jasmine. 'He seems very bitter about the accident, but you can't really blame him, can you?'

'I suppose not, but I'm not sure why he was so angry with Penelope. He might disapprove, well, he obviously did. But in the end, it's none of his business, is it? I assume it didn't affect her singing, and it wasn't as if she was missing rehearsals or not turning up for concerts.'

'I've only talked to one member of the choir, but she didn't remember seeing Bruce Hunter after the concert in Malmesbury, so it must have been him on the train with Penelope.'

'We should check that,' said Katya. 'He may have flown back to Australia. Wouldn't his family have missed him if he hadn't returned? You'd think they would have started making enquiries.'

'Perhaps they did, but he wasn't exactly a vulnerable missing person. It probably just got filed away somewhere and forgotten about.'

'We need to contact the family,' said Katya. 'You have details for the hiking company, don't you?'

'Shall I email them?'

What would be the best way to approach them? Katya wondered. If they worked out the time difference, either Katya herself or Jasmine could call and ask to speak to Bruce. But if he had gone missing, would they say so, or would they just tell them he was out, or unavailable? It could stir up all kinds of misunderstandings. An email might just disappear into an inbox and be ignored, but it was the best option, at least to begin with. 'We'll start with an email,' she said. 'We'll go back to the office now and put something together. We want to be persuasive so they reply, but not too alarmist. If Bruce has disappeared, we don't want to upset them.'

'And we can't jump in and say we think he was killed in a train crash. We'll have to be very careful how we phrase it.'

'Yes,' said Katya. 'You're right. And of course, we might discover he's been at home all along and we wouldn't want to stir things up for him there. He might have a wife and kids, so we need to be tactful.' Katya would be the first person to admit that tact wasn't one of her best qualities. She wasn't too certain of Jasmine's tactfulness either. She was a sweet girl whose heart was definitely in the right place, but she did tend to jump in with both feet and get a little too emotionally involved. 'Tell you what,' she said. 'We'll get Jonny to help.'

18

Jonny sat down at the computer and opened a new Word document. Katya was leaning over his shoulder, chomping on a flapjack. 'Why don't you sit over there and make a few notes?' he suggested, worrying about crumbs falling onto the keyboard. Messy keyboards were hell to clean up. 'Make a list of what you want to say to these people and then we'll tweak it and copy it into an email.'

'And what are you going to do while I make my list?' asked Katya, licking her fingers and draining a cup of coffee.

'I'm going to set us up with a detective email. I'll add it to the Breakfast Club account. I guess we're going to be using email quite a bit, and we'll get into a muddle if we use our personal ones. Also, there are going to be problems with data protection and spam filters if it's not affiliated to a website.'

That brought back memories. When she was working, Katya was forever in trouble for using the wrong email, sending them off from her personal account or without using blind copies. But at least she was in good company. Hadn't a recent home secretary been in trouble for something like that? 'I'll leave that to you,' she said. Then she had an idea. 'Can you do something with a nice little logo at the top?'

'That's more Jasmine's forte,' said Jonny. 'But it's a great idea. I can add a detectives page to the Breakfast Club website as well, if you like.'

Not a bad idea, although she wasn't certain about the ethics of advertising themselves and so far it hadn't been necessary. She'd think about it. 'Jasmine will be up when she's finished the lunches,' said Katya. 'I want her to read through what we've written before we send it.'

They were hard at work when Ivo and Harold appeared. 'What's up?' Ivo asked as Harold edged towards Katya and her plate of crumbs. Katya recounted her visit to the Applewoods and showed him the notes she'd made. She explained the plan to email the Hunters in Australia.

'Cool,' said Ivo. 'If you don't need me, I thought I'd drop in on Jason.'

'Be careful,' said Jonny. 'Don't start accusing him of knowing where his father was all along. If he thinks he's now a suspect, he might do something stupid.'

'I'll just have a snoop around,' said Ivo. 'We don't know for sure that he did know where Hugo was. All Hugo told Betsy was that he had to meet his son. He could have been planning a surprise visit.'

'You're both right,' said Katya. 'It's too soon to start making accusations. Like Lugs said, we don't know that it wasn't an accident. But we've been neglecting Jason a bit recently and we are supposed to be supporting him. You might try to find out what he knew about his mother's goings on. We know Hugo had a roving eye, but we don't know if Penelope made a habit of going off to hotels with strange men. We're assuming the man on the train was Bruce Hunter, but apart from a couple of witnesses seeing them together in Bath, we've no evidence. For all we know, Bruce is safely back in Australia and Penelope picked up someone else.' She dabbed the last of the crumbs off the plate with her fingers and wiped them with a tissue. 'And check with that neighbour. She would probably have seen more of Penelope.'

'Okay,' said Ivo. 'I can drop in on Poppy. She usually has jobs for me to do.'

BY THE TIME JASMINE APPEARED, they had both an email address of their own and a text to paste into it. 'What do you think of this?' Jonny asked, as Jasmine sat at the computer next to him.

WE ARE *a group of private investigators based in Windsor UK and currently working with Thames Valley Police, who require information concerning the deaths of local residents Hugo Walsh and his wife Penelope. We understand that Mr Bruce Hunter had been travelling in the UK last year and could well have been in contact with Mrs Walsh shortly before she was involved in the train accident that caused her death.*

We would be most grateful if Mr Hunter could contact us with any information that might progress our enquires.

THEY SIGNED themselves off as *BC Investigations* which they agreed was more businesslike than either adding all their names or using the affectionate name of Breakfast Club Detectives, which made them sound like a group of busybodies who talked about murder over the cornflakes and coffee. Jasmine put together a logo with a silhouette of four people in a circle, adding *BC Investigations* around the edge.

'Shouldn't we add a dog?' Jonny asked, laughing. 'Ivo keeps reminding us of Harold's crime detecting history.'

'We don't want to look like a group of dog walkers,' said Katya, dismissively.

'But we don't want to hurt Ivo's feelings, either,' said Jasmine. She added a few dog paw prints. 'How's that?'

'It's okay,' said Katya.

'It's great,' said Jonny, using it to edit the Breakfast Club email by replacing the coffee and croissant motif with Jasmine's new one and saving it as a template. He copied in the draft letter to the Hunters and clicked send.

'How long do we wait for a reply?' Jasmine asked. 'And what do we do if there isn't one?'

'If we don't hear anything in a few days, I'll get Lugs to call the Australian police and get them to investigate,' said Katya.

'What do we do while we're waiting?' Jonny asked, scratching his head and wondering if it wasn't all becoming rather confused. He stood up and, finding a clear space on the board, began to make a list:

Hugo – whereabouts discovered but why did he return when he did?
Penelope – overheard planning to murder Hugo?
Dead man on train – Bruce Hunter? If not, who?
Boot prints on riverbank – link to Bruce or coincidence?
Jason – did he genuinely think both parents were dead?
Malcolm Applewood – hated Bruce Hunter

'Have I missed anything?' Jonny asked.

'There's enough there for Jasmine to type up a report for Lugs,' said Katya. 'But wait a day or two. We might find out that Bruce Hunter is alive and well in Australia.'

'Then we'd be back to square one as far as the man on the train goes,' said Jasmine.

'We would,' Katya agreed. 'But unless we can tie it up with someone on the mispers register I don't think much more can happen. They'd just have to let it go.'

'Which would leave Jason paying for both funerals?' Jonny asked.

'I've really no idea,' said Katya. 'But I don't think that will be our problem. Jason would need to get legal advice.'

Jonny was just wondering who would break that particular bit of news to Jason when the email pinged. He looked at the name of the sender and was surprised to see it was from Hunters' Hikes. What time was it in Australia? It must be the middle of the night. Perhaps the Hunters stayed up late, or got up very early, to keep on top of their admin. Assuming they were stomping around rugged bits of the Australian outback during the day and didn't have time for paperwork. He clicked to open it and Katya and Jasmine peered over his shoulder while he read it.

WAS WONDERING when I'd hear from the UK authorities. I reported my father missing over a year ago. He failed to return from a European trip. Not unusual for him not to keep in touch but when he still hadn't returned after the expiry date on his open ticket I began to worry and reported it to our local police, who lodged an enquiry in the UK. We were told that he had been added to a list of missing travellers but that active searches would not be made as my father is neither vulnerable nor suspected of committing a crime and therefore free to come and go as he wishes. Needless to say, my mother and I are not of the same opinion.

I would be extremely glad of any news you have or can find about my father. You will understand the stress this has caused the family.

Regards

Mervyn Hunter

'Wow,' said Jonny. 'How do we respond to that?'

'Well,' said Katya. 'It looks likely that our dead man on the train *was* Bruce Hunter and someone will have to break the news to the family. I don't think we can go much further until I consult with Lugs.'

Jonny printed the email and stuck it onto the board with Blu Tack. 'I don't envy whoever gets that job.'

'It's hell breaking that sort of news,' said Katya. 'I'd imagine it would be handed over to the Australian authorities to deal with, if it wasn't for the fact that there's no actual proof that it *was* Bruce on the train. The evidence is all circumstantial.'

'I think we all need a strong cup of tea,' said Jasmine, 'while we try to assess what's going on.'

Jonny and Katya agreed that when in doubt about what to do, a cup of tea was the go to answer and Jasmine headed for the stairs. 'Won't be long,' she said. 'I'll see if there are any pastries left.'

JASMINE WAS STILL busy in the kitchen when Ivo and Harold burst into the office. 'I've found something really, really important,' said Ivo, sinking into a chair and putting a shoebox down on the table while Harold, picking up on his mood, sped round the room bumping into furniture, his tail wagging furiously. Ivo opened the shoebox and took out a photograph of a group of young people. 'Look on the back,' he said.

Katya took it from him and stared at it. Then she turned it over and tried to read what was written on the back. 'What on earth is it?' she asked. 'It's too small to make out the words. It just looks like a list of names.'

'That's exactly what it is,' said Ivo. 'And it changes everything. Give it to Jonny. He's got better eyesight.'

'I doubt it,' said Jonny, mostly because he didn't want Katya getting into a huff at what she might assume was a dig at her advanced years. He turned on a desk lamp and shone it on the writing, which was, as Katya had said, very small and hard to read.

'What's going on?' Jasmine asked as she arrived with a tray of tea and pastries.

'Take a look at this,' said Ivo. 'Put the tray down first, though.'

Jasmine put the tray on the table, poured the tea and handed round the buns. Then she stared at the photo. 'Turn it over,' said Ivo. 'It's too small for the two oldies to read.'

Jasmine squinted at it. 'It's tiny,' she said, and Ivo admitted that he'd borrowed a magnifying glass from Poppy to read it. 'We've got one,' said Jasmine, opening a drawer and picking up a small torch with a folding magnifying lens attached. 'It was in a cracker last

Christmas. I knew it would come in handy one day.' She aimed it at the letters and then sat down suddenly. 'Wow,' she said.

'Could one of you please tell us what it says?' said Katya impatiently.

'*University of South Berkshire Innovation Summer School 1990,*' Jasmine read. '*Professor Hugo Walsh presenting a certificate to winning student Alexander Pike.*'

'Hugo was a university professor?' Jonny asked. 'Quite a career move, professor to carpenter.'

'That's not all,' said Ivo. 'Read the names of the other students, Jasmine.'

Jasmine read a list of names, then stopped suddenly. 'Oh my God. Ivo's right. This changes everything.'

'Go on,' said Katya.

'The next two names on the list are Bruce Hunter and Malcolm Applewood.' She turned the photo over and stared at it. 'Hugo's recognisable but I can't make out the other two.'

'So Malcolm and Bruce didn't just happen to meet on the same rock climbing holiday. They knew each other before and may have been good friends,' said Jonny. 'That was long before the train crash.'

'And before Penelope and Bruce got together,' said Katya. 'We need to rethink our whole enquiry.'

'Where did you find the box, Ivo?' Jonny asked.

'It was in Jason's loft. He's got mice up there and he asked me to get rid of them. It's one of those roof spaces with a ladder that drops down. Jason showed me how it worked, and we went up there together. He spotted the box and realised there was a bit more paper-work about his dad that he'd forgotten about. He said I had better take it with me and add it to the rest of Hugo's stuff.'

'Did Jason know about the photograph?' Katya asked.

'He didn't say anything about it, and I didn't look in the box until I was next door at Poppy's.'

'There's more in here,' said Jasmine, tipping out the contents.

'There's probably a mixture of stuff,' said Ivo. 'Jason told me he'd got a bit overwhelmed with everything and just piled it into the box and shoved it into the attic. He didn't think any of it was urgent and he thought he'd come back to it later. Then he forgot all about it.'

Katya flicked through a collection of newspaper cuttings, a couple of birthday cards, a receipt for a printer and an address book with lists of local tradespeople: a window cleaner; a garage; a washing machine repair company and a dentist. Then she pulled out a silver bracelet, a disc with a symbol attached to the thick chain.

Jonny took it from her and looked at the red cross over which a snake twisted around a rod. 'Something medical, isn't it?'

Katya nodded. 'It's worn by people with epilepsy,' she said. 'Recognising things like that is part of police training.'

'Do we know if Hugo suffered from epilepsy?' Jasmine asked.

'I don't think it was Hugo's,' said Ivo. 'Before I left Poppy's, I called Jason and asked him about it. He said it was among things rescued from the debris of the train crash. They thought it could be Penelope's but he said he'd never seen her wearing it.'

Katya picked up a pen and started writing on the whiteboard. 'As I said, we need to rethink our enquiry.' She wrote a list:

1. *Find out about Hugo's university career and the innovation summer school.*
2. *Did Penelope suffer from epilepsy? Ask Poppy and woman from choir – Juliet. If they don't know get Lugs to find out from her GP.*
3. *Was Bruce Hunter a student in the UK? Did he invent something for the innovation thing?*
4. *Where did Malcolm study and why was he at the summer school. Ask his sister?*

'FOUR OF US AND FOUR TASKS,' said Katya, putting the pen down. 'That's handy. Who wants which?'

'I'll do number one,' said Jonny. 'Hopefully it will all be online and if I get stuck, I can go to one of our HR people for advice. They know how to find out stuff like that.'

'I'll do the second,' said Ivo. 'I can ask Poppy. I don't know the woman from the choir, though.'

'No problem,' said Jasmine. 'I can go and see Juliet at the church when her daughter's practising there, and I'll do number four as well. I've already met Malcolm and his sister.'

'Which leaves me to find out all about Bruce,' said Katya. 'I may need to go through Lugs to check visa records, so I'm probably the best one to do that anyway. And Ivo, if you don't have any luck with Poppy, let me know and I'll ask Lugs about contacting the GP.'

Jasmine picked up the bracelet and felt the weight of it. 'It doesn't feel like a woman's bracelet,' she said. 'It's too heavy.'

Jonny took it from her. 'I agree,' he said. 'We should find out if Bruce suffered from epilepsy. I can email his son again.'

'Do it tactfully,' said Katya. 'We don't want to scare him. Make up something about a possible sighting of a man fitting Bruce's description and wearing a bracelet. You can send a photo if you like. If it was his bracelet, it will probably be time to hand it all over to the Aussie authorities to ask further questions.'

Of course Jonny would be tactful. He always was, wasn't he? Belinda teased him about it, telling him it wasn't always an asset in business. And if anyone on the current team was lacking tact... well, it was obviously not him. Then something occurred to him. 'What if it turns out not to have been Bruce on the train?' he asked. 'Even if he did own a bracelet like this, it doesn't confirm one way or the other that it was him. It's not as if there would be any DNA after the fire.'

'I'll take another look at the crash scene photos and see if I can spot anything helpful,' said Katya.

'Then we've got two real headaches,' said Ivo. 'If it wasn't Bruce, who was it? And where is he now?'

'He's right,' said Jasmine. 'We're making assumptions because Penelope and Bruce were in Bath together, but they might have quarrelled and left separately.'

'I'll get the mispers list from Lugs and we'll meet again tomorrow evening,' said Katya. 'Compare notes on our searches and talk about where to go from there.'

Jonny tapped on the list he'd made earlier. 'We should revisit this,' he said, feeling his contribution had been forgotten.

'We will,' said Katya. 'You had some useful ideas. We'll go over everything tomorrow and try to tie it all together.' She stood up and put on her coat. 'I'm off to see Lugs,' she said.

'And I need to get back to work,' said Jasmine. 'I'll go and see if Juliet and Gracie are at the church this evening after work. Do you want to come with me, Ivo?'

He shook his head, then stood up and took Harold's lead out of his pocket. 'I need to be on site this evening. There's a residents' meeting about litter on the footpath. I'll pop in and talk to Poppy now and see you all tomorrow.'

'I think I'll stay here,' said Jonny. 'I can use this computer and call through to CPS if I need help.'

'I'll bring you something to eat,' said Jasmine. 'See how you're getting on.'

Jonny watched them head off and sat down to start his searches, surprised by how quiet it seemed in the office on his own. Good for the concentration, he supposed, typing in *South Berkshire University* only to discover that it no longer existed. It had merged with two other establishments in the early nineties. Was that why Hugo had stopped working there and become a carpenter? It still seemed an unlikely career move. He found no mention of him on any university websites, past or present. Looking at the back of the photo again reminded him that Hugo was apparently *Professor* Walsh which made him wonder if he'd ever published anything. Wasn't that essential for professors? But again he drew a blank. Hugo's website was still there, headed *Hugo Walsh – carpenter of style in business since 1991*. A busy year for him, apparently. It was also the year of his marriage to Penelope and Jason's birth. Was there a connection? Had Hugo ditched his academic career in favour of carpentry in order to support a family? But that made no sense. University professors were well paid, weren't they? Starting up a carpentry business must have meant a few lean years even if it had ultimately been successful.

Jonny was getting nowhere, so he turned to South Berks University's innovation summer school. There had only been two of them, one in 1988 and a second in 1990. They'd not run after that through lack of funding. This was not the only project to have been cut. Times were hard in the nineties. *Arguably not a lot better now,* Jonny thought, remembering Belinda's hard work trying to keep educational projects going. But what he did find was a mention of Alexander Pike, who had won an award at the 1990 summer school for creating a simple but ingenious device for assisting wheelchair users. He clicked through to Pike's own website and found a diagram that left Jonny baffled but which had clearly been a success. After finishing university, Pike set himself up in a shed at the bottom of his father's garden, where he started mass producing the device and selling it. He'd successfully pitched the idea on Dragon's Den and five years later was running a thriving production plant.

Fate was on Jonny's side. He discovered that since 2016, his own company, CPS, had been providing them with ethical recyclable packing materials. *Marcus would know about that,* Jonny thought, picking up his phone and tapping in his son's number. 'Are you busy or can you spare a moment?' Jonny asked.

'Just on my way home,' said Marcus. 'Want to pop round? Justin would love to see you.'

Why not? Jonny hadn't seen his grandson for a while. He looked at his watch. 'See you in about twenty minutes?' That would give him time to drop into a newsagent and stock up on chocolate. His daughter-in-law would disapprove, but it was not long until Easter and what was the use in being a grandad if you couldn't turn up with chocolate?

He had just put his coat on when Jasmine appeared with a cup of tea and a bun. He had forgotten that she'd said she would bring him something to eat. But that was fine. He'd time for a cup of tea and he could take the bun with him to eat in the car.

Jasmine put the cup down and handed him the bag with the bun.

'I'm just on my way to dole out soup at the food bank. I can see if Juliet and her daughter are at the church. I thought I'd copy that photo for when I go back to talk to the Applewoods. See what Malcolm can tell me about Professor Hugo. I might see if Juliet recognises anyone as well.'

'Good idea,' said Jonny, getting out his own phone and scanning the photo. Marcus might recognise Alexander Pike. He wasn't sure how useful that would be, but it couldn't do any harm.

19

Jasmine opened the door of the church and listened. *Good,* she thought. *Someone is playing the organ.* Stevie had not mentioned anyone other than Gracie practising there. Except himself, of course, and she knew it wasn't Stevie because this was soup kitchen day, and he'd be outside doling out Styrofoam mugs of spicy pumpkin soup. She knew that's what it was because she had cooked it herself in an enormous cauldron in the kitchen at the back of the church hall the previous evening.

She stood for a moment and listened to a piece of music she thought might be Bach drifting from the organ loft. Gracie was good, Jasmine could hear that. In fact, she was better than Stevie. But that wasn't a surprise. Gracie had been practising the piano since she was three. Half an hour every day from then until she finished junior school, her mother had said, increasing to an hour a day at secondary. Then two hours once she'd been accepted by the Royal College. Stevie, according to his father, had grudgingly spent an hour or so a week at the piano when he had an exam coming up. And Jasmine could hear the difference. Not that Stevie was a bad player. He just tended to go for easy options, hymns and familiar pieces for when newlyweds were signing the register. And of course, he'd played the wedding march so often he could probably manage it in his sleep. But Gracie was working her way through something intricate and dramatic. She'd be there for a while, Jasmine guessed.

She looked around and spotted Juliet sitting in a pew halfway down the aisle. She was knitting something pink and fluffy and Jasmine hoped it wasn't destined for Gracie. The poor girl was reaching the age of ripped jeans and grey hoodies, or indecently short skirts and black tights with holes in them. Not fluffy cardigans that her mother would probably team with frilly dresses.

Jasmine slid into the pew next to Juliet with what she hoped was a friendly smile on her lips. Juliet looked up and smiled back at her. 'Hi,' she said. 'Nice to see you again.' She put her knitting to one side. 'And nice to have someone to chat to. It gets a bit lonely sitting here.'

Then why don't you go home? Jasmine wondered. She didn't think the precious Gracie could come to much harm playing the organ in a church. Or was Juliet worried that Gracie wouldn't stay here practising, but might wander into town and meet up with friends? Jasmine had never spoken to Gracie, but she really hoped the poor girl's life wasn't as cosseted as her mother made out. Wasn't it possible to be a gifted musician and have a bit of a social life as well? But she wasn't here to talk about Gracie or express her views on parenting. She wanted information from Juliet. She turned on her phone and scrolled to the photo of the innovation summer school. 'I just wondered if you could take a look at this,' she said. 'Tell me if you recognise anyone.'

'More police investigation?' Juliet asked, taking the phone from her.

'We're working on some leads,' said Jasmine. 'The train crash inquiry is coming up soon.' Lucky she'd noticed that in the news. It had been a long time since the accident, and people had forgotten about it unless they were directly involved.

Juliet squinted at the picture. 'It's very small,' she said.

Jasmine pinched the screen to enlarge it. 'That's Malcolm,' she said, handing the phone back to Juliet and pointing to a young man on the left of the photo.

'So it is,' said Juliet. 'I can see that now, but I'd never have recognised him if you hadn't told me.'

'This was taken more than thirty years ago,' said Jasmine. 'He will have changed a lot.'

'He's still recognisable, though. I was caught out at first because he's not in his wheelchair. I suppose it was before his accident.'

'Just a few months, I think. He would have been about twenty when this was taken.'

'Such a dreadful thing to happen to a young man,' said Juliet. 'And such a blessing that he had his music. It must have been very comforting for him. And of course, he was able to make a career of it.'

Jasmine took the phone from her and moved the photo to the right, homing in on the picture of Bruce. 'What about this man?' she asked. 'Have you seen him before?'

'I'm not sure,' said Juliet, peering at the screen. 'He does look slightly familiar, but I can't think why.'

'You might have seen him listening to choir rehearsals a year or so back.'

'There was a man listening a couple of times – it could have been him, but I think I've seen him more recently.'

Jasmine scrolled to the photo she'd downloaded from the Hunters' Hikes website. 'Is this better?'

'That's the same man? Yes, I can see it is. And I'm sure I've seen him recently. I just can't remember where. Perhaps he lives in the town and I've seen him at Waitrose.'

'Can you let me know if you remember?' Finding Bruce Hunter in Waitrose would be a surprise and most unlikely. Jasmine found a slip of paper and scribbled down her number. 'It might be important for the inquiry.' That was an understatement. If Juliet had seen this man recently, it couldn't have been Bruce on the train. 'And this one,' she said, scrolling to the photo of Hugo. 'Do you know him?'

Juliet shook her head. 'No, I don't recognise him.'

'This is what he looked like a couple of years ago,' she said, finding a more recent photo of Hugo.

'No, never seen him before.'

So it wasn't Hugo she'd seen picking Penelope up after rehearsals. More than that. It probably meant Hugo had shown no interest at all in the choir, never picked Penelope up after rehearsal, never been to a concert and never been introduced to Penelope's friends. Perhaps he didn't like music, or, and this was more likely in Jasmine's opinion, perhaps Penelope's involvement with the choir gave him the opportunity he needed to spend time with other women. Like Betsy Blake. 'There's just one more thing,' she said, finding the picture of the medical alert bracelet. 'Did Penelope wear one of these?'

'I don't think so. I don't remember seeing it, but I didn't always notice her jewellery. I can't say she never wore it.'

'She'd have worn it all the time,' said Jasmine. 'Or something else with a similar symbol.'

Juliet looked at it again. 'What is the symbol?' she asked.

'It's a medical alert. You can't see on this photo but on the back it says EPILEPSY. Do you know if Penelope suffered from epilepsy?'

'No,' said Juliet. 'I'm sure she didn't. I would have known because I volunteered to check the forms we all had to fill in for the insurance. We had to declare any medical conditions that could affect performances.'

'Really?' said Jasmine. 'Is that usual?'

'I've no idea, but Malcolm said it was in case we had to cancel mid-performance if someone was ill. I suppose they wouldn't pay out if anyone collapsed on stage because of a condition they hadn't declared.'

'Is it different if they collapse from something they had declared?'

'Yes, it is. A risk assessment would have been done before every concert, and actions outlined for anyone at risk.'

That's interesting, Jasmine thought. Not very helpful though, except that it confirmed the bracelet wasn't Penelope's. 'Well,' she said as the organ finished its piece. 'That's really helpful. Thank you so much.'

'My pleasure,' said Juliet. 'I shall follow the inquiry with interest.'

20

'Grandad!' The front door flew open, and a small boy hurled himself into the living room, dropping a school bag onto the floor, casting off a striped blazer and kicking off a pair of black lace-up shoes. He flung his arms around his grandfather's waist. 'We won,' he shouted.

'Did you, champ?' said Jonny, returning the hug while trying to keep his balance. 'Well done.'

'Rugby match,' explained Marcus, who had followed his son into the house and was carrying a sports bag. 'Hi, Dad. Been waiting long? The traffic was bad.'

'Not long. Jenny let me in. She's just making some tea.'

Marcus handed the sports bag to his son. 'Run and give this to Mum,' he said. 'It can all go straight in the washing machine.' He turned to Jonny. 'You won't believe how muddy they get playing rugby.'

'Oh, I do remember how muddy you used to get,' said Jonny. 'I wouldn't imagine it's changed much.'

'You'd be surprised, Dad. It's not the game it was when I was a kid. It's all health and safety now. The schools are too scared of being sued if the little darlings hurt themselves.'

Not such a bad thing, Jonny thought. When Marcus was Justin's age, he was forever coming home with bruises, a bleeding nose and on one occasion missing a front tooth.

'Anyway,' Marcus said, 'it's good to see you. Not been in the office much recently, have you?'

'It's easier to do my charity stuff at home,' said Jonny. 'I'll be there for next week's board meeting, but there's something I wanted to ask you.'

'Oh yeah, missed the board meeting agenda?'

'No, it's not to do with the company. Well, only marginally.' He opened his phone and found the innovation photo. 'I wondered what you could tell me about this guy. The one at the front holding the trophy. He's probably changed a lot. This was taken thirty years ago.'

He passed the phone to Marcus, who stared at the picture. 'Yeah, I know him. Alex Pike. Known him for years. We do his packing for him, or rather his company. He's fairly hands off these days. His wife and Jenny are best mates, though.'

'I'd like to talk to him. Do you think he'd mind?'

'As long as you're not about to accuse him of a crime, I don't suppose he'd mind.'

'I just want to find out what he remembers about a couple of other people in the photo.'

'You think he'll remember them thirty years on?'

'It must have been very significant for him, winning that award. I'm hoping he'll at least remember this man.' Jonny pointed to Hugo Walsh.

'Why? Is he important?'

'Not any more, he's dead. It says here on the back that he was a professor at the university, and it looks as if he was running the summer school. The trouble is, I can't find out anything at all about him now. The university merged with a couple of others soon after this was taken, and I can't find any records. I'd also like to ask Alex Pike if he remembers this man.' Jonny pointed to Bruce Hunter.

'Is he dead, too?'

'We're not sure.'

'We? Oh, you and your detective club.'

'We're actually working with the police on this.' Jonny sighed. He knew the family would never take him seriously.

Justin came into the room carrying a plate of biscuits, followed by his mother who carried a tray of teacups. Justin plonked the biscuits down on the table and Jenny kissed Jonny on the cheek. 'We don't see enough of you,' she said. 'How's Belinda?'

'Busy preparing for the election,' said Jonny. 'And after that the coronation.'

'Is Granny going to the coronation?' Justin asked. 'We're watching it on the telly.'

'She won't be at the abbey,' said Jonny. 'But there are lots of local events she needs to go to.' One of which was a street party in her ward. With the coronation only two days after the election, Jonny wondered what would happen if Belinda lost her seat. It would be embarrassing if she had to share a slice of quiche with voters who had just kicked her out of office. But everything was organised and invitations had been issued, so he supposed it wouldn't make any difference. Belinda would be there because she was respected for the work she'd done locally, not just as a council member. And she was extremely unlikely to lose her seat. On the whole, local councillors were elected for what they'd done rather than which party they belonged to. He sat down and picked up a cup of tea.

'Dad wants to talk to Alex Pike,' said Marcus.

'He married a friend of mine,' said Jenny. 'They've a couple of boys who go to the same school as Justin. Jeremy and Charlie.'

'Charlie's in my class,' said Justin. 'He's super good at Minecraft.'

'Do they live in the area?' Jonny asked.

'They've got a big house in Sunningdale,' said Marcus.

'With a swimming pool,' said Justin. 'Why don't we get a swimming pool, Dad?'

'Maybe one day,' said Marcus vaguely, while scrolling through his phone. 'There you go, Dad. I've sent you his details.'

'Great,' said Jonny. 'I'll give him a call.'

'Are you going to talk to him about detectives?' asked Justin.

'Probably,' said Jonny. 'I'm hoping he can tell me about a couple of people he knew once.'

'Cool,' said Justin. 'Are they baddies?'

'We're not actually looking for baddies,' said Jonny. 'The police have asked us to check up on someone who they thought was killed in a train crash and then died over a year later.'

Marcus looked puzzled. 'Why... No, I won't ask,' he said.

'It's complicated,' said Jonny, realising he'd explained it very badly.

'Alex wasn't involved, was he?' Jenny asked.

'No, not at all,' said Jonny. 'He might just know something about someone we think was.'

'Someone he met thirty years ago,' said Marcus with a derisive laugh. 'If you ask me—'

'He didn't,' said Jenny, looking at Jonny affectionately. 'Leave him alone.'

Feeling grateful to his daughter-in-law, Jonny finished his tea and said his goodbyes, promising that they'd get together again soon. They only lived a few miles apart, but when Jonny gave it some thought, they really didn't see much of each other.

He returned to his car and headed for home. Belinda was out, so he poured himself a drink, opened the message Marcus had sent and clicked on Alex Pike's number.

ALEX PIKE HADN'T SEEMED PARTICULARLY surprised when Jonny called and asked if he could talk to him about the innovation summer school. He guessed that Marcus had called to warn him. Jonny could hear it now. Marcus with an embarrassed laugh, apologising for his old duffer of a dad and his weird ambition to be a detective. It may have been more than thirty years ago, but Jonny assumed it had been a significant moment in Alex's career. Perhaps if he hadn't won that trophy, he would never have developed his invention and would not have become the rich man he obviously was now.

Alex would be passing through Windsor the following day, he told Jonny. He would need lunch between meetings and would be happy to chat about old times. CPS had been a big hit with his shareholders, Alex told him. They had recently developed eco consciences and CPS had won awards for their recyclable products. Jonny modestly pointed out that it was Marcus who had developed their ethical packaging. He suggested meeting at a pub called the Rising Sun, a small, half-timbered building tucked away in some lanes near Old Windsor where they did good old-fashioned home cooking. Jonny arrived first and ordered a pint and a cheese ploughman's.

Alex Pike was easy to recognise. As Marcus had said, he'd not changed very much in the last thirty years. The biggest difference, as far as Jonny could see, was the designer suit that had replaced the jeans and sweatshirt he'd been photographed in.

'Thank you for agreeing to meet me,' said Jonny, shaking his hand and handing him a menu.

'I've not got long,' Alex said, ordering a seafood sandwich and a bottle of sparkling mineral water. After paying for his drink, he joined Jonny at a table by the window. 'Marcus tells me you're a detective now. I'm intrigued.'

'Kind of,' said Jonny. 'I'm part of a team working for the police as civilian investigators.'

'Fascinating,' said Alex. 'How can I help you?'

'I was hoping you could tell me a bit about the innovation summer school you attended back in 1990 at South Berkshire University. You won an award, I believe.'

'That's where it all started, I suppose. Until then I was just a nerdy kid inventing gadgets in my bedroom. That summer school was the first time anyone took my ideas seriously. I've never looked back.'

Jonny looked out of the window at the shiny Porsche in the pub car park. And there was the big house in Sunningdale with a swimming pool, private schooling for his children, probably a nice holiday home tucked away somewhere in Tuscany. Yes, if all that began with the success of his first invention, he'd definitely never have looked back. 'What do you remember about the other students?'

'Not a lot, to be honest. It was a good many years ago.'

Their food arrived and Alex took a bite of his sandwich while Jonny picked up his phone and scrolled to the photo of Hugo Walsh handing over the award. He passed his phone to Pike.

Alex took the phone from him and smiled. 'Ah, yes,' he said. 'I still have that trophy. I was only supposed to keep it for two years, until the next summer school. But by then the university had merged with a couple of others and no one seemed to know who wanted it. I told them to let me know when they'd decided but I've not heard a word since then.'

Jonny pinched the picture and zoomed in to Hugo. 'What do you remember about this guy? Professor Walsh. I can't find any record of him as an academic. What was he a professor of?'

Pike laughed. 'Nothing. He wasn't a professor. We just called him that because he fancied himself as an academic.'

'But he was on the university staff?'

'He taught some classes on the adult outreach programme. A history of furniture, I think was one of them. Can't remember what else.'

'How did he come to be running the summer school?'

'Probably because no one else wanted to do it. It was a joint project run by the university and local industry. Basically, just a way to bring new graduates and employers together. Hugo was part of the admin team. There was no teaching involved. We produced blueprints for our projects and they were judged by a panel of boffins from tech companies.'

'What was Hugo Walsh like as a person?'

Pike shrugged. 'A bit full of himself. Like I said, he fancied himself as an academic. He used to strut around trying to look learned and starting earnest discussions. He had this fixation with what he called the philosophy of invention. Used to sit in the bar in the evenings and challenge people to kind of verbal duels. He became a bit of a laughing stock. We used to bait him with more and more outrageous propositions.'

'Do you know what happened to him after the merger?'

'No idea, but things got very tough financially around then. I think a lot of the non-degree courses were cut so I guess he was out of a job. To be fair, he was good at making stuff, wooden toys, that kind of thing. He sold some during the summer school to the visiting techies. Even took some orders, I think.'

That tied in with what Jonny knew about Hugo Walsh. That he'd started his carpentry business around then. That was also when he'd married Penelope and Jason was born.

'I'll tell you one thing, though,' said Pike, finishing his drink and pointing to a trio of young women at the back of the photograph. 'There were only three girls at the summer school, and he couldn't keep his hands off them. He was a bit of a menace, they said. They used to go around together, make sure they were never alone with him. One of them said she was going to write and complain about him.'

'And did she?'

'I don't know. I didn't keep in touch with the other students.'

But it could be why he no longer taught courses there. Perhaps financial constraints and the merger were just an excuse not to contract him any longer. 'Do you remember which one she was? The one who complained about him?'

Pike squinted at the photo again. 'This one,' he said, pointing to a girl with a jaunty blond ponytail.

Jonny scrolled to the picture he'd taken of the back of the photo, the list of names. He enlarged them so that they were big enough to read. 'Do any of these names ring a bell?'

'Of course,' said Pike. 'It's coming back to me now. The three 'H's: Helen, Harriet and Hazel. They were very close, all in the same hall at uni. The one with the ponytail, the one who was going to complain about Hugo, was Harriet Angel. That one,' he pointed to the girl on the left, 'was Helen Robertson. She had a boyfriend there with her, so she felt a bit safer.'

'Can you show me the boyfriend?' Jonny asked.

'This one here. He was a musician, working on an electronic tuning device. He came second.'

That's very interesting, Jonny thought. Pike was pointing to the picture of Malcolm Applewood. 'And what about him?' Jonny pointed to Bruce Hunter.

'Australian guy, right?'

'Yes. Did you get to know him well?'

'Not really. He was a bit of an outdoorsy type. He'd invented some bit of kit for rock climbing and spent most of his time in the gym. He was another one with an eye for the women, though. Spent his evenings chatting up the girls who worked behind the bar.' Pike looked at his watch. The kind that cost two or three thousand, Jonny guessed. 'Look,' said Pike, 'I need to get going. I've got a meeting in Basingstoke this afternoon. But give me a buzz if there's anything else you need to know. It's been good to meet you.'

21

After leaving the church, Jasmine went to help with the clearing up at the soup kitchen, only to find it was all done. She must have spent longer talking to Juliet than she thought. Stevie was just hanging out the tea towels to dry, having, Jasmine was relieved to notice, scoured the soup pot until it was sparkling. She hated having to make soup in a pot that still clung to the remains of last week's recipe. Some of the volunteers were not too careful about the finer details of washing up. But then they weren't professional like Jasmine, who had regular inspections by the food hygiene people to consider.

'Sorry,' said Stevie, when Jasmine suggested going for a drink. 'I've promised to help Dad with the garden. We've been putting it off for weeks and now everything's started growing after the winter. We won't be able to get into the house if we don't do something about it now. Another time, okay?'

'Sure,' said Jasmine. It was too early to just go home, and she wondered if Ivo was at a loose end. They could take Harold for a walk along the river and get a coffee at the shack near the bridge. But then she remembered that Ivo had a residents' meeting. Even if the

meeting had finished, Ivo was likely to be out. Since Poppy had introduced him to her brother, Ivo seemed to have developed a social life
that didn't include her.

So socialising was out, but she did have Katya's list to get on with.
No time like the present. She'd drop in on Malcolm and Clara Applewood and find out what they remembered about the innovation
summer school.

It was a short walk from the church. There was only one car on
the drive when she arrived, which probably meant Malcolm wasn't
teaching and would have time to chat to her. Clara answered
Jasmine's ring at the doorbell and invited her in. There was no sign of
Malcolm and his wheelchair. 'I'm afraid Malcolm's not here,' said
Clara when Jasmine said she'd like to talk to him. 'He won't be back
until tomorrow afternoon. It's one of his regular check-ups at the
Stoke Mandeville Hospital.'

'I hope everything's okay,' said Jasmine.

'It's no big deal. He goes every couple of years. The house seems
quiet, though, while he's away. Did you want to see him particularly
or is there something I can help you with?'

'I just had a few questions about the innovation summer school
back in 1990.'

'I remember it,' said Clara. 'I was still at school and too young to
go to it. Not that I ever invented anything. But I dropped in a few
times. I felt very grown up, mixing with students, and my parents and
I were all rather excited by Malcolm's invention. Come in and have a
cup of tea. I'm sure I've got some photos somewhere.'

Clara led Jasmine into the kitchen, a room Jasmine found less
stark than Malcolm's studio. It had obviously been adapted for his
wheelchair, but it was still a cosy room with a pine table littered with
sketches and watercolour paintings. Clara pushed them to one side.
'My little hobby,' she said with a nervous laugh.

Jasmine picked up one of the paintings, a black cat asleep on a
cushion next to a jug of daffodils. 'It's lovely,' said Jasmine. 'It looks
like much more than a hobby. They'd make beautiful birthday cards.'

'I do sell one or two,' said Clara modestly. 'The library in town sometimes shows them and there's an annual watercolour exhibition at the Guildhall. I do have a website but really I don't have the time to produce all that much. I never got to study art so they're a bit amateurish. I was planning to go to art college, but... well, you know.'

Caring for Malcolm must be a full-time job, Jasmine thought. 'And I've interrupted your free evening. I'm so sorry.'

'Not at all,' said Clara. 'I'm glad of your company.' She boiled a kettle and made a pot of tea, pouring it into two pottery mugs. 'Now, where did I put those photos?' she said. 'Probably in my bedroom. I'll just pop upstairs and get them.'

She bustled out of the room, leaving Jasmine to flick through more of her paintings. She wondered if Clara would have time to paint some for the café. There were plenty of blank spaces on the walls and these had a nice, homely feel to them. She might even be able to sell some.

Clara returned carrying a box of photos, which she put down on the table. She picked out some of herself and Malcolm as children and put them to one side. 'Here we are,' she said. 'This is one of Malcolm's electronic tuner. He was disappointed that it didn't win the award.'

'Did he develop it any further?' Jasmine asked.

'I think he always planned to, but he'd chummed up with Bruce Hunter and went to Australia as soon as the summer school ended. Then, of course, the accident stopped him doing anything for a long time. Once he started getting his life back together again there were other electronic tuners on the market, and he felt there wasn't room for his.'

She picked out more photos and passed them to Jasmine. 'Here they are together.' She picked up a picture of two young men and a girl. 'Malcolm and Bruce, and that was Malcolm's girlfriend, Helen Robertson.' She looked at the photo and sighed. 'They broke up soon after that.'

'After the accident?' Jasmine asked. 'That's sad.'

'I'm not sure they were that serious about each other. But what do I know? I was just a teenager. But it's even sadder. Helen died the following year. I don't think they'd seen each other for a while. Malcolm would have been in hospital at the time, and as far as I know Helen didn't visit him there.'

Jasmine opened the photo on her phone. 'There were three girls at the summer school,' she said, pointing them out. 'Did you know the others as well?'

'Not really. They were quite close, all at uni together. They didn't have a lot of time for a schoolgirl like little old me.' She pointed to the one with the ponytail. 'That's Harriet Angel. She was very clever, destined for a first and a dazzling career.'

Jasmine recognised Helen as one of the girls in the group photo from Jason's attic. She opened the photo on her phone and showed it to Clara. 'And this one is Hazel Corruthers?' she asked, pointing to the third girl.

'Hazel was the quietest. A bit of a dreamer, but I liked her the best. I always hoped Malcolm would dump Helen and take up with Hazel instead. But I was fifteen and no one took me seriously.'

'And do you remember Hugo Walsh?'

'The director? I was warned to keep away from him,' she said with a nervous laugh.

'And did you?'

'Did I what?'

'Keep away from Hugo Walsh?'

'They said he was evil,' said Clara, staring into her tea. 'When Malcolm was let out of hospital and moved back here with Mum, Dad and me. The last thing he wanted was to find Hugo Walsh had moved into the area. And on top of that, his wife joined Dad's choir just a year or so later.'

'How did Malcolm react to that?'

'Oh, it scared me but Malcolm didn't care. I think after all he'd been through, Hugo Walsh and the summer school were just a distant memory. Malcolm had been through a lot by then. But I think he was fond of Penelope.'

'She must have been in the choir for a very long time.'

'She was, but there are others who've been in it for longer. Members are very loyal.'

Jasmine accepted a second cup of tea. 'I was talking to Juliet earlier. She said she thought she'd seen Bruce recently.'

'God, I hope for Malcolm's sake she didn't. He was upset enough last time Bruce showed his face.'

'You've not seen him recently?'

Clara shook her head. 'And it's not likely Malcolm has either.'

How did she know that? As brother and sister, they lived together and were close, but surely they didn't tell each other everything. Malcolm wasn't housebound. There must be times when he went out and met people and didn't have to account for every second of his time to his sister. She had a sudden memory of the last time she was there, seeing Malcolm watching them from the window.

It was time to go home. She stood up and carried her mug to the sink. 'Thank you for the tea,' she said. 'And for showing me your paintings. Would you be interested in displaying some of them in our café? We get tourists dropping in. You might be able to sell some there.'

Clara looked at her in surprise. 'How kind of you,' she said. 'That would be wonderful. Most people I meet only think of me as a carer.'

'Then we must make sure people see your work,' said Jasmine, kissing her on the cheek.

Clara showed her out. The door to Malcolm's studio was open and Jasmine was able to glance in. Something was puzzling her about the window. It was a normal-looking window, and that was what was bothering her. From wheelchair height they'd only have been able to see Malcolm's head and shoulders. But they'd seen more than that. Malcolm had been standing at the window. That must have been a huge effort for him, so what was it about her and Katya that had made him pull himself out of his chair and stare at them? Were there things he hadn't told them? Was he worried about what they'd discover? She wondered why he'd not mentioned the summer school when they'd visited before. If he blamed Bruce Hunter for his accident, surely that was important. He let them think that he and Bruce were acquainted only through the rock-climbing holiday. No mention of them having spent the week together at a summer school just before that. Was Malcolm covering something up, or had she and Katya just asked the wrong questions?

22

'This is better,' said Lugs, handing Katya a pint of beer.

Lugs was off duty for the day and he and Katya had driven out of town to a nice country pub that sold real ale and proper bar meals – sausage and mash, plaice and chips or cauliflower cheese.

'It's good of you to take the time on your day off,' said Katya. 'I hope Mrs Lomax didn't have plans for today.'

'Just a few hints about getting the lawnmower out. But the weather's not up to that today. Anyway, she's off to get her hair done and she was only too pleased not to have to worry about my lunch.'

'Well, I'm very grateful,' said Katya. 'I just hope all my questions haven't taken up too much of your time.'

'Not at all. They're all relevant to the research I asked you to do, although you seem to be uncovering way more than we'd anticipated. We expected it to be a simple enquiry about where Hugo Walsh had spent the last eighteen months and why he didn't come forward after the train crash.' He put a thick folder down on the table, just as a woman came to take their food order. 'There's stuff that will interest you in here. But before we look at it, what would you like to eat?'

'Bangers and mash,' said Katya without hesitating. She'd already made that decision and was just waiting for Lugs to ask. He ordered the plaice and chips.

The woman wrote it down on her notepad. 'Ten minutes,' she said. 'Another drink while you wait?'

They both shook their heads. Too much beer at lunchtime and Katya would spend the afternoon asleep. Lugs too, probably. He opened the folder, took out a photograph and handed it to Katya.

It was a still from some CCTV footage of a man going through a ticket barrier at a train station. It was no one she recognised. 'Should I know who it is?' she asked.

'His name is Barry Brent. A thirty-seven-year-old delivery driver from Wolverhampton. He was reported missing by his family a few days after the train crash.'

Katya looked at the picture again, trying to identify the station. She could just make out the First Great Western logo on a wall behind the barrier. It was a First Great Western train that had caused the accident. 'Shouldn't that have been flagged up after the crash?' she asked.

'It should,' said Lugs, taking a swig of beer. 'The family did query it, but everyone had been accounted for, so it wasn't taken any further.'

'Like I said before, the local police did a slovenly job. What brought it to your attention now?'

'It was your suggestion that Bruce Hunter had been seen recently in Windsor and that it might not have been him on the train.'

'Just speculation,' said Katya. 'We're not sure this particular witness is reliable. It's not supported by any other sightings.'

He shrugged. 'All the same, after you asked for the mispers list, I thought I'd better go through it again myself.' He pushed the photo towards her again. 'Take a look at the man's wrist.'

Katya stared at it. 'He's wearing a bracelet,' she said. 'But I can't really see what kind.'

'I took a photo of the one that Ivo found in Walsh's attic and emailed it to a mate in Wolverhampton, who showed it to Brent's father. He identified it as identical to one his son wore. He'd had it made for Barry when his epilepsy was first diagnosed.'

'That can't have been an easy conversation,' said Katya. If one of your family goes missing, the last thing you want to hear is that one of his possessions has turned up in the wreckage of a train crash. Worse still, that you'd asked about it and been told your nearest and dearest was out of the picture. 'Can you be sure Barry Brent was on the train? Just because his bracelet was found in the wreckage, it isn't proof.'

'No, but he was seen going through the barrier at the right time to have been catching that particular train. I would expect a coroner to accept that as enough evidence to grant a death certificate.'

'I'm surprised the CCTV footage is still available. I thought it was usually overwritten after a month or two.'

'It would have been, but everything was kept for the inquiry which is due to open next month.'

'Yes, of course. It's a long wait for the bereaved, isn't it?'

'Heartbreaking, I'd imagine.' Lugs stared sadly into his beer.

'So why was he holding hands with Penelope Walsh? Is there any evidence that they knew each other?'

'None that I can find, but take a look at this.' Lugs took out another photograph from his folder. 'Rather gruesome, I'm afraid.'

He wasn't wrong. Lugs had cropped out the two charred bodies, but the picture of two badly burnt arms was enough. Katya was glad their food hadn't arrived yet. But there was something not right about the image. 'They're not holding hands,' she said.

'Well spotted,' said Lugs. 'I think that was just a bit of journalistic hype.'

Just the kind of thing Katya's freelance journalist friend, Teddy Strang, might do to tug at his readers' heartstrings. As if being burnt alive wasn't enough. 'So what is going on here?' she asked.

Lugs used his pen as a pointer. 'I think this is Penelope's arm,' he said. 'Hard to tell when it's burnt that badly, but of the two bodies found together, this one was slighter. I'd say she was sitting with her arm resting on a table. This is her right arm. The other arm is a left arm. It has grabbed her just below the elbow. Not an affectionate gesture, I think.'

'No, you're right,' said Katya. 'He was probably clutching at whatever he could out of fear. They'd have felt the crash and had a few seconds before the train plunged off the rails and caught fire. My God, it must have been terrifying.' Katya shuddered and pushed the photo back in Lugs' direction. 'But he wasn't wearing a bracelet.'

'Take another look at the CCTV picture.'

Katya looked at it again. 'He's wearing it on his right arm,' she said. 'So we assume Penelope and Barry were travelling in the same part of the train, sitting at a table opposite each other. There's nothing to suggest they knew each other. That answers one question but leaves another much more difficult one. What happened to Bruce Hunter?'

'Well,' said Lugs. 'You know he was in Bath with Penelope just before the crash, and that he might have been in Windsor recently. I suggest you pick up the trail from there. A bit more work for you and your team, I think.'

That was an understatement if she'd ever heard one. What were they going to do? Take it in turns to loiter outside Waitrose with a picture of Bruce Hunter on the off chance someone might have seen him there? 'Do we get an extended contract?' she asked.

'I guess I can arrange that,' said Lugs, laughing. 'So let's turn to your other question.'

'Hugo Walsh and the girls. Did you discover anything?'

Lugs shook his head. 'It's too long ago. If one of them did make a complaint, there's no record of it. There would only be a police record if it had gone to prosecution. The sex offenders register started in 1997 so even if there had been a successful prosecution, he wouldn't be on it. You'd probably do better to try and trace the girl, Harriet Angel, and ask her. It's an unusual name so you could be lucky.'

How much work was he going to send in their direction? Anyone would think the police did no work at all. But that was unfair. Lugs was a grafter and he'd done a lot to help her with this case. And times were hard. Police numbers were well down on what they should be.

Teams like hers were much cheaper and she was hardly one to complain.

Their food arrived and Katya attacked it hungrily. All this work had given her an appetite. Life was good right now. It had a purpose that retirement had never given her. She was also sleeping better, and her clothes felt a bit looser. *Swings and roundabouts,* she thought. Austerity was a nightmare. But it had given her a new lease of life. She was one of the lucky ones.

Lugs drove her home and she sat down with a cup of tea and began making plans. The three girls would be a good place to start. Jasmine had discovered that one of them, Helen Robertson, had died not long after the summer school. She put the notes Jasmine had made from information Clara had given her to one side. Death at such a young age was always upsetting, but it was unlikely Helen had anything to do with where Bruce was right now. They needed to find Harriet Angel and Hazel Corruthers.

She turned to Jonny's notes. *He should be the one to research Harriet Angel,* she thought. He could carry on from where he'd got to with Alex Pike. If, as Jasmine had noted after her talk to Clara, Harriet was the high flyer of the three, she had probably made a mark for herself and would be easy to find. She might even know what had become of Hazel Corruthers. If the two of them were still in touch, it could save a lot of searching. Katya picked up her phone and called Jonny.

'I'm on it,' he said when she asked him to find out all he could about Harriet Angel. All Katya had to do now was sit back and wait for Jonny to call back.

23

Jonny drove through an open five bar gate and up a gravel drive, parking outside the front door of a well-maintained cottage with dormer windows and a red-tiled roof. It was chocolate-box perfect: a lawn yellow with primroses, a brick patio with a set of wrought iron garden furniture and small wooded area vibrant with daffodils. There was obviously money in IT consultancy.

Harriet Angel had been easy to find. Jonny was only surprised that he'd not heard of her already. She was a frequent broadcaster; a pundit who was apparently the go-to person for any newsworthy technical developments. He found her in the archives of the more respected news outlets, offering her opinion on everything from proposed supercomputers for the civil service to advanced surveillance systems patrolling global markets.

He called Katya.

'That was quick,' she said. 'Do you have contact details?'

'All on her web page,' he said. 'She lives a few miles the other side of Reading.'

'Email her,' said Katya. 'And follow it up with a phone call to arrange a meeting.'

. . .

THE FOLLOW UP phone call hadn't been necessary. Harriet had replied at once, saying she'd be happy to talk to him. Must have been the way he worded the email, he thought. Casually friendly, with a tantalising touch of intrigue. Jasmine's logo probably helped as well. No one could resist friendly detectives with a dog, could they?

After parking his car on the gravel driveway, Jonny was greeted at the door by a woman he recognised from YouTube videos he'd watched of her recent broadcasts. Her hair was still blond but now expensively bobbed to shoulder length and in contrast to the well-tailored outfits she wore on TV, she was dressed for the country in jeans and a padded Barbour gilet. 'Come in,' she said, leading him into a low-ceilinged living room with oak beams, an open fireplace and two Chesterfield sofas. A golden retriever was stretched out in front of a log fire. It stared lazily at Jonny, then sunk its head back onto its paws and closed its eyes. 'Can I get you a tea or coffee?' Harriet asked.

Jonny shook his head. 'I'm fine, thank you, and I won't keep you long.'

'I was intrigued by your email,' she said, inviting him to sit on one of the sofas and seating herself on the other one. 'You're trying to trace people who were at the innovation summer school. May I ask why?'

There was no reason not to be straight with her, he supposed. 'You know that the Swindon train crash inquiry begins in a week or two?'

She nodded.

'Well, I'm working as a civilian investigator with Thames Valley Police. There has been a case of mistaken identity that they would like to clear up before the inquiry starts.'

'Very interesting,' she said. 'But I don't see what that has to do with a summer school that took place more than thirty years ago.'

Jonny opened his briefcase and took out the photograph Ivo had found in Jason's attic. He put it down on the coffee table and turned it in Harriet's direction. 'You remember this man?' He pointed to Hugo Walsh.

'God, yes. Dreadful man. I complained about him to the organisers, but nothing came of it.'

'It may have done,' said Jonny. 'He never worked again at the university.'

'That's something, I suppose. Why is he of interest now?'

'It was believed that he died with his wife in the crash.'

'I'm sorry for them, but I don't see—'

'The thing is, his body was found in the Thames recently. He'd not been in the river for long and DNA identification confirmed it was him. He'd disappeared around the time of the crash, but we have since established his whereabouts for the intervening eighteen months.'

'Interesting,' said Harriet. 'So who was it on the train and how had the identification gone so wrong?'

'I'm sure you know a lot more than I do about the technicalities of identifying bodies. But in this case, I guess there was a lot going on and people just made assumptions. Hugo's wife, Penelope, was identified. There's no question about that. She was with a man and Hugo was nowhere to be found after the crash, so they jumped to the obvious conclusion.'

'Dreadful,' said Harriet, with a suitably shocked expression. 'With all the technology available they should be able to identify someone, however badly damaged their remains.'

'This man is also of some interest to us.' Jonny pointed to Bruce Hunter.

'Bruce,' she said, sounding surprised. 'You think he was on that train? Why?'

'We knew he'd been seeing Penelope both near her home in Windsor and then at a hotel in Bath. We also know that he didn't return home to Australia when expected and his family are unable to give us an address for him.'

She looked down at the dog lying at her feet, as if trying to decide how to react to this piece of news. Then she looked up at him. 'Bruce is not dead,' she said.

Really? She was still in touch with him, then. 'How can you be sure?' he asked.

She paused again, as if not knowing what to say. 'Because I saw him last week.'

'You did? Where?'

'Right here.'

'He came to visit you?'

'He actually came to visit my son.' She reached for a photograph in a silver frame of a young man wearing an academic gown and clutching a rolled-up scroll. 'Damian,' she said. 'This was taken some years ago when he graduated from Corpus Christi. A first in biochemistry. He's thirty-two now and working at Porton Down.'

'You must be very proud,' said Jonny, doing a bit of quick mental arithmetic and coming up with some interesting answers.

'I can see how your mind is working,' said Harriet. 'I had better tell you the whole story.'

'It started at the summer school?'

'Yes, but possibly not in the way you think. Damian is my adopted son. His mother was Helen Robertson. She died soon after Damian was born. Suicide.'

'I'm so sorry,' said Jonny. 'Can you tell me what happened?'

'Helen discovered she was pregnant just before Christmas 1990. Her parents wanted nothing to do with her and of course it was too late for an abortion. I was a few months into my postgraduate work and I had a small flat in Oxford. I took her in, and she stayed with me until Damian was born. She was completely unprepared for mother-hood. Well, she'd not even known she was pregnant until well into the pregnancy. She was always rather vague and unworldly. She suffered from what we now know was postnatal depression. She refused to see anyone after the birth, so it was never diagnosed. I came home one evening when Damian was about three weeks old. He was screaming his head off. Helen had taken an overdose.'

Jonny was speechless. Shocked and horrified by what he'd just heard. That poor girl. Where the hell were her parents when she needed them? And the baby's father? Oh yes, he'd gone off rock climbing in Australia and come back paralysed.

Harriet disappeared into the kitchen, returning a moment later with a glass of water, which she handed to him.

Jonny took a sip and recovered some of his composure. 'And I suppose Damian's father wasn't able to do much? He would still have been in hospital.'

'I'm sorry, I'm not following you,' she said. 'Who was in hospital?'

'Malcolm Applewood.'

'Malcolm?'

'Yes. He was Helen's boyfriend, wasn't he?'

'Ah,' said Harriet. 'I can see why you are confused. Yes, Malcolm had been going out with Helen. But he wasn't Damian's father.'

Jonny wondered how many more twists there were going to be in this sad story. 'Then who was?'

'Malcolm left for Australia with Bruce when the summer school finished because... well, because of what Helen told him.'

'Which was?'

'That Hugo Walsh had seduced her. I would have said he raped her, but Helen denied that. She said it happened one evening when they'd both had too much to drink.'

'So Hugo... Hugo Walsh was Damian's father?' This was getting more shocking by the second.

Harriet nodded.

'Did Helen tell him?'

'She refused to have any more to do with him. I went to see him because I thought the least he could do was stump up some cash. But he was quite abusive, and he denied it had ever happened. Helen refused to take it any further. Hugo had just got married himself and there was a baby on the way. Another baby, I suppose I should say. Helen told me she couldn't bear to ruin another woman's life and to let it go.'

So Jason has a brother. Jonny couldn't imagine how on earth they were going to break that to him. He wondered if Damian knew he had a brother or whether Harriet had kept that secret. Did he even know who his father was? Not something Jonny was prepared to get into. Then there was the other bit of shock news. Bruce Hunter was alive. But where the hell was he? 'Do you know where Bruce is at the moment?' he asked.

'He's lying low,' said Harriet. 'I don't know where.'

'But he keeps in touch?'

'By email and phone, yes. But he doesn't have a work permit or an extended visa so he shouldn't be in the country.'

'Then why stay? He owns a thriving business in Australia.'

Harriet sighed. 'He has personal reasons for staying. I'm afraid I'm not at liberty to say what they are.'

'Can you give me his contact details? There are some questions I'd like to ask him about his visit to Malcolm last year.'

'Not without asking him. If he gets in touch again and agrees, I'll let you know.'

He was unlikely to get more than that from her, so he scribbled down his phone number and handed it to her. 'Thank you for your time,' he said.

He'd learnt a lot. A pity he couldn't top it off with an address for Bruce, but what she had told him was explosive. He wasn't sure what they would do with it, but Katya would know. And they were all meeting the next morning.

It was only after Jonny had turned out of Harriet's drive that he realised he had forgotten to ask about the third girl, Hazel Corruthers. But that wasn't really a problem. He could drop Harriet an email to thank her for seeing him and ask about Hazel at the same time.

One more thing struck him on the way home. When you tell people a body has been found in the river, most are curious about the cause of death. There is a gruesome interest in whether it was an accident, suicide or murder. And yet Harriet hadn't asked. Could that be because she already knew the answer?

24

'We should go on a pub crawl,' said Katya.

That was not quite the expected answer to Jonny's question about what they should do next. 'Why?' he asked.

Katya wiped the board clean and drew a circle, in which she wrote Hugo's name. 'We know he'd been drinking the night he died. He wasn't staying with Jason so it's not like he would have gone into an off-licence and stocked up for a boozy evening with his son. And I don't think he would have sat on a park bench drinking. He was in Windsor for a reason, and I don't think it was to get drunk and throw himself into the river. Which means?' She looked round hopefully.

'That he was in a pub?' asked Jasmine.

'And why would he go to a pub?'

'Aren't we going round in circles a bit?' said Ivo. 'He went to a pub to get drunk.'

'But why here? There are perfectly good pubs in Banbury, probably on a lot of other stretches of canal. He must have had a reason for coming here.'

'Betsy told us he wanted to see his son.'

'But he didn't, did he?'

'Not if Jason's telling the truth,' said Jonny. 'But perhaps he's lying because he was the one that pushed Hugo into the river.'

'It's possible,' said Katya. 'But we don't think he's got the right sized feet to match the prints, and we don't know if he has a motive.'

'He does,' said Jasmine. 'Once it was known that Hugo was alive, he'd lose the house and anything else he'd inherited.'

'Maybe,' said Katya. 'But Hugo had kept quiet for eighteen months. Why turn up now?'

'Sick of living on a canal boat?' Ivo suggested.

'We won't rule it out,' said Katya. 'But let's think in a different direction. What exactly did Betsy say was his reason for leaving her?'

'He told her he wanted to see his son.'

'No,' said Katya. 'He said he needed to *meet* his son. And we assumed that was Jason. But think about it. What have we just discovered?'

Jasmine and Ivo looked puzzled. Jonny suddenly realised what Katya was getting at. 'He had two sons,' he said. 'It was Damian he was meeting.'

'But how did he know Damian even existed?' Jasmine asked. 'And what made him think he was in Windsor? Who would have known that Hugo was Damian's father?'

'Harriet, obviously. Bruce, and possibly Malcolm,' said Jonny. 'We need to find out which of them had an alibi for that night.'

Ivo had been sitting quietly doodling on a sheet of paper. 'How about this for an idea?' he asked, holding up the paper on which he'd drawn a mind map.

Katya took it from him and fixed it to the board with a piece of Blu Tack. 'It's good,' she said. 'Very much what I was thinking myself.' She pointed to Ivo's drawing of a small building, which he'd labelled *Pub* and which had three stick figures outside it. He'd labelled them *Harriet, Bruce* and *Malcolm*. On the left of the page, he'd drawn a figure being pushed into the river and labelled *Hugo*. He'd drawn a question mark over the pusher. Katya picked up the pen again and wrote *Suspects – Motives,* and listing the three names:

Harriet – revenge for Helen's death.

Malcolm – payback for Hugo having seduced Helen.
Bruce -?

'What about opportunity?' asked Jonny. 'I don't see how it could have been Malcolm. Even if he was able to meet Hugo in town, how could he have lured him to the river and pushed him in?'

'It's not impossible,' said Jasmine. 'He can get out of the wheel-chair. I saw him standing at the window at his house. They might have gone to look at the river and when Hugo wasn't expecting it, he got out of the chair and pushed him in.'

'And then walked across the bridge, leaving footprints on the bank? We need to find out more about how mobile he is before we start accusing him of anything. It's not impossible though, I suppose.'

'Bruce could have managed it easily,' said Ivo. 'And he was likely to own the right sort of boots.'

'But we've no idea how to find him. What makes you think Hugo knew where he was?'

'Or for that matter, how Bruce knew where Hugo was,' said Jonny.

'What about Harriet?' Jasmine asked. 'Would she have been strong enough?'

'If she'd taken him by surprise, it might have been possible,' said Jonny. 'She looks like she spends time in the gym.'

'Which brings us back to the pub crawl,' said Katya. 'We'll print a photo of Hugo. It was only a couple of weeks ago. Someone will remember seeing him and whoever was with him. I'll go this evening. Who's going to join me?'

None of them wanted to be left out.

'We'll meet at the Royal Station at seven,' said Katya. 'And work our way round to the Riverside.'

Jonny opened Google Maps. 'There are five pubs between the station and the river,' he said. 'All of them just a short walk from the bridge.'

'That's manageable,' said Katya. 'Just go easy on the drinks. We don't want to end up in the river ourselves.'

∿

THEY DECIDED to start with the pub closest to the station. They assumed that Hugo would have stayed on the canals for as long as possible. He could have travelled all the way to Slough by boat, taking the train for the last few miles.

'That's not a very quick or reliable way to travel,' Ivo pointed out. 'If he was going to meet someone, how would they know what time he'd arrive?'

'That's a good point,' said Katya. 'But even if he caught a train from, for example, Banbury, he would still have finished up in Slough. The only trains that go to the Riverside Station are commuter lines from Waterloo.'

'So,' said Jonny as they found a table in the first pub, not too far from the bar. 'What's everyone having?'

'Just a shandy for me,' said Katya. 'I need to keep a clear head.'

Neither Ivo nor Jasmine drank alcohol, so Jonny ordered Katya's shandy, half a pint for himself and orange juice for Ivo and Jasmine. 'Do you work here regularly, Paul?' he asked, noticing the name badge worn by the young man behind the bar.

'Most evenings, yes,' said Paul.

'Can you remember if you were working the Thursday before last?' Jonny asked, giving him the date.

'Yes, I would have been.'

Jonny showed him the photo of Hugo. 'Do you remember seeing this man?'

'What time would that have been?'

Jonny had to think about that. It probably hadn't been a long, sociable meeting and pushing people into rivers was likely to be a late-night activity. But on the other hand, whoever intended doing the pushing would need to allow plenty of time to get their victim wobbly on his feet. Jonny had never had to make this kind of decision and hadn't realised what a fine balance it was. Too drunk and they'd not have been able to stagger to the river. Not drunk enough and Hugo would have been aware of what was going to happen and put up a fight. 'Most of the evening, I think,' he said. 'He probably stayed until closing time and he did have a lot to drink.'

Paul stared at the photo. 'Was he on his own?' he asked.

'I don't think so,' said Jonny. 'He would have been with at least one other person.'

'Don't remember him,' said Paul.

'Is there anyone else you could ask? I assume you weren't on your own here.'

'Here, Tim,' said Paul, waving the picture at the man serving drinks further down the bar. 'Do you remember this bloke, Thursday before last?'

'Nah,' said Tim, barely looking at the photo.

Jonny carried the drinks back to the table, shaking his head. They finished their drinks quickly and headed to the next pub on the list, where the result was much the same. As it was at the next two.

It was nine-thirty by the time they arrived at the last pub on Katya's list. 'Last chance saloon,' she said with a laugh.

'What if no one saw him here?' Ivo asked.

'Then we have to think again. There are more pubs in Windsor, but I think we'll have had enough for this evening.'

Jonny went through his routine of ordering at the bar and showing the photograph, this time to a young woman called Serena with dark hair. 'Yeah, I remember him,' she said.

'Was he alone?' Jonny asked, trying to keep the excitement out of his voice.

'No, he was with a woman,' said Serena.

'Really?' he said in surprise. 'One minute. I need to ask my friends something.'

He rushed back to the table where the others were waiting. 'Any of you got a photo of Harriet?' he asked. Why hadn't they thought of printing one?

'Here,' said Jasmine, handing him her phone. 'There's one on her website.'

Jonny headed back to the bar and paid for the drinks. Then he handed the phone to Serena. 'Was this the woman?' he asked.

'No,' said Serena. 'Nothing like her.'

'Can you describe her for me?' Harriet in casual wear might look very different from the glossy photo on her website.

'She was middle-aged, quite tall, plumpish, greying hair.'

'Okay,' said Jonny, disappointed. 'Thanks for your help.'

He carried the drinks to the table and sat down. 'Good news and bad,' he said, taking a gulp of beer. 'Hugo was here that night, but not with any of our suspects.' He repeated Serena's description of the woman she'd seen.

'It doesn't sound like anyone we know,' said Jasmine.

'What about Poppy?' Katya suggested.

'No,' said Ivo. 'She's tiny and probably not a day over thirty.'

'It's disappointing,' said Jonny. 'We've found another suspect but without any idea who she might be. But at least we know Hugo was in town that night.'

'We already knew that,' said Ivo. 'He died here, didn't he?'

'Let's go home and sleep on it,' said Katya. 'We'll regroup in the morning.'

As JONNY WALKED HOME, he had an idea. He quickened his pace and, arriving home, turned on his computer and typed a name into Google.

KATYA WAS ALREADY in the office the next day when Jonny finished his washing up duties and headed upstairs. He was carrying a plastic wallet, which he put down on the table in front of her.

'Considering last night's disappointment,' said Katya, 'you are looking rather pleased with yourself.'

'I'm feeling pleased with myself,' said Jonny, unfastening the wallet and pulling out some sheets of paper. 'This,' he said, pointing to a photo of a woman with grey hair, 'is someone we all overlooked. I'm surprised the rest of you didn't think of trying to find her.'

Katya stared at the photo. 'I'm not following,' she said. 'Who is she?'

'You remember that Clara told Jasmine there were only three girls at the summer school. They were close friends, all at uni together?'

Katya nodded.

'Well, this is the third girl. Hazel Corruthers. Don't you think that if Harriet and Helen stayed closely in touch, they would have included Hazel?'

'Almost certainly,' said Katya. 'Jonny, you're brilliant.' She sifted through the pages Jonny had printed from Hazel's web page.

'She runs a goat farm in Wiltshire,' he said, pointing to a photo of a run-down farmhouse. 'It's about ten miles this side of Salisbury. An isolated spot up in the Downs.'

Katya took the picture and pinned it to the board, just as Ivo and Jasmine arrived with Harold wagging his tail enthusiastically at the sight of Jonny. 'You two recovered from last night?' Jonny asked.

'It's left me feeling a bit flat, to be honest,' said Jasmine. 'Where do we go from here?'

'Right,' said Katya. 'No need to feel like that. Jonny's found a new lead.' She tapped on the photo. 'Hazel Corruthers,' she said. 'Fits the description that girl Serena gave of the woman who was with Hugo in the pub.'

'We should confirm that,' said Ivo. 'She's a fairly ordinary-looking woman. There could be lots that would fit that description.'

'I'll go back and check,' said Jonny. He picked up his phone and found the number for the pub where Serena worked. After a short conversation he ended the call. 'She's just started her shift,' he said, looking at his watch. 'I'll pop round there and catch her before it gets busy. I can be there and back in ten minutes or so.'

'While Jonny's doing that,' said Katya, 'we can plan what to do next. What are our priorities?'

'Finding Bruce,' said Ivo. 'Do we know if he's even in the country?'

'We know Harriet keeps in touch,' said Katya, reading the notes Jonny had sent her after his visit. 'She said he was lying low because he's not supposed to be in the country. She was going to let Jonny know if she could pass on his phone number. As far as I know, Jonny hasn't heard back from her.'

'She was probably just saying that to get rid of him,' said Jasmine. 'If Bruce is lying low, why would he give anyone his details?'

Katya cast her mind back to her policing days. How did they find people who'd gone under the radar? With difficulty, she remembered, but there were ways. Although when she thought hard about it, most of them were things only the police could do. Lugs, helpful as he was, was unlikely to help with that unless he was sure there was a crime involved. And if there was, he would take over the case himself.

Fifteen minutes later Jonny returned, clattering breathlessly up the stairs. 'Serena thinks this might be the woman she saw,' he said, putting the photo down on the table and sinking into a chair.

'Brainstorm time,' said Katya, handing out sheets of paper and pencils. 'Write down all your thoughts about the case and we'll pull them together into an action plan. Ten minutes, then we'll discuss it over coffee and sandwiches.'

'Not the best way to spend my time off,' Jasmine muttered. 'It's like being back at college.' She wrote for five minutes then folded her paper and stuffed it into her pocket. 'I'm not sharing until the rest of you have finished,' she said crossly.

'I'll put the kettle on,' said Katya. 'Then we can put a plan in place and you young ones can all get off and enjoy yourselves. I wouldn't want to impose on your fun.' She slammed her folder shut and stared grumpily out of the window.

'We're not getting at you, Katya,' said Jonny, looking up from his paper.

'No, we really like doing this, don't we, Ivo?' said Jasmine, kicking Ivo in the shins.

'Of course,' said Ivo. 'Harold as well.' He nudged Harold with his foot, an action that always made him wag his tail. 'See?' said Ivo as the dog's tail thumped against the floor. 'He agrees.'

'Hmm,' muttered Katya. 'I'll go and get the coffee.' She pushed her folder into her bag and headed for the door.

'Have we upset her?' Jasmine asked, as they listened to Katya's feet clomping on the stairs.

'She gets a bit touchy about her age,' said Jonny. 'We both do. Why should two youngsters like yourselves want to spend time with a couple of oldies? Must be a bit dull.'

'Like when we were set upon by a mad murderer in the park?' Ivo asked.

'Well,' said Jonny. 'That was a one off.'

'It was our first case,' said Ivo. 'And we solved it. And then we found the body in the river, which was exciting. What's not to like?'

'Perhaps she thinks you should both be going to parties every night,' Jonny suggested.

'We're planning a barbecue at *Shady Willows*,' said Ivo. 'Soon as the weather warms up a bit.'

'Not sure that's what Katya had in mind,' said Jonny. The average age of *Shady Willows* residents was around seventy-five. Although he shouldn't be ageist about it. They could probably all party like rock stars.

Katya pushed the door open with the edge of a tray containing a cafetière of coffee and a milk jug, which she'd filled too full and was spilling onto a plate of biscuits. She put the tray down on the table and poured four cups of coffee. 'What didn't I have in mind?' she said.

'We're just discussing the generation gap,' said Jonny.

'Jonny thinks because Ivo and I are young we should be partying every night,' said Jasmine.

'That's so last generation,' said Ivo.

Jonny and Katya laughed.

'Well then, you two serious Gen-Z types, let's get down to it and solve this mystery.' Katya picked up a pen and wrote *How to find Bruce* on the board. 'Any ideas?'

'Start with the obvious,' said Jasmine. 'It all goes back to that summer school, doesn't it?'

'I wrote that down,' said Jonny, opening his sheet of paper. 'It's the one thing that links all our suspects. And the final link in that chain has to be Hazel.' Jasmine and Ivo nodded in agreement.

'What I wrote,' said Ivo, 'is that Bruce is lying low and where better than an isolated farm in the Downs? We should go there and look for him.'

'Hold on,' said Katya. 'We're getting ahead of ourselves. Are we accusing Hazel and Bruce of murdering Hugo? If so, we've a couple of gaps that need filling.' She picked up the pen again and wrote *Motive*.

'They were both Helen's friends,' said Jasmine. 'So revenge for Hugo's attack and her death.'

'Do we include Harriet and Malcolm in that?' Katya asked. 'If so, how do you explain Malcolm's part in it? He hated Bruce, and in any case he's wheelchair bound.'

'Malcolm's the only one who lives locally,' said Jasmine. 'If it wasn't for Malcolm, they could have lured Hugo anywhere. There are loads of other rivers they could have pushed him into.'

'We need to go further back,' said Katya. 'How did they find Hugo? And who told Hugo he had another son? Was it the thought of meeting Damian that brought him back here?'

'Do you suppose Damian knew who his father was?' said Ivo. 'He might have only recently found out and then gone searching for him.'

Jonny had been busy writing something. 'How about this?' he asked, copying what he had written onto the board.

Damian starts asking Harriet questions about his father and decides to find him.

Around the same time Bruce turns up. He wants to put things right with Malcolm but isn't welcomed with open arms.

Bruce realises Penelope is married to Hugo and starts an affair with her. He assumes that Hugo was on the train with Penelope when she was killed but then discovers that he is still alive and that Damian knows where he is.

Bruce's visa expires and he needs somewhere out of the way where he can lie low. Harriet suggests staying with Hazel.

They plan to confront Hugo about Helen's death. They write to him telling him about Damian and arranging for Hazel to meet him in Windsor.

'We still don't know how they found Hugo,' said Jasmine. 'They didn't have as much information as we had. Like the details about his car and how he met Betsy at the craft fair.'

'Malcolm might have known about the craft fair and asked around,' Ivo suggested. 'But only once they knew he wasn't dead. Perhaps Bruce saw Penelope onto the train and knew she was on her own. When he heard about the accident, he'd have realised that Hugo hadn't been killed.'

'It's all speculation,' said Katya.

'And we might not have much time left,' said Jonny. 'If the four of them were conspiring to kill Hugo as revenge for Helen's death, then they've got what they wanted. There's no reason for Bruce to stay here any longer. He can go home. Perhaps he's already left.'

'Is there enough there for Lugs to investigate?' Jasmine asked.

Katya looked at Jonny's summary. 'I don't think there's any evidence there that a crime was committed. There's nothing particularly threatening about meeting someone in a pub.'

'Except when that person was fished out of the river just a few hours later.'

'I think Lugs will still say there was not enough evidence at the scene.'

'Even the boot prints?' asked Ivo.

Katya was in two minds. She didn't particularly want to hand the case over to Lugs. On the other hand, proving that it had been murder would mean that not all their hard work had gone to waste. 'I suppose if we could prove that Hazel owns a pair of similar boots it might help.'

'They are more likely to be Bruce's boots,' said Jasmine. 'And if he has been staying with Hazel, they might have planned it together – met outside the pub after Hazel got him drunk and then forced him down to the river.'

'That makes sense,' said Katya, a plan beginning to form in her mind. 'Who fancies a trip to Hazel's goat farm?'

'Won't that make them suspicious?' Jonny asked. 'We don't want Bruce to go to ground.'

'Not necessarily,' said Katya. 'We'll say we're looking into the train crash. We know Bruce was in Bath just before it, and was with Penelope, who was killed. We need to establish that Bruce was not among the dead.'

'What if Bruce asks how we found him?' asked Ivo.

'We can say we're looking into all his known contacts. We've already spoken to Harriet and Malcolm – he might know that already – and Hazel was with them all at the summer school.'

'That sounds believable,' said Jonny. 'When shall we go?'

'Tomorrow morning?' It was probably better if she and Jonny went without the other two, more authentic somehow. 'Are you two okay with that?' she asked Jasmine and Ivo. 'You will both be working, won't you?'

'Fine by me,' said Jasmine. Ivo nodded. 'We can track you. Make sure you're both safe.'

'In case we get thrown into the nearest river?' Jonny laughed.

'It's not a bad idea,' said Katya. 'We can't be sure they won't be armed with shotguns. Farmers are famous for protecting their property.' Did she really expect that? Or was she just worried that she was leaving Jasmine and Ivo out of any possible action? A bit of both, she supposed.

25

'I hate to think what this is doing to my suspension,' said Jonny as he narrowly avoided yet another pothole. They'd left the A30 some miles back and had turned onto ever smaller and less well-maintained lanes. 'Are you sure we're still going the right way?'

Katya looked at the map folded on her lap. Swinson Farm, according to Jonny's satnav, was well away from any kind of beaten track. He'd zoomed into Google Earth and found it was approached by an unmarked lane. Not only unmarked, but uncared for. He wondered how the goats came and went from the farm. Herded by lads in leather shorts and knee socks, perhaps. Or maybe they didn't come and go but were born and bred on the farm. Goat meat wasn't a particularly popular commodity, but their milk and cheese were and that would have to be transported somehow, wouldn't it?

The farm buildings appeared over the brow of a hill. A stone farmhouse that could do with some care and attention. Notably a new roof and replacement of door and window frames. There was a sprawl of outbuildings that ranged from a timber barn to some brick and corrugated iron sheds. Parked outside one of the sheds was a tractor and trailer. The answer, Jonny assumed, to how goods were transported.

'Not much money in goat farming, I suppose,' said Katya. 'And I thought my flat was shabby.'

'It's probably cosy inside,' said Jonny, noticing smoke drifting out of a chimney. He opened the car door and stepped cautiously out onto a muddy driveway. Katya followed him and they headed towards a door covered in blistered black paint. Katya, looking for a doorbell, spotted a knocker in the shape of a lion's head and rapped loudly. A black and white dog appeared from the side of the house, barking and snarling at them. Jonny was about to grab Katya and hurtle back to the car when the dog was jerked to a sudden halt by the chain that was fastened around its neck. It stopped barking abruptly and bared its teeth at them.

The door opened and a woman appeared. 'Pack it in, Sarge,' she yelled.

Katya blinked and stared at her before realising that it was the dog being yelled at. The dog sank onto the ground and cowered.

'What do you want?' the woman, presumably Hazel Corruthers, asked.

Was this the woman Serena had seen in the pub? Jonny was sure *tall* had been part of the description. This woman couldn't be more than five one, although what she lacked in height she made up for in girth, something that hadn't really shown on her website photo.

'Hazel Corruthers?' Katya asked. The woman nodded. 'I'm Katya Roscoff. This is Jonathan Cardew. We're investigators. Could we come in and have a word with you?'

'I suppose,' said Hazel, standing back and ushering them into the house. The door opened into an open plan living room, with a kitchen visible through a door at one end and a staircase at the other. 'Take a seat,' she said.

Jonny eyed the threadbare sofa suspiciously and chose a wooden wheelback dining chair. Katya seemed happy to settle for the sofa.

'Tea? Coffee?' Hazel offered.

'We're fine, thanks,' said Jonny, before Katya had a chance to accept. God only knew what state the kitchen was in, and he'd never had tea with goat's milk and didn't intend starting now.

'What's this all about, then?' Hazel asked. 'What is it that you are investigating?'

'We're working with Thames Valley Police,' said Katya. 'You know the inquiry into the Swindon train crash is due to start soon?'

Hazel shrugged, with an expression that suggested anything not in the immediate vicinity of the goat farm was of little interest.

'We have reason to believe that you may be in contact with Bruce Hunter. He was seen in the company of one of the victims of the crash and we just want to establish that he is alive and well and was not also involved.'

'You're not from immigration, are you?'

'No,' said Katya. 'I told you, we're working with Thames Valley Police. We're not in the least interested in travellers who may or may not have outstayed their visas.'

'Then I can assure you that Bruce Hunter is both alive and well,' said Hazel, looking up at the ceiling, where there had been a sudden thump and the sound of footsteps heading down the stairs. 'In fact, you can see for yourselves.'

Jonny and Katya looked towards the stairs, where a man was clumping down in his socks, a pair of boots in one hand. He stopped on the third stair from the bottom and looked at Hazel with an expression of concern. 'Who...?'

'It's okay, Bruce,' said Hazel. 'They're just here to check that you are alive.'

Jonny stood up, walked to the foot of the stairs and shook his hand. 'I'm Jonny Cardew,' he said. 'And this is Katya Roscoff.'

'It's something to do with a train crash,' said Hazel.

'What train crash?'

'It was not far from here,' said Katya. 'Eighteen months ago.'

'Eighteen months,' said Bruce, with an expression that suggested he was in the middle of a complicated calculation. 'Well, as you can see, I'm alive, so what makes you think I might have been involved in the crash?'

'We believe you were in the company of Penelope Walsh around then.'

'What if I was?'

'Well...' Katya started. Jonny suspected what she was going to say would be less than tactful.

'I'm very sorry to tell you that Mrs Walsh died in the crash.'

Bruce sat down suddenly, his boots dropping to the floor with a thud. 'Penny's dead?' he said, staring at Jonny open-mouthed.

'I'm afraid so. I'm so sorry for your loss.'

'Walsh?' said Hazel. 'Anything to do with Hugo Walsh?'

'His wife,' said Katya. 'You didn't know?'

'Why would I? Bruce, is there something you haven't told me?'

'Bruce and Penelope were having an affair,' said Katya, bluntly.

'I wouldn't exactly call it an affair,' said Bruce. 'It was more of a fling. We agreed, didn't we, that I should call on Malcolm and ask if he knew where Hugo was.' He turned to Jonny. 'Hugo Walsh had a son he didn't know about. Damian asked our advice. Damian is...'

'We know who Damian is,' said Katya impatiently.

Hazel looked at Bruce and sighed. 'You were supposed to find out where Hugo was. You never told us about finding his wife, never mind having a fling with her. Did Hugo know about that? And why didn't you tell us you'd found him?'

'I lost him again. I thought I knew where he lived, but when I called on him no one could tell me where he was.'

'Why not just ask his wife?' Hazel asked.

'We'd broken up by then.'

Jonny was getting confused. 'Let's get this clear,' he said. 'You and Bruce were looking for Hugo to tell him about Damian. Why couldn't Damian do that for himself?'

'Bruce,' said Hazel. 'Go and make some coffee. We'd better tell these people the whole story. They may be able to help us clear things up.'

Jonny was even more confused. He thought they were there for information that could lead Lugs and his team to open up a murder inquiry. Now it all seemed to be about a hunt for a missing father.

'Mind if I make notes?' said Katya, delving into her bag and finding an exercise book and a pen.

'Please do,' said Hazel. 'I've no idea what you already know, but I gather one of you spoke to Harriet so you will have a little of the background.'

'Harriet told me she adopted Damian when Helen Robertson died, and that Hugo Walsh was his father.'

'That's right,' said Hazel. 'Harriet resisted telling Damian about his father for a long time, but as soon as he was eighteen, he was able to see his birth certificate. I don't think it meant much to him at the time, but about three years ago Damian met a girl, Suzette. They moved in together and decided to start a family, but Suzette had trouble conceiving and they started going for a lot of tests. Questions were asked about their families, which of course Damian was unable to answer.'

'So he decided to find Hugo,' said Katya.

'He'd no idea where to start,' said Hazel. 'Plus he was very involved with some new project at Porton and had little time to spare.'

'I don't understand where Bruce comes into things,' said Katya.

'We all became very close at that summer school,' said Hazel. 'Malcolm was upset about Helen and what he saw as her betrayal with Hugo. We tried to tell him she'd been coerced, but as she wouldn't report him for rape, Malcolm never really believed her. He jumped at Bruce's offer of a long visit to Australia and they flew back there together the day after the summer school ended.'

'That's when Malcolm was injured?' asked Jonny.

Bruce returned with a tray and handed round mugs of coffee and slices of cake. 'That was hell,' said Bruce. 'A faulty piece of equipment and Malcolm fell forty feet onto rocks. He was lucky to survive. He blamed me for the accident, but honest to God, it wasn't my fault.'

'And you were cleared of all blame,' said Hazel.

'Why did you decide to come to the UK when you did?' asked Katya.

'I needed to get away,' said Bruce. 'I'd fallen out with my wife. She was pushing for a divorce, but I couldn't face all the hassle. I'd been away before and things had always settled when I returned.'

'Did you always stay away for as long as this? It's been eighteen months,' said Katya.

Bruce shrugged. 'Sometimes longer,' he said. 'My wife and son are more than capable of running the business without me. In fact, I'm a bit of a spare part most of the time.'

'Bruce has been helping me here on the farm,' said Hazel. 'I've really needed him.'

'You do realise your family have no idea where you are,' said Katya. 'Until some vital evidence came to light, we thought you'd died in the train crash with Penelope. The authorities here were about to begin discussions with the Australian embassy about breaking the news of your death to them.'

'Sorry to disappoint them,' said Bruce. 'My death would probably have been cause for some celebration back home.'

'We're getting off track,' said Jonny, wondering if he could expect to get home in time for supper. 'You decided to come to the UK to get away from the family. What made you visit Malcolm?'

'I wanted to tell him about Damian.'

'Malcolm wanted nothing to do with Damian when he was small,' said Hazel. 'But Harriet and I knew how guilty he'd felt after Helen died, and we thought after all this time had passed, it might be time for him and Bruce to patch things up. We knew by then that Hugo and Malcolm both lived in Windsor, which was quite a coincidence and we wondered if their paths had crossed.'

'He wouldn't have anything to do with me when I visited,' said Bruce. 'Then I discovered Penelope sang in his choir. I knew Damian wanted to find his father, so I thought by getting to know Penelope I would be able to bring them together.'

'So you told Penelope about Damian?' Katya asked.

'No. Well, I couldn't just suddenly tell her that her husband had a son he knew nothing about, could I? Anyway, Penelope and I had a bit of a bust-up while we were in Bath. She planned to go home after the concert, and I came here to see Hazel.'

'And made yourself at home, apparently,' said Katya.

'Hazel needed help on the farm, so I stayed on.'

'And you've been here for eighteen months?'

'We had to keep quiet about it,' said Hazel. 'His visa expired, but with all his experience in Australia I really needed his help here.'

'You didn't go back to Windsor at all?' Katya asked.

'No. Why would I?'

'I don't know,' said Jonny. 'But someone thought they saw you in Waitrose.'

'Not me, mate. Your someone made a mistake.'

Juliet must have got it wrong, Jonny thought, looking at Bruce's mud-spattered trousers, a jumper with holes in the elbows, matted hair grazing his shoulders. He'd have stood out like a sore thumb in Waitrose. And after all, Juliet had only seen an old photo of him. She was probably just anxious to help Jasmine. It was all getting too complicated for Jonny. 'So how did you discover where Hugo was?' he asked.

'After a year of unsuccessfully looking for him, Harriet hired a private detective, who found his address and email. It took him three months.'

'And Damian contacted him?'

'No. He wanted someone to break the news to Hugo first.'

'Very considerate of him,' Katya muttered.

'We thought Malcolm might be the one to tell him,' said Hazel. 'Since he'd been close to Helen. Harriet and I went to see him, but he said he wasn't willing to act as a go-between.'

'So you contacted Hugo yourselves?'

'We haven't yet,' said Hazel. 'Harriet and I are discussing the best way to do it. We still don't agree about it.'

This was definitely not making any sense. 'You contacted Hugo on your own?' Jonny asked Hazel. 'And arranged to meet him at a pub in Windsor?'

'What?' said Hazel. 'No, I'd never do that without telling Harriet.'

'Damian, then. Did he contact Hugo? And you turned up to the meeting?'

'I've no idea what you are talking about,' said Hazel. 'All we have for Hugo is an address in Banbury. I told you – we hadn't decided what to do next.'

'But you were seen in a pub in Windsor. The barmaid described you and then identified you from your website photo,' said Katya.

Bruce laughed suddenly. 'That photo? Doesn't look anything like her.'

Not as she was now in her farming gear, perhaps. But with her hair tidied and without the grimy jumper, possibly. Although, Jonny suddenly remembered, there was the matter of her height. He'd taken Serena's word for it that this was the woman she'd seen and now he felt distinctly foolish. He fumbled with his coffee cup. 'I'm sorry,' he said. 'I seem to have made a dreadful mistake.'

Katya reached over and patted his arm. 'Case of mistaken identity,' she said. 'It can happen to anyone. But not a wasted journey. We can let the inquiry people know that Bruce has been accounted for and I suggest you also contact your family,' she smirked at Bruce, 'before they set up an international search. However, we do have some news for you. I assume you haven't spoken to Harriet in the last few days.'

Hazel and Bruce shook their heads.

'It's bad news, I'm afraid. At least for Damian. Hugo Walsh is dead. Drowned in the Thames the Thursday before last. Perhaps Hazel, you or Harriet might break the news to him gently. That's if Harriet hasn't already done so.'

'Harriet knew?' asked Hazel.

'Jonny told her a couple of days ago.'

'I'm surprised she hasn't been in touch,' said Hazel. 'But I know she's very busy right now.'

'You say he drowned?' Bruce asked. 'Can you tell me, was it an accident or suicide?'

'Our enquiries are ongoing,' said Katya. 'But murder is also a possibility.'

'Can't say I'm surprised,' said Bruce. 'He was a bit of a bad apple.'

'Bruce,' said Hazel sharply. 'That's no way to speak of the dead. And for God's sake don't say that in front of Damian.'

Bruce scowled at her. 'Good riddance, in my opinion.'

'Shut up, Bruce,' said Hazel. 'Or these two will think... Oh God, that's why you're here, isn't it? You think one of us killed Hugo.'

'You specifically,' said Bruce. 'Since you were spotted in a pub in Windsor. Was that the night he died?'

'It was,' said Katya.

'Well, I can assure you that it wasn't me,' said Hazel.

'And were you anywhere near Windsor that night?' asked Katya, turning to Bruce.

'Not been near the place in months,' he said, looking smug.

'I assume you both have an alibi for the night in question. Apart from each other, of course.'

Bruce looked rather less smug now, Jonny thought.

'Actually, yes,' said Hazel. She walked over to a roll-top desk and picked up a diary. 'I had a meeting with the AI man in Salisbury to discuss our, er, needs, for this spring.'

'The goats' needs, really,' said Bruce with a smirk.

'Bruce and I drove there together and after our meeting we went for a meal at the Golden Lotus restaurant. I daresay someone will remember us. We arrived back here at around midnight.'

'Bloody good meal,' said Bruce. 'Butter chicken and peshwari nan, washed down with Kingfisher beer.'

'We've not been away from the farm since. It's a busy time of year and we've both been working flat out.'

Katya shut her notebook and pushed it back into her bag. 'Thank you for your time,' she said, standing up and buttoning her coat. 'Just one more question, Mr Hunter,' she said. 'Do you always wear those boots?'

Bruce stared down at his boots. 'Always wear this make,' he said. 'Have done for years. In fact, Malcolm and I bought our first pair together when he was in Australia with me.'

'So you've been wearing the same boots for thirty years?'

'Give or take,' he said. 'Got a problem with that?'

Katya picked up her bag and headed for the car, Jonny scuttling in her wake.

'WHAT DO YOU THINK?' Jonny asked as they headed back to the main road. 'Do you believe them?'

'I think I do,' she said. 'Can't say I liked Bruce Hunter much, and we'll need to check their alibi, but it does make sense.'

'So who was it in the pub with Hugo? And who pushed him into the river?'

'Blessed if I know,' said Katya. 'But while we figure it out, do you fancy an Indian meal in Salisbury?'

26

Jasmine looked around at the café walls. *Six paintings,* she thought. She wanted to brighten things up a bit, not overwhelm people. Clara had sent her a link to her website where she'd uploaded some of her paintings. Jasmine looked at it and had a pretty good idea of which ones she wanted. But they still needed to talk about frames and prices, and that would be better done face to face. She'd just finished her afternoon shift so now would be as good a time to go as any.

She arrived at the house to the strains of piano music and stopped in the driveway to listen. One of Malcolm's better students, she guessed, as the faultlessly played piece drifted out of the window. It seemed a shame to interrupt, but it was not Malcolm she'd come to see, and if he was busy teaching, she'd be able to talk to Clara without disrupting his lesson.

She pressed her finger to the bell and the music stopped abruptly, making Jasmine feel insensitive and guilty. The door was opened by Clara herself and Jasmine apologised for interrupting the lesson.

'It wasn't a lesson,' said Clara gruffly. 'Malcolm's out. What do you want?'

Not exactly welcoming. 'It was you I wanted to talk to,' said Jasmine.

'Can't you come back another time?'

'It won't take a moment,' said Jasmine. She really didn't want to keep trekking back and forth. It was a fifteen-minute walk from the café and she had work to do as well as a mystery to solve.

Clara hesitated for a moment as if trying to decide whether it would be better to deal with Jasmine now or later. 'You'd better come in,' she said with a sigh. 'I'm used to my playing being interrupted.'

'That was you playing?' Jasmine asked, trying not to sound surprised. Why wouldn't Clara be a musician as well as her brother? 'It was beautiful,' she said.

Clara frowned. 'I could have been good once,' she said, leading Jasmine towards her workroom at the back of the house. The hallway was tidier than when Jasmine had last visited, although she couldn't work out what was different. There were coats piled onto pegs near the door and below it, a rack with boots and shoes. She noticed a pair of hiking boots. That was odd, wasn't it? The day she'd visited with Katya, Malcolm had been wearing soft shoes with wide Velcro straps. It couldn't be easy getting one's shoes on and off when paralysed, so stout, lace-up hiking boots didn't seem like something Malcolm would wear. But what did she know? Perhaps Clara put them on for him. In cold weather maybe, or just when he wanted to look a bit more rugged. Anyway, she'd seen him standing at the window, so perhaps he could walk short distances. Into the garden, maybe. Malcolm might still be able to take a few steps, but he could hardly go hiking. So he might keep them for sentimental reasons. Or perhaps Clara wore them. She was tall so she probably had quite big feet. Jasmine tried to catch a glimpse of Clara's feet, but she was already heading for the back of the house and the lighting in the passage was not good.

Clara led her through a set of double doors at the back of the house and down some steps into a studio with big windows and a view of the garden. The sun was streaming into the room, the light catching on a glass bottle that was standing open on a windowsill, close to a pile of sketches on flimsy paper. There was no ramp, so presumably Malcolm had no need to come in here.

'This is where I work in the warmer weather,' said Clara. 'I assume you've come to select the paintings you want for the café?'

'It's a lovely room,' said Jasmine. 'It would be nice to have a garden room at the café but there isn't the space.' *And if there was, I'd keep it a lot tidier than this.* She looked round at shelves stacked untidily with pots of paint, tubes of glue and aerosol cans. In front of her was a long trestle table covered with Clara's paintings. Clara was hurriedly piling them up and from the glimpse Jasmine caught of them, they were very different in style from the ones on her website. These were uncomfortable images of angry faces staring up from watery surfaces, twisted limbs and broken bodies. Jasmine didn't look too closely. Clara obviously didn't want them to be seen, and the darker side of her work didn't interest Jasmine right now.

'These are ones you liked,' said Clara, grabbing some paintings she'd piled onto a shelf at the back of the room and spreading out some of her happier images on the table in front of Jasmine.

Jasmine moved closer to look at them. They were not great art, but Jasmine liked them. The bright colours and undemanding images would suit the walls of *Jasmine's* very well. They were more impressive in reality than on the website and would be popular in the café. 'Have you decided on prices?' she asked. 'Once they've been framed, I thought we could put a small price sticker on the glass. Or if you prefer, I could run off some leaflets.'

'I don't mind,' said Clara, clearly not interested in their selling potential. 'I'll leave that to you.'

'Oh, well, there's no hurry. We need to decide about frames first. Do you know anyone who can make them for you?'

'I think there's someone in town you could ask.'

Was she really not interested? Jasmine thought that was strange. Who wouldn't want to see their work framed and hanging in public? Clara seemed nervous and started fidgeting with the bottle on the windowsill, and then pulling more bottles and cans from the shelves. If she was trying to tidy up, she was not making a good job of it.

Jasmine wished she would sit down and relax. She was sorry to have disturbed her playing, but if she'd just settle down and talk about the mini exhibition in the café, then she could be on her way and Clara could get back to the piano. 'What does Malcolm think about your work being in the café?' Jasmine asked, hoping Clara would say that he was impressed and that it might encourage her to talk about it.

'He's not that interested. Stupid to think he might actually care, but he's never had much time for his little sister's interests.'

I should probably go, Jasmine thought. Leave Clara to whatever she was fretting about. But maybe she needed help, someone to talk to, a sympathetic ear. 'You've given up so much to care for him. Surely he must realise you need your own interests.'

'No one thinks I have any interests,' Clara said bitterly, looking anxiously around the room. 'And he's barely been able to look me in the eye since...'

'Since?'

'I don't want to talk about it. You should leave.'

Something was wrong. *The stress of being a carer,* Jasmine thought. No one to talk to about it, no sign of support from anyone else. This woman needed help and shouldn't be left on her own. 'Why don't you sit down and tell me about it? Sharing it might help.'

'You think so?' Clara shook her head and sighed. 'Well, if you must know, it was at the summer school.'

'But that was years ago.'

'Yeah, and you don't get over something like that.'

She wasn't making much sense. Was she talking about her brother's accident? But that was after the summer school finished. Then she remembered that Malcolm's girlfriend Helen Robertson had been there with him. 'That was when Malcolm and Helen split up, wasn't it?'

Clara nodded.

'But that was nothing to do with you, surely?'

'Malcolm blamed me. My parents, too. They said I must have led him on.'

'Who?' Jasmine asked, with a horrible feeling she already knew the answer.

'Hugo Walsh,' said Clara, with an odd expression on her face. Almost one of pride, Jasmine thought.

'What happened?'

'I'd been hanging around with the students quite a bit. We lived close by and I was bored at home that summer. My parents encouraged it. I was about to start sixth form and they thought mixing with students would be good for me. I started going to the bar in the evenings. Hugo was always there, having what I thought were very grown-up, learned discussions and I wanted to be part of that. I didn't think he'd ever noticed me but one evening he did. He wanted to buy me a gin or vodka, but the bar staff said I was too young to be drinking. Hugo put his arm around me and laughed at them. He said something like, "She's a big girl, isn't she? Don't you think she looks eighteen?" But they asked for proof, so he said we'd go to his room for a drink instead.'

'But you were what, fifteen?' Jasmine asked. And Hugo Walsh must have been in his thirties.

'I was just sixteen and I was oh so flattered when an important man like Hugo Walsh said I looked eighteen.'

'So you went to his room. Then what?'

'He poured me a glass of wine, then he made me stand in front of him while he sat and stared at me. He said I had such a beautiful body it was a shame to keep it covered up. He just wanted to look, he said.'

'And you believed him?'

'Like I said, I was flattered, sixteen, completely inexperienced and trusting. And he watched while I slipped out of my sandals, took my cardigan off and unbuttoned my dress. He didn't touch me. He just lounged back in his chair and stared at me. He told me I should show more of my body, that I could be a model. But then Helen burst in and called me a stupid little girl. She grabbed my clothes, bundled them into my arms and told me to get out. Hugo's room was up a flight of stairs in a kind of attic. I ran down the stairs, thinking

Helen would be close behind me, but she wasn't.' Clara stared at Jasmine, her eyes blazing. 'I was cross with her. She'd made a fool of me.'

This was horrifying. Jasmine didn't know whether Clara had been angry or frightened, or even jealous. 'What happened next? Did you get help?'

Clara shrugged. 'I got dressed and took a taxi home.'

'And you didn't tell anyone about it?'

'Not then, I was too upset. It was me Hugo wanted, not Helen. They'd warned me about him, but I'd ignored them. Helen wanted him for herself, but it was me he'd asked. He only wanted to look at me and buy me a drink. Helen seemed fine the next day. I assumed she got what she wanted, which was a night with Hugo. It was only months later when we heard that she'd had a baby and then died that I told my parents and Malcolm what had happened. Malcolm was in hospital by then and he said it was all my fault. If I hadn't gone with Hugo, he would never have attacked Helen, and Malcolm wouldn't have gone to Australia with Bruce.'

A sudden thump from upstairs made Jasmine jump. Clara was on her own in the house, wasn't she? Did they have a cat? Or perhaps the sound came from the house next door. 'What was that?' she asked.

'Nothing,' said Clara.

It obviously was something, but Clara was looking edgy and nervous. And then Jasmine remembered the empty hallway. Empty because the stair lift wasn't in its usual place at the bottom of the stairs. And if it wasn't there, it must be at the top of the stairs and that could only be because Malcolm had gone up in it. He was still in the house.

'Can Malcolm walk at all on his own?' Jasmine asked. 'I thought I saw him standing by the window when we were here before.'

'With support he can pull himself out of the chair and walk a step or two. Why do you want to know?'

'Just wondering about those hiking boots in the hall...'

Clara glared at her.

'I'm sorry. I didn't mean to pry.' It was time she got away from there. 'Well,' she said, trying to sound breezy and carefree, 'I'd better be on my way. Let me know when—'

She didn't have time to finish her sentence. Before she knew what was happening, Clara had grabbed her by the arms and pinned her against the kitchen wall. 'Not so fast,' she said. 'You know too much. Now you have to stay here.'

As Jasmine struggled to escape, she heard the doorbell ring. 'Ignore it,' Clara hissed as it rang for the second time, and the thumping from upstairs became more insistent. Jasmine tried to wriggle free, but Clara was bigger and stronger. She followed Clara's gaze towards the untidy pile of paper on the windowsill, on top of which was the open bottle – turpentine, she could now see from the label. The sun was still glinting on the glass of the bottle. You could start a fire that way. Was that Clara's plan? Burn the house down with Malcolm trapped upstairs? She'd probably had it all planned. Claim on the insurance money and escape to a new life. But Jasmine had blundered in and ruined it. Knock the bottle over, strike a match and it would be a matter of seconds before the whole room, then the whole house, went up in flames. The only small comfort was that Jasmine couldn't see any matches. But she shouldn't count on there not being any. If Clara had planned this, she would probably have a box of matches or a lighter in her pocket.

The door from the studio into the garden was just a few feet away, but there was no way of knowing if it was locked. If she did manage to escape Clara's hold on her, she could probably make it to the door before there was time to strike a match, but if the door was locked there would be no escape. It would be better to head for the other door, the one into the house, but that was further away. She had to make a decision before Clara gathered her thoughts. Another thump from upstairs distracted Clara for a second. She didn't loosen her hold on Jasmine, but she did shift her weight to one side, allowing Jasmine to bend her right leg behind her and deliver a sharp kick to Clara's kneecap. With the shock of the pain Clara loosened her grip and bent down to rub her knee with one hand. Jasmine pushed her to the floor and headed for the door into the hallway, but before she could reach for the handle Clara grabbed her by the ankle, tripping her up. Jasmine lost her balance and, knocking her head on a corner of the table, she fell to the floor.

IN THE OFFICE, Ivo was fixing a new whiteboard to the wall. They had so many notes and photos now that they'd run out of space. Ivo's plan was to cover the whole of one wall with white melamine. He removed everything from the old whiteboard and laid it carefully on the table. Then he unscrewed the board from the wall and moved it along to the end nearest to the door. He'd already measured up and had bought a new panel to fix next to the old one.

Harold was sitting under the table watching him with his head on his paws, but emerged with his tail wagging when Jonny arrived carrying a box. He put it down and made a fuss of Harold. Then he looked up at what Ivo was doing. 'That looks awkward,' Jonny said. 'Can I help?'

'You're just in time,' said Ivo. 'Can you hold this up for me while I fix the first screw?' Holding the board against the wall while he marked out where the screws were to go was no problem. Trying to do the same while using a screwdriver was awkward, but with Jonny's help they soon had it fixed and ready to use. 'What's in the box?' Ivo asked as he stood back to admire his work.

'I thought we could do with a printer,' said Jonny. 'I picked this one up for half price.'

'I'd better get all this stuff back on the board,' said Ivo. 'There's not much room to unpack it at the moment.'

'Maybe wait for Katya,' said Jonny. 'I'm going to type up the notes we made yesterday, and she might want the board organised differently.' He gave Ivo a summary of what they discovered.

'You mean the woman in the pub with Hugo wasn't Hazel?' said Ivo.

'Seems not. Unless Hazel was lying, but Katya and I both thought she wasn't.'

'I thought the barmaid identified her.'

'She told me she thought it was the same woman,' said Jonny. 'She must have been mistaken.'

'Perhaps it was Harriet she saw,' Ivo suggested.

Jonny had turned on the computer and was typing up his notes. Then he unpacked the printer and connected it. He needed a test print, so he clicked into Hazel's website and sent her photo to the printer. Then he found a photo of Harriet and printed that as well. They lined them up, side by side on the board, and studied them.

'There's no way you could mistake them for each other,' said Ivo.

Jonny agreed. 'Even if they changed their hairstyles and tried to look similar, they couldn't. Hazel's much shorter and plumper. And Serena at the pub was sure it wasn't Harriet.'

'Which means we have another suspect,' said Ivo. 'Another woman, and we don't have any idea who she is.'

Katya puffed through the door and caught what Ivo had just said. 'Been wondering about that,' she said. 'Hazel told us that they'd hired a private detective to find Hugo's current address. They were going to contact him about meeting up with Damian but hadn't got around to it yet, but what if someone else had seen the detective's notes and contacted Hugo themselves?'

'Who else would have it in for Hugo and want him dead?' Jonny asked.

'What about Damian's girlfriend?'

'I can't see that she'd have much of a motive,' said Katya. 'Damian wanted to meet his father, and as far as we know it was purely to find out a bit more about him. He was after a family medical history because his girlfriend Suzette was having trouble conceiving. No malicious intent.'

'Anyway,' said Ivo, 'she'd be a lot younger than Hazel. Hardly likely to be mistaken for her. Even on a dark night in a pub.'

'She might be older than Damian,' said Jonny. 'Hazel told us she was having trouble getting pregnant. Perhaps she was getting worried about her body clock.'

'I suppose she could be in her early forties,' said Katya. 'Damian is thirty-two so it's not impossible.'

'But we don't know her last name or what she looks like,' said Jonny.

'I'll see if Damian has a Facebook page,' said Ivo. 'She might have been tagged in a photo with him.' He took Jonny's place at the computer and logged into Facebook. He tapped in some details and sighed. 'We need Jasmine for this,' he said. 'She'd get there much quicker.'

'Keep trying,' said Katya. 'Where is Jasmine, anyway?'

'She's gone to see Clara Applewood,' said Jonny. 'About some paintings for the café.'

'Here,' said Ivo, looking pleased with himself. 'I've found them.' He clicked open a photo he'd found after searching for Damian and Suzette.

Jonny leant over his shoulder and read the caption, *Porton Down Christmas Party 2022*. 'Sounds jolly,' he said. 'Wouldn't fancy the punch, though. No knowing what might have been slipped into it.'

'It was in a pub,' said Ivo. 'The Golden Hind near Dorchester.'

'You're getting off topic,' said Katya. 'What does Suzette look like?'

Ivo enlarged the photo and printed it. 'It's fun having a printer,' he said.

'Maybe,' said Katya. 'But you might want to be mindful about the cost of ink cartridges.' She picked up the photo as it emerged from the printer.

Jonny took it from her and stared at it. 'Can't be her,' he said. Katya and Ivo had to agree. This was a woman in her twenties, with curly, auburn hair and freckles. Even a grey-haired wig and layer of concealer wouldn't make her look anything like Hazel.

'Let's have another look at the summer school photo,' she said. 'Perhaps we missed someone.'

Jonny opened it on the computer and enlarged it. 'No,' he said. 'There were only the three girls. And one of those is dead.'

'No,' said Ivo, suddenly. 'There was another girl there. I remember from Jasmine's notes.'

He grabbed the mouse from Jonny and clicked desperately on their browsing history. It was a site Jasmine had been looking at earlier that day. Was she using this computer or her laptop? Ivo was fairly sure it was this one. She'd been sitting at the table with a cup of coffee, right here in this room. He found what he was looking for and launched the site triumphantly. 'Here,' he said, showing them the photo he'd found.

Katya looked at it and turned pale. 'Print it,' she said, grabbing it the moment the printer finished. She pinned it up on the board next to Hazel's picture.

'Well, I'm damned,' said Jonny. 'Clara Applewood. She's taller than Hazel, but apart from that and with similar hairstyles they could be sisters. And you're right, Ivo, Clara did hang around at the summer school.'

'And Jasmine's gone to see her,' said Katya. 'We need to get round there. Now!'

~

THEY RANG the bell twice and then Ivo tried Jasmine's phone. No reply to either, but they knew someone was in because they could hear thumping from inside the house. It was coming from upstairs, Ivo thought, looking up at the first-floor windows. 'Can we break in?' he asked.

Katya shook her head. 'There's no way we can break the door down,' she said. 'And the windows are all double glazed. Anyway, we could be arrested for breaking and entering.'

'We should call the police,' said Jonny. 'We know Jasmine's inside and we can hear suspicious noises from upstairs.'

'There's no time,' Ivo wailed. 'I'm going round the back.' He headed for the gate at the side of the house, which he assumed would lead him to the back garden. The gate was locked so he took a few steps back, took a running jump at it and vaulted over, leaving Harold straining at his lead, Jonny having some trouble stopping him from following.

Ivo landed on a path that skirted the side of the house. He crept along, knees bent, until he came to a window, where he stood up and peered inside. Just an empty living room with nothing to see. Next to that was a garden room with big windows. Ivo crawled along on his stomach, making sure he stayed below the level of the windows, until he came to a door with glass panels. He looked cautiously through it in time to see Clara grab Jasmine by her ankle, crashing her to the floor, knocking her head on the way down. Clara gave her a kick and then reached for a bottle. Ivo couldn't see what it was but watched as she poured the contents onto the pile of papers, then reached into her pocket and pulled out a box of matches.

Ivo turned round and spotted a very large garden gnome seated on a toadstool and holding a fishing rod. He prayed that it wasn't concreted into the patio on which it stood and was in luck. He lifted it over his head and hurled it at the glass door, which caved inwards with a satisfying sound of shattering glass. Ignoring what Clara was doing, Ivo rushed in, hefted Jasmine onto his shoulder and carried her out into the garden, lying her gently on the grass. She opened her eyes to the sound of the gate crashing back against the wall of the house and Harold rushing up to them, barking furiously. He was followed by Katya and Jonny. Jonny knelt at Jasmine's side while Katya climbed through the broken door into the studio, to be confronted by Clara holding a lit match. She gazed at Katya as if in a trance. The match had burnt down almost to her fingers as Katya stepped forward and blew it out. 'You don't want to do that, love,' she said. 'You'd set fire to yourself. It's not a nice way to go.' She reached into her copious pocket and found a length of twine. Then she led Clara out of the conservatory and sat her in a garden chair, binding her hands together behind her back. Clara was clearly in shock and offered no resistance.

27

In early May, two brothers sat either side of the coffee table in Jason's lounge and stared at the urn that contained Hugo Walsh's ashes. Ivo had found the other urn, the first one that had Hugo's name on it. Penelope's ashes had been scattered in the Saville Garden Lake as requested in her will. Jason couldn't remember what had happened to Hugo's remains until Ivo suggested he might have put it in the workshop, eventually uncovering it from where it was hidden in the clutter Jason had pushed aside eighteen months earlier. This urn had now been given to Barry Brent's father, following the formal identification of Barry as a victim of the train crash by the chairman of the inquiry.

The problem now was what to do with what remained of Hugo Walsh. It had been a very small funeral attended only by Jason, Damian, his visibly pregnant girlfriend Suzette, Hazel and Harriet – Bruce having now returned somewhat unwillingly to his family in Australia. After a very short service at the crematorium, they were joined by the breakfast club detectives for a small wake in Jason's house. Ivo had scrubbed and polished until the house gleamed, Jasmine had made sandwiches and cakes and Jonny had provided a crate of beer. Katya hadn't known what to bring until Belinda offered her the best of the early summer flowers from her garden.

Damian had taken the news of his father's murder calmly. Even the short, unflattering resume of Hugo Walsh's character provided by Harriet hadn't upset him. 'I never knew the guy,' he said. 'And discovering I have a brother is actually kind of cool.' He grinned at Jason, who had put on a suit and clean shirt for the funeral. He had taken on a new lease of life since learning about Damian. He may have suffered an unusual loss of parents, but he had gained a half-brother and would soon be an uncle. He had family after all, and it made all the difference to him.

Clara was in custody awaiting trial for Hugo's murder. Malcolm had been discovered tied by his arms to a chair in his bedroom, but had refused to bring charges against his sister. He was now in sheltered accommodation close to where his parents lived. He felt partly to blame, he told the police, for allowing Clara access to his computer. She had intercepted the emails from Harriet, which had disclosed Hugo's whereabouts as discovered by the private detective she had hired, as well as the news that Hugo was Damian's father. Clara had set up an email in Damian's name and lured Hugo to a meeting at the pub in Windsor where he would meet his 'son'. She was claiming his death was an accident, although the police rejected her story that Hugo had drunk heavily at their meeting, and she had suggested a walk by the river to sober up before she introduced him to Damian – a meeting of which Damian, when interviewed by the police, denied all knowledge. Her explanation was not enough to convince the police that Hugo's death was not premeditated. She had been charged with murder.

Katya was still tutting about the private detective. Who was this man who had effortlessly uncovered Hugo's whereabouts? A quick word with Harriet told her the man's name, but also the reminder that it had taken him three months to find Hugo. Katya's team had done it in three days.

She carried some empty teacups into the kitchen, where she found Jonny gazing out of the window. 'All done and dusted,' she told him, rubbing her hands. 'Onwards and upwards to the next case,' she said.

'Do you have one in mind?' Jonny asked.

'A new case will turn up,' she said. 'Lugs will keep us up to date. There's bound to be something soon, so don't look so glum.'

'It's not that,' said Jonny. 'I'm sure there will be more cases.'

'Something's wrong, though.'

'Belinda lost her seat on the council,' he said. 'Bit of a shock, to be honest, to both of us.'

'Well, I would have voted for her,' said Katya. 'If I was in her area. It's a damn shame if you ask me. She was so good.'

'She'll get over it,' said Jonny with a sigh. 'She's had approaches from a number of charities, so she won't be short of things to do.'

'And she'll be voted back in next time. Sure to be.'

Jonny laughed. 'If she's not too busy by then.'

Katya patted him on the shoulder. 'Shall we go and see if they've decided where to scatter Hugo's ashes? Where are Jasmine and Ivo?'

'They've gone next door,' said Jonny. 'Ivo's hoping to see Poppy's brother and Jasmine is going to ask Poppy to do some quilted pictures for the café.'

'She doesn't fancy the paintings of a suspected murderer?'

'They'd probably sell like hot cakes, but she doesn't want to be reminded of that day.'

They returned to the gathering in the lounge, where the discussion was still ongoing. They'd rejected the river as ghoulish and hadn't been able to think of anywhere else that Hugo liked.

'What about a canal?' Jonny suggested. 'Hugo spent a lot of his time on them recently.'

'Why not?' said Damian. 'I can't think of anywhere more suitable.'

Jason nodded. 'I'll just be glad not to have him in the house any more.'

'Let's go now,' said Harriet. 'All of us. We'll give him the send-off he deserves.'

Jonny wasn't sure what that meant and didn't like to enquire too deeply. He just hoped they weren't about to find any more bodies.

≈

For the Breakfast Detectives' next case read **Death on the Carousel.**

Launching 20th November 2023
Pre order your copy here:
https://books2read.com/u/4D8Pee

ACKNOWLEDGMENTS

I would like to thank you so much for reading **Death in the River.** I do hope you enjoyed it.

If you have a few moments to spare a short review would be very much appreciated. Reviews really help me and will help other people who might consider reading my books.

I would also like to thank my editor, Sally Silvester-Wood at *Black Sheep Books*, my cover designer, Anthony O'Brien and all my fellow writers at *Quite Write* who have patiently listened to extracts and offered suggestions.

Discover more about Hilary Pugh and download the Breakfast Club Detectives prequel novella **Crime about Town** FREE at www.hilary-pugh.com

ALSO BY HILARY PUGH

<u>The Ian Skair: Private Investigator series</u>

Finding Lottie – series prequel

<u>Free</u> **when you join my mailing list:**

https://storyoriginapp.com/giveaways/61799962-7dc3-11eb-b5c8-7b3702734d0c

The Laird of Drumlychtoun

https://books2read.com/u/bwrEky

Postcards from Jamie

https://books2read.com/u/4X28Ae

Mystery at Murriemuir

https://books2read.com/u/mgj8Bx

The Diva of Dundas Farm

https://books2read.com/u/bMYMJA

The Man in the Red Overcoat

https://books2read.com/u/4DJRge

Printed in Great Britain
by Amazon

36676344R00136